For
Ma.

# The Yawning Veil

all my
love!

OTHER NOVELS BY E.M. KNOWLES

*Diary of Mimosa Creek*
*Iona*

# The Yawning Veil

## Book One of The Four Holds

# A Novel by E.M. Knowles

Despoina Publishing Co.

MMXV

# Table of Contents

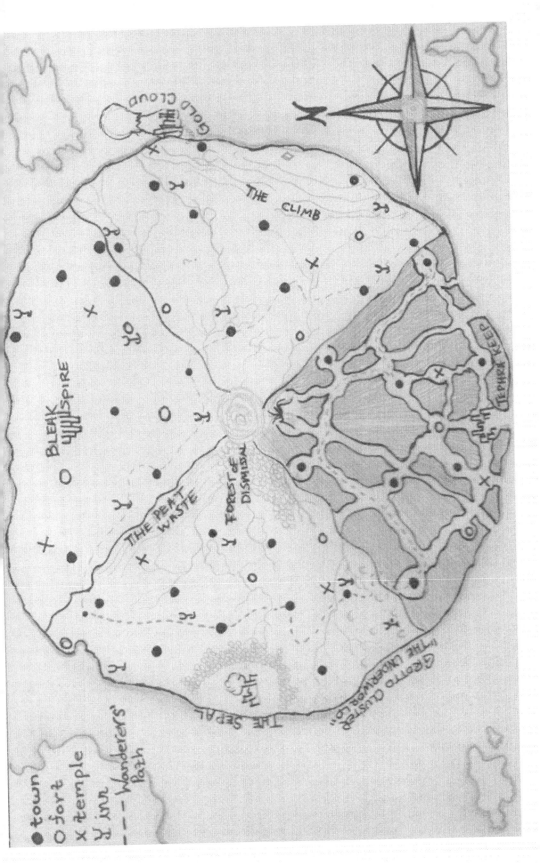

# Prologue
## *Of The Veil: All Returns*

There was suction to the air in The Veil. Winds blew in reverse, rushing away and always racing. All was barren: ash and smoke. If the ground was disturbed by movement, the particles would hover and glide, hesitant to resettle against the harsh and lonely field of emptiness. But rare was the visitor: eons of silt upon untouched silt waited and slept. The Veil was a cage of oblivion.

The world began from a spot at the peak of The Nameless Mountain that shot through the core of the land. Where there was once nothing, a parent-less seed appeared. As spontaneous as an idea, it came into being and rooted itself into ground that had just enough substance to give it life. It willed itself to survive and it fought to thrive. And eventually, a most unusual tree grew.

The expansion of trunk and branch spread outward. For a long time it grew in the vacuum of nothingness within The Veil. Yet, even the slightest development of the tree translated into inches, before yards, before miles of energy escalated out from the core. The scope stretched exponentially. Until finally, the reach of the branches of that most unusual tree alone on The Nameless Mountain outgrew the space that The Veil could contain. It supplied lands in all directions and birthed life that would never look upon its distant and secret majesty.

The side of the tree that faces the far-away North Hold was made of brittle branches shining of ice and snow. The east of the tree was dry and orange: leaves caught in a gossamer flux of ruby and gold. The side situated toward the South Hold was charred and has eternal smoke and ember pouring from its bark. The west of the tree glimmered a bright green canopy with a prism of flowers. The unknown and unusual tree was the only point at which all Four Holds exist as one.

The old fables are too far from the lonely tree to know its tale. The bard songs about The Veil sing of a land where the beloved dead congregate, but fail to realize that the tree draws the souls to hang from the splayed branches as bells on their respective seasons. The path is arduous. Many lose their way and are forced to drift and linger among the other inhabitants of The Veil.

The tree, while forming the world, shifted the conditions of The Veil just enough for a great many beasts to appear and roam. Some kind, some cruel. Some still living, some long destroyed. Of the ones who were eventually destroyed, there were four spectacular and unique horses that quickly became cherished by the early people for how precious and rare they were. Unlike the epic legends of ballad sung at the glory of each Hold, they were not slain during battle or in the midst of an honorable action. They were hunted by the very people who should have loved them. People saw that the land varied and began to believe that the differences in the horses signified some natural form of division between otherwise average people. The horses vanished and with them, unity. Those of opportunistic disposition among the people of the freshly segregated Four Holds elevated themselves to the rank of hero before claiming the title of divine-born. Their rise was on the back of chaos and in the wake of vengeance.

Other creatures, known collectively as Veilkith, crept about The Veil. Keeping to darkness and away from the bright clashing of humans who would do anything to assert their dominance, the occasional tale would spread of rogue Veilkiths prowling outside of The Veil, causing havoc and leaving wreckage in their wake. The Veil was growing weak and the tether of travel had begun to lessen. Some had a hunger for the robust world outside of the dream-state timelessness into which they had been born. Some rushed to flee the vicious time-eater, Malotetch, who rumor claimed had become agitated in his fitful slumber and threatened to wake by the omens and signs. Still others enjoyed their attempts to commingle with the human realms. They were entertained by the fragility and mortality of people and made comfortable lives for themselves just far enough from populations to remain largely unnoticed.

It was this very fragility and mortality that made these humans of The Four Holds so unusual and compelling.

We give this land to our children.
To our children, loved and true.
We give this land to our children,
and all the destruction children do.
We have made them, through-and-through.
And we must love them, through-and-through.

For in the wake of chaos,
little children always know:
in dreams live countless ethos
in countless ethos, they may grow.
But, do children wish to grow?
But, will children want to grow?

To the South, the children of fiery Pyrois.
Flickered flames, fierce ablaze.
Across black crag and rigid coast,
across volcanic ash and mineral maze.
The strongest of our children.
Scorched South, they are the strongest of our
children.

To the East, the children of lofty Pegasus.
Cautious clouds, clever wisps.
Atop the gold and orange, Autumnal eloquence,
atop the traps, teeth, and trips.
The proudest of our children.
Windy East, they are the proudest of our children.

*To the West, the children of trickster Unicorn.*
*Seductive stealth, secret minds.*
*Among the vivid forest and flower-crowned newborn,*
*among the poisons and the pines.*
*The cleverest of our children.*
*Fertile West, they are the cleverest of our children.*

*To the North, the children of elegant Hippocamp*
*Hyperborean hearts, hiemal chill.*
*Within the blue belly of the ice-lamp,*
*within the hollowed arms and frozen shrill.*
*The most vigilant of our children.*
*Wintery North, they are the most vigilant of our children.*

*Now here, at our heart, is an ancient foul thing,*
*At our core does the rage beast wake.*
*Recoiling the veil with wide-ranged wing,*
*Suffocation and ash will it make,*
*And shut closed the doors of time,*
*And seal fast our doors of time.*

*-Ballad of the Divine Four. Traditional*

# Chapter I
## *Of Pegasus: Otver's Arrow*

The children of the East, those of Pegasus' care, were nestled aloft the world, in lingered and tethered districts high above an autumnal canopy. The culmination of the land banishing the heat from its face coupled with intricacies of well-engineered blimps, balloons, and anchors were a testament to the ingenuity and needs of the people of the East. The rising heat protected the principalities' upper districts from plummeting while the elevation protected the majority of her people from predators. Shining well above the capital of the East, GoldCloud Castle hovered and from that vantage the Autumn hold was governed by King Voreto of Pegasus, and Queen Etvera, the auburn and fair.

"What infinite foolishness manned your bow, boy? What weakness failed your clutching fingers and let fly that forsaken arrow? Right to the heart of our doom!" The frothing and snarling of the court adviser, Marvis, boomed through the elevated corridors of GoldCloud Castle. A young boy, named Otver, shook and trembled as the old man in dark green robes circled the lad like a hawk. The King and Queen sat upon their golden thrones and watched on with scowls and fear dripping from their silent faces. The matter at hand was a grave one, and deep consternation could not sway the inevitable outcome: it was a crime and as the leaves fall, swirling motions had beset all around GoldCloud, all by a hungry little boy's mistake.

The autumnal East learned within a few generations, eons ago, that life lived under the orange, red, and gold tree canopy would be riddled with hardships and danger. The East was the native home to many predators and would be perilous enough without the push of the North's own large animals. Easterly boars and panthers were often tracked by the bears and wolves of the North, and failing that obstacle to security, raiding parties would commonly encroach from the fiery South. The ingenuity of survival lifted the people, as if on wing, over the majestic trees and to the tips of the mountainous crowns, from which they developed a great skill of watching, waiting, and archery. It was from the tip of an eastern arrow that these hardships began.

"What you've done is treasonous! Do you have any concept of how the people of the glacier will react to this? Of how Bleak Spire will react?" Marvis demanded as if the weeping of Otver enraged him further.

Finally, Queen Etvera, who had come to the sudden hearing with an already heavy heart and loud mind due to unrelated concerns, steadied herself to address the traumatized youth, "What is your age, my boy?"

Otver kept his walnut eyes low and bowed his head deeper at the song of her words, "Eleven, Queen."

King Voreto sunk deeper into his slick and glimmering chair of opulence. No part of the incident was pleasing or easy, two attributes which he valued above all else. His heart grew heavy as mourning threatened to set in. Awarded his crown by the legends of man, he was revered as a descendant of great Pegasus. As the steed fell from the sky in its final mortal death, feathers danced away, and where they landed sprang forth the people of the Eastern hold. The King's ancestors were born of the blood of the beast's broken form. These were the beloved laws of appointment and origin for GoldCloud, older than memory. He was not a poor king, but far less a ruler than his mother had been and fortunate to have found a wife with an administrative mind balanced by a warm heart.

"His youth is not an excuse for this act, my Queen," insisted Marvis, still enraged. "Think what the Queen of the North will think of this boy's age! It will be of no consequence! Should it be? Would it be for you?"

"You rant and shout as if you'd see this boy killed, Marvis," Voreto remarked before offering the youth a sigh. "Boy? Where are your father and mother?"

"I have neither, King," Otver's voice cracked. His hands, weathered and dirty, clenched and rubbed in some faint effort to silence his own dread.

"Who looks after you? Do you live at Ruby Brook?" The Queen quickly asked.

"The orphanage, Ruby Brook, they turned me out when my big sis died. Been a birthday already." The three adults shared glances of anger filled curiosity before Otver continued, "She was gone. She couldn't work. She wouldn't make them coin anymore. They turned me out."

Cautiously, Marvis questioned, "It has no sway on the thing you did that has you here, but, what manner of work did your sister at Ruby Brook? Cooking? Cleaning? What manner of thing did they not find you fit to do? Why turn you out, young man?"

Otver shook his head. Clearly he didn't wish to answer and with the bold petulance of a child, he refused. His reaction made the case against Ruby Brook clear: there had been reports of the orphanage turning out the

8

younger children to make room for the older ones for the purchase of pleasure. The matter was severe and a spur on the sweet Queen's hide. But that matter had to wait till this one met a resolution.

"Tell us what happened, young Otver. Express it to us to make it clear," requested King Voreto, who, aware of his Queen's growing rage at the abuse of the orphanage, became even more eager to quicken the pace.

Otver nodded and wrung at his small hands, "I was alone and under the canopy. I was hunting. I was hungry. All morning I followed a doe deeper and deeper west and deeper and deeper. I watched as the sun led me, through the leaves, deeper and deeper. I came close upon the border of the Kingdom: that point at which on the horizon to the left began the realm of southern fires, and to the right, the white and cold. My sis would read me stories when I was small about that place in the world that a giant-boy could be in three places at once because his arms were long enough. And he would sleep deeply in three holds while the fourth grew nightmares. But where I was, that place, it was the most magic I had ever known and only after a good while did I notice that I had lost the doe. Forward I looked and for some time I watched the swirling black center of the lands, the Veil. I never knew you could look into it. I never knew my eyes would look into it. But I did, and I saw my doe, locked in place, locked in mid-stride: still, like a statue. It gave me fright, such a horrible, deep, dark fright, that I ran. I stopped and looked behind and saw a figure in black and out of fear for what had followed me, I drew my bow and shot."

"How close to the Veil was the Prince of the North when you killed him?" asked Marvis.

9

"I don't know, really. I ran for some time. I thought... I thought he was a thing, come to take me. It had grown dark. He had a hood high and his mouth was covered."

"As is their custom in dress," muttered Marvis spitefully.

"You brought the Prince back here?" softly the Queen questioned.

Otver again lowered his eyes and nodded.

"By yourself? You carried the limp body alone?" the King asked with some pride in the honor and strength of even the most unfortunate of his kingdom. "Prince Edgar was what, twenty years?"

"Twenty-two, my King," Marvis sighed with a dismissal of the importance of the choice made by small Otver to face the crime, body in-tow.

"Do you know that this may start a war, young Otver?" said the King. "What shall we do? What would you do were you faced with this decision? Hide the body? Execute the killer? Celebrate the killer and make them a general: Ice-Slayer? The Steed knows we'll be in need of fighters in the near future. What would you have us do, were you faced with it all?"

"Sire, please. Execute him and send his remains to Bleak Spire with the carefully preserved Prince and be done with it. It is the only way to avoid the worst possible fallout," begged Marvis.

"The boy really is a fine shot, is he not darling King?" chimed the Queen with hopes to add some dignity to Otver's heart. "Tell us, sweet Eastern son, what shall be done with you?"

"I have no coin."

"Bribery will win you no favor," snarled Marvis as he

10

clutched his dark green robe as thunder crashed.

"I would...buy a carriage and bring him back to his family. If I had to say what someone like me ought to do... I would say that would be the right thing," Otver whimpered. "I should not have killed him. I thought he was a monster come to take me to the Veil."

"You? You would return the Prince to his home?" the King asked in amazement as Otver quietly nodded, "Yes, Sir."

"What keeps you from hiding the body and running away?" remarked Marvis, who was quickly interrupted by the impressed and protective Queen.

"A million times that thought must have crossed his mind between the choice to first pick up the dead Prince and the moment he stood before us. The boy did not falter. This act has my blessing. You shall have a horse and a funerary cart. But know this: the scent of a dead prince is just as appetizing and attractive to a bear as the scent of a dead orphan. You may well die next to him whom you shot."

Otver knelt and with all the gratitude his little body could muster, he could find no words of thanks for the decision. Adviser Marvis, vexed and fuming, grabbed the boy up, offered an obedient bow of his head to the King and Queen and was near to departing the great hall of GoldCloud Castle when Queen Etvera lifted a soft, breeze-kissed hand, and with a voice wispy and faraway, demanded, "Hold."

Marvis extended a quickly closing fist and gripped the scruff of Otver's dingy tunic while dutifully turning back from the ivy-arched portal. "Yes, Queen?"

Both the King and Queen had begun to feel, as

individuals and in the very human fashion, the sudden and unavoidable weight of fear and panic over the repercussions of the whole of the tragedy. They both had, in their own way, and largely independent of one-another due to the silence held while the case had been presented, processed the path that led from the terrified orphan, to the orphan that killed a prince, to the probable death of the orphan for his role in every part of the affair. While the King mused on how he would have better preferred honoring the boy for his bravery in honesty and, had it been a war-time, the kill of the oft-enemy of the North would have been an occasion for splendid celebration, the Queen held concerns which ran in other directions in her mind.

Etvera closed one rust-colored eye and with a sweet exhale, withdrew her hand to rest over her heart, and, with measured caution, spoke to that which darkened her soul, "Isobella, the Queen of the North, Queen of the Bleak Spire: I would ask if the boy knows anything of her, but I am certain he does not."

King Voreto stroked his bearded chin while refocusing a knowing gaze of lament down to Otver, who, after receiving a shove from the frowning Marvis, finally remarked, "Um, no, I do not, Queen."

"Queen Isobella is not only as cold and unforgiving as the territory which she, with King Alistair, controls, but also a fiercely protective and deeply attentive mother. She has likely sent parties of Grimms out in search of her beloved second son. You can not go alone, little Otver. Brave Otver, we can not allow this." Her maternal anguish evidenced itself over her creasing features of sorrow.

"I do not know what a Grimm is, my Queen," whimpered Otver as he shook and did his best to stand as tall as possible.

"The Grimms are the royal guard of the North, kind boy," Voreto remarked while dabbing storm-summoned sweat from his brow. "They are to Bleak Spire as The Magpie are to GoldCloud. Young Prince Edgar was, in fact, a Grimm. Has no one taught you these things?" With an exhale he continued while the Queen placed a grip onto his forearm to motion that she had a thing to say, "North: Bleak Spire, The Grimms. West: The Sepal, The Satyrs. South: Tephra Keep, Red Spines. Here, home, East: GoldCloud, Magpies. How have you so aptly avoided such a basic education?" the King concluded.

"Darling King, one wonders what our role in the crime would be should we let this poor child of our own kingdom venture alone?" Etvera's voice was nearly a birdsong.

"Your Majesties are well beyond reproach for the senseless act which robbed Prince Edgar of life. I would not worry with claims of assassination, if effort is made to deliver the royal corpse," Marvis quickly replied. "This is why I have so strongly suggested the execution of this foolish cliff-dweller. It would be a sign of good-faith to deliver to Bleak Spire not only the Prince, but also, the Prince's assailant!"

"You misunderstand the question, Marvis," the Queen quickly corrected with a terse and harsh frown. "You wish the boy to die for the alleged crime, while I wish for him to live. Were he to perish in the act of a journey that the Eastern Crown had set him on, then the Eastern Crown would be guilty of the spilling of his blood.

As we are now, we are but an unhappy observer of a horrid and troubling accident. An accident! Are we a people who issue children death-march orders?"

The King rested his fist into his cheek with a sigh while Marvis stood in silent stupefaction. Otver trembled and badly wished to make sense of any of it while casting an over-shoulder gaze to the gauze covered body of the Prince which lay in the adjoining corridor.

"We are not," Etvera demanded. "The death of a Northern Prince is not worth half of the life of an Eastern pauper. The journey is set. The boy professed to wishing to do that which he felt the right thing to do: it is set. He will travel North, but he will not travel into the North defenselessly. May great Pegasus guide his eyes, for the first Magpie his sight lands upon will be his companion. I decree this. With all the severity of the Queen of the East, I demand this. We will not lose a child of our lands to this mistake made in a sliver of a moment of fear without some belief that we gave him a chance at survival." Her commanding impetus flooded the room and for the smallest of moments, Otver felt hopeful.

"You will have the funerary cart, a fine horse, precious few supplies, a royal missive, and a Magpie. If you should make it to the throne room of Bleak Spire, I do not wish you to admit that it had been you to end the Prince, but I can not, I will not command you to lie. These things you have reported: the doe turning to a statue, and the Prince in our lands, these things are dizzying in their unusual nature. Hardly could top or bottom be made of what to do or how to react. If only The Wanderers, in their constant pilgrimage, were somehow in the lands of the East or the North." She desperately looked to Marvis for some clarification on the status of the guild of scholars, The Wanderers, who orbited the map unhindered, and unvexed, in a perpetual cycle, for the collection of knowledge, legends, and tales.

Marvis, authentically remorseful to disappoint the Queen, shook his head and offered, "They would be leaving the East and entering into the South according to the celestial clock. They could not offer escort for some time. Too much time to preserve the Prince and keep him from his homeland."

Etvera stood and shook her head, "This is as it is, then. Marvis, set aside your incessant hatred for compassion and kindness and outfit the boy as I have instructed. Give the first Magpie he encounters the orders to travel with him, and express that the most fair method of selection was to allow Pegasus to guide his eye. Neither the King nor I would compel such a task. No, nor could we have compelled little Otver to do that which he wishes."

Marvis placed a hand to his chest and lowered his head, "As you wish, Queen."

The King spoke, "And handle the boy more gently from here to there. It may be the last of his homeland he would know. Were times different, and circumstances swayed, I would have you as knight, young man. While likely doomed, this path of yours is admirable. It is an honorable journey. Go with Our love and know that thoughts of you will stay with your King till the end of days. Truly, I wish I had half the stuff you have when I was your age. May the Winged One guide you."

Gracefully, the Queen stood from the golden throne as, like aged leaves, the layers of her warm hued dress rippled and swayed. After a passing thought of decorum, she slightly lifted the hem of the gown and descended the few steps from the royal stage to the ground on which both Marvis and Otver stood.

Marvis drew a step away, aware that the unusual nature of her approach was an event keenly linked to the boy. A thousand matters had he brought before the Crown and none before the one at hand had ever witnessed such a proximity. Almost ashamed to look upon her as she knelt before the boy, Marvis lifted his eyes to the King, who silently observed with an obvious sorrow for both the ill-fate of the child and the heartache of his wife.

Queen Etvera held out both hands and softly clasped at Otver's shoulders, "You are a good boy. You would have made your father and mother very proud. You would have made you sister very proud. I know so few who would claim their mistakes so bravely. And it was a mistake, dear child. We know you meant no harm. You saw a thing that should not have been there. It was a mistake. You are not a killer. You are my champion, and my little hero."

Otver, overwhelmed with honor, fear, amazement, and all other things, sucked in his tears and offered a single nod, as grown-up as he could muster. He tried to speak, but could hardly let escape a strangled crack of a sound.

"There may be a gamble," remarked Marvis toward the King as he continued to give the Queen the respect of space, "There may be a trick to implement to better assist the child."

"Assist the child? Has the Queen lit a candle in your

dark heart?" Voreto sadly chuckled.

"If you require a response to the royal missive, Bleak Spire would be dubious about sending a Northerner; especially if they had the boy and the Magpie killed. Therefore, the only safe option for a return missive is the very messengers with the original news," Marvis claimed while folding his arms in thought.

"Why would they respond at all?" the King asked of Marvis with a renewed interest.

"A response would have to be compulsory. In the spirit of, 'Here is your trespassing son, slain in an accident, our apologies. Truly, it must be a deep hardship, and not an unfamiliar loss to what our own crown has endured with the recent troubles with the Princess, and in parental grief, let us be friends.'"

King Voreto glanced at the shaking head of the Queen before quickly remarking "I do not care for involving the loss of the Princess. The wound is too fresh a thing."

"And I apologize, my King... and my Queen, for my blunt and quick mention of such a dreadful topic, but solidarity and common-ground is the enemy of loss. It could serve to protect the child," Marvis nodded in Otver's direction.

"I fail to see how the response is compulsory, Marvis," the King said while contemplating the proposal.

"That would be the gamble, Sire."

"How so?"

"If the terms are set that a lack of response is an indication that the crime is too deep a cut to overcome, then a war is understood as the only satisfaction the Crown of the North would accept."

"War? You would have us go to war? Were you not,

17

just a handful of moments ago belittling this boy for causing a war? And now you would have us pen a note to declare that 'war would be a reasonable response' and 'we shall sit and await word, and if none comes, await your army?'" Voreto shouted.

"That is the nature of a gamble, my King. That said, I do not think they will go into a war with a Kingdom prepared enough to mention it. Contrarily, I believe that the mere act of mentioning it will serve to greatly reduce the likelihood of both a war and the death of our pair of unfortunate Eastern kin."

"Do you speak honestly, Marvis?" asked the Queen.

"Eternally, my Queen."

"I don't want to be the cause of a war," whined a very troubled Otver.

"Silence!" demanded the King harshly. "Few ever are what they truly wish to be." He drew in a deep breath and looked to the Queen. After unspoken communication, he stood, shaking his head, "It will be decided as I write. I can think no more without a reprise. A messenger will find you with the note, Marvis. Stay with the boy until it arrives." While turning to exit the hall, he extended a summoning hand to the Queen and muttered, "All of this over a trespasser."

# Chapter II
## *Of Unicorn: The Missing Flowers*

The West Hold contained the rolling hills, shining springs, and fertile valleys of the children of Unicorn. The warm western nights were illuminated by fireflies of yellow, green, and blue while the days welcomed the lush growth of flora in carpets of luxury and intrigue. Homes in settlements and villages were built into the trunks of trees and sometimes featured subterranean living areas as well as stairways which spiraled up along the mighty wooden body of the trees to other living quarters. The style of decoration in the West consisted of deep jewel-toned fabrics and rugs, crystals, hanging pendant candle holders of vibrant coloring, the carefully distilled fragrance of floral oils and herbs, an abundance of hammocks and pillows, and the low tables and furniture were often carved right from the wood, in place, as simply part of the natural environment. So clever were the people of the Unicorn that even their forts, manned by The Satyrs, were strategically built over sources of spring-water. Wars of attrition were never winnable affairs when set against the Westerners in their homeland with fresh water and fish always an arm's reach away. The air sang with the scents of rain, soil, and flowers while birds, hare, sheep and butterflies bounded about in the forest mist and the deer-fawns soundly slept in the high ferns.

Amid blankets of poppy, buttercup, hyssop, and narcissus, on a slight meadow knoll, in the carved heart of a grand and mighty tree was situated the seat of power in the Western hold: The Sepal. The complexities of the palace, the etched wood-works and great intertwined braids of the arched passages were the cultural standard expressed by her people. Within everything there was to be an equal division of three: beauty, danger, and enigma. The Sepal boasted an entire set of rooms specifically designed for unwelcome dignitaries: beyond winding corridors were hidden false doors to the exterior of the tree for a steep drop, or bedchambers decorated in flowers which contained succulent yet fatal aromatic poisons. The design was intentional and often echoed in every establishment and home throughout the region.

He sat in the luxurious administrative hall, his two thumbs pressed against the sides of his long, thin nose as he waited. Sighing from nerves and tension, the freshly appointed Prince Regent, Nyseis, grew restless and uncomfortable. He sank his elbows deeper across the wood surface of the meeting table, and rubbed at his face with more groans, while his eyes, dazzling jade and mischievous, pointed his attention to the set of three hanging lamps overhead: a pink one, a blue, and a red.

"They will be along. Shortly, surely. They will be along, my Liege," marked the oldest of the attending group, Honeios, with much anxiety. The Purpureus Council, the administrators of the Crown's will in the West, were a group of five in total. Of those five, three stood around the table where Prince Nyseis sat, awaiting the delayed pair. Honeios, sweating, offered his two colleagues unsure and dissatisfied frowns.

"I was summoned," Nyseis, with a quiet and short tone, remarked.

"Yes, Sir," Honeios replied, shifting his vivid robes

and clasping his boney hands.

"At this hour," the Prince continued with disbelief.

"Yes, Sir. It was made clear that any hour would be acceptable if news of your regal parents came? If we misunderstood..." Honeios sniffled while feigning some subservient apology.

"News? Yes, news I would welcome. Yet, I find it incredible that The Purpureus would call for me while they, themselves, were not already assembled. Is it an amusing thing, Honeios? It is amusing to playact at missing persons in this dark time?"

Unwilling to allow Honeios' jaded tone to speak for the whole of the group, Reileus, a member near in age to the Prince, cleared his throat and interrupted any window of opportunity for the old man to respond, "We have received the same summons as you, Prince Nyseis." His voice was intentionally smooth and comforting. "Messengers brought word that we three, in your company, should await the arrival of both Loritia and Brasios. They are traveling together and left The Satyrs stationed at the fort at Briar Bay hours ago. They will, barring tragedy, arrive very shortly."

The third Purpureus member in attendance took a step into the corridor and removed her gem-hued hood before calling over a servant, "Bring wine and berries for the Prince and Council. And bread as well."

Prince Nyseis directed his voice toward her. "Is this what you understood to be so? That we're to sit and wait for Loritia and Brasios, Mytio?"

"It is as I understand it, yes," Mytio replied with a slight shake of her head. She had spoken against the selection of Brasios in the endeavor to investigate the

21

disappearance of the King and Queen, citing his usual belligerence and incompetence, and quickly assumed that was some of what the Prince had been asking, "I would be very pleased if news comes of your parents, Prince. I would be surprised, and still very tired considering the hour, but very happy."

"I would like to see you happy, Mytio," Prince Nyseis muttered before lowering his hands to the table. "Why have you three not sat? Just sit."

"We were waiting for..." Honeios grumbled while painfully lowering himself into a chair.

Nyseis interrupted, "Yes, I know who we're waiting for. And look, we wait still, even with you sitting."

Lightly, Reileus chuckled while claiming the seat to the Prince's left, "We're not to sit until you tell us to."

"Well, then, you're very welcome," Nyseis, having very little knowledge of how these things worked, remarked flatly.

A young page followed quickly on the heels of a servant who brought in a jug of honey-wine. He nearly tripped when turning into the entrance of the meeting hall while Councilor Mytio lingered unexpectedly in the archway. "Oh! My apologies. I am so... so, I am so...," his labored breath was a struggle to maintain. Clearly, the boy had run some distance in a small amount of time.

With a warmness eclipsed by concern, Mytio recovered quickly and leaned to the page to help him steady himself, "You've caused no harm. Are you alright? Has something happened?" As he heaved and nodded, she directed her request to the servant, "Bring water."

"I have word from Councilors Loritia and Brasios. They...they are close and coming as quickly as they may.

They..."

"Take time to breathe, child. We'll stand a few more moments of delay to see that you're able to speak without fainting," Nyseis proclaimed while pointing to the bread in an indication to Reileus to offer it to the page. "I do hope this news isn't as dramatic as your entrance."

The young boy again nodded while accepting both bread and water. The bread he placed in a pouch which was tied at his hip, but the water he quickly drank, "We work the stables at Briar Bay. In training to serve as Satyr, me and my friend, Caradis. My name is Quamios. Her mother and father, Caradis' parents, I mean, were Wanderers before settling at Thorn Bush, a small village near to the bay."

"Very nice to meet you, young Quamios. Has something happened to your friend or the Councilors?" Nyseis urgently asked. "I am familiar with Thorn Bush, and likely know the parents of Caradis."

Frantically, Quamios shook his head and lifted a hand as if he had gotten embarrassingly off-track, "Councilors Loritia and Brasios tasked both Caradis and me with a job. I was to travel here, to The Sepal as quickly as I could while Caradis shot off for her home. She is trying to catch The Wanderers, who make Thorn Bush a stop on their journey, and ask them to send someone to meet up here with all of the Purpureus and the Prince. They are due to move on to the South, I overheard a Satyr say."

"I say! With what, by the great horn, would we need a Wanderer to assist?" protested Honeios with a slam of his fist to the table.

"Clearly, either Loritia or Brasios, or both, feel there

is a need, Honeios," Nyseis grumbled.

"How did the Councilors seem, young Quamios?" Reileus questioned while leaning toward the exhausted youth.

"Very noble, Sir."

Reileus chuckled and shook his head, his sapphire eyes twinkled as an eyebrow rose in gentle jest, "That was not a trick, little boy. Did they seem...worried? It would need to be a thing very worrisome to send two baby Satyr off into the woods in different directions with messages."

Quamios nodded, then shook his head, again ashamed and embarrassed, "Oh, Sir. Yes, Sir. I misunderstood. They were very worried; it seemed they were frightened by something. Both had their hoods up and to just look at them: they were very pale and I thought sick, until they spoke to me and Caradis. It was clear that something was wrong when they spoke." He chewed at his lip and glanced around the room to take in the alarm and dread. With hopes to ease some of the growing tensions before leaving, he stood and commented, "The path from Briar Bay to Thorn Bush is a short one, I'm sure someone will be along soon. So will the Councilors, they only sent me to run ahead of them to explain why a Wanderer would turn up."

"We will remember the names: Caradis and Quamios," smiled Reileus. "Once we've all had a good night's rest, we'll send along good word to Briar Bay to praise how well the two of you helped the Purpureus Council, The Prince Regent, and all of the West."

The three counselors and the Prince offered the boy the most silent and false of smiles while holding their hurricane thoughts muted until the awkward boy had exited and traveled a good distance down the corridor.

"What kind of trick is this?" demanded Honeios. "What are those two up to?"

"I knew they couldn't do it. Loritia would have been better partnered with an alligator. If she failed, then it was surely because of Brasios' bumbling!" chided Mytio.

Nyseis sunk deeper and deeper into despair, "Involving the Wanderers... Something is clearly wrong."

"It could just be an inquiry, Prince. Perhaps Loritia and Brasios wish to know if they've seen anything, or heard anything about the King and Queen?" Reileus offered.

"So frantically?" questioned Nyseis skeptically. "With such a panic as to think of it only as they are to depart our lands?" Prince Nyseis' handsome features, fine and unusual, while attractive and personable, melted into a hopeless and distraught frown. "The Wanderers have been in our realm for three full moons. It was the one before this last that found no King or Queen return from a hunting party. Of what number, Honeios, do you know? How many were in the King and Queen's entourage in total?"

"Sixteen, Prince Nyseis," Honeios quietly grumbled.

"Sixteen! Sixteen western bodies, including the two crowns never came home! Sixteen of Unicorn's beloved are...what? Lost? In their own homeland? Lost? Twenty-nine horrible days and nights have I thought that the next day would see the guffawing fat face of my drunken father through the throne room doors. And now, so suddenly there is a need to involve a departing troupe?"

Loud and serious footfalls approached as the glistening lamps overhead flickered and danced. The

Prince narrowed his eyes while glancing to Mytio; he felt interrupted by the sound, he had much more to say on the topic, but instead sighed and sulked.

Around the corner came first the middle-aged and bulky Brasios followed by like-aged and far smaller Loritia.

"By the horn and hooves, the show that preceded your arrival was a spectacle. I do hope the news you bring is less foreboding than the news that a Wanderer has been summoned to this illustrious hall?" Honeios remarked with an exhausted whine of antiquity. "Come and have some wine. If it is either too late or too early, the fault for that is yours alone." With a nod he indicated toward the prism-cut crystal carafe of purple liquid, but did not make any motion to pour.

"Are your mistresses unable to keep each other company, old Honeios?" Gruff Brasios questioned as he reached to the table to take up a chunk of bread. "Those little Satyrs, they're due commendations."

"We met the boy just as he was leaving. Thought better of letting him venture back to Briar Bay till morning and so had him put up in the kitchens for the night," Loritia mentioned while removing the hood of her ruby colored cloak and letting loose her hair of wild golden locks. Her face read of severity which made the flippancy of Brasios' false mirth all the more evident.

Still sulking and glaring, Prince Nyseis groggily proclaimed, "You would have a Satyr sleep in a kitchen, Loritia? They are the Royal Guard, not the royal dogs."

"We were keen to find a quick solution, Highness. The boy had done more than enough."

"The boy? His name is Quamios. I wonder how he

26

would be awarded his commendations if his name is a forgettable one." Nyseis shook his head and lifted his open palms from the table top. "This is all neither here-nor-there. I'm obviously woefully ignorant of the way in which things go around here. So, I'll just sit here and continue to wait for someone who could offer any ray of insight as to why my ass is in this uncomfortable chair at all rather than in bed. Apparently, that savior will be a Wanderer?"

Reileus, with his legs crossed and arms draped to the side smiled at the Prince and while moving little else, extended a hand to the Prince's wine and carefully inched it closer as if it would help with Nyseis' obvious discomfort and dissatisfaction.

"In truth we have much to report but would rather wait until the Wanderer arrives, yes. These matters are...I have no words for what I feel these matters are. But a Wanderer should assist and a retelling is not something I care to ever have to do," Loritia offered while sitting at the table. "I apologize, Prince Nyseis. It is well known how long you've waited for word on the King and Queen. It is also well known that the position that their absence puts you in is not at all a desirable one for you. We here at the Purpureus understand and want you to know that we are steadfast in our fidelity to the hold and to you."

With a scoff and a faint chuckle, Nyseis began a retort, "That is so comforting in an absolutely condescending and smug fashion. You do know you have that way about you, yes, Loritia?"

Quietly, a young woman peeked into the room from the corridor. Prince Nyseis, and the Purpureus Councilors Reileus and Honeios were situated facing the entrance and were among the first to see her. Her bright gray eyes and shining black hair marked her as a daughter of the wintry North, but her pale skin decorated nearly completely with inked swirls, patterns, and runes identified her clearly as a Wanderer. She wore the customary gray cloak, black mid-shin trousers, tunic shirt, and boots. "There was no door on which to knock," she softly apologized.

Prince Nyseis stood and bowed his head to her entrance. While Westerners were a scheming sort, they were never short on suspicions for others. But The Wanderers were an ancient and honored guild. They were a border-less tribe: the keepers of the myths and legends. As much as he disliked involving a Wanderer in a Western affair, he was in awe of her presence. "I am the Prince Regent. Please, sit. Have a drink."

She smiled and offered a slight nod to the Purpureus members before speaking as she sat, "My name is Morigan. We received word that your Council requests assistance?"

"Forgive the hour, Morigan," Mytio requested while offering a glass of wine.

"Not at all. We were sharing drink and smoke and making merry. You disturbed nothing." She pleasantly received the wine with a kind nod. "On what may I assist? The child - oh, she's a delight, have you met her? Caradis, I believe her name was Caradis. Excellent girl, good family, too! – Caradis mentioned that those who sent her seemed gravely concerned and insisted that someone hurry along. I was not sleeping, or drunk, or in the middle of any grand tale or anything, and so here I am. What seems to be the matter, my Western friends?" Her lively and charming ways struck the room silent for some time. "Does the matter relate to the King and Queen?"

"How did you know?" asked Reileus.

She laughed softly, "What greater matter could possibly be afoot in your realm? Missing what now? Thirty days?"

"Twenty-nine," Nyseis quietly lamented. "What do you know of this? Have you heard anything?"

"I have heard what any have. The full-moon festival before this most recent they left with a hunting party of fourteen others. None have been found or heard from. I tell you, your people are talking of scarcely else."

Old Honeios, full of schemes and curiosity, leaned to the Wanderer of Northern descent and questioned, "What have you heard about the Prince? What do the people say?"

Surprised and disgruntled by the inquiry, Nyseis scoffed while remarking, "What? What a silly thing!" Uncomfortable with nervousness, he glanced to Brasios and noticed the large man intentionally swallowing massive amounts of wine as if to steady himself: the facade of calm confidence was clearly taxing to uphold.

"While it may well be pertinent to this matter which we have before us, I doubt any Wanderer would feel comfortable discussing something so clearly tangential," Reileus quickly remarked. For as severely as Honeios wanted a thing verbalized, Reileus seemed to stand on the opposite end. "Unless I've been mistaken and The Wanderers have gone into the business of espionage? Informing the Capital on her people's whims seems at odds with the role of the esteemed scholar."

Morigan traced her thumb over a swirl of skin ink on

her wrist. Her demeanor had shifted slightly from jovial to concerned over the possibility of finding herself ensnared by a conspiracy. "Commonly, we do not advise any ruler of the Four Holds. This is so." She found that the Western people seemed to feel generally in favor of the Prince Regent and had developed a closeness to his recent suffering as they too suffered the uncertainty surrounding the loss of their King and Queen. But as sympathetic as many of them were, they were still the children of Unicorn, and the inheritors of the natural scheming suspicions of the spring-lands.

The Prince was viewed by all as a radiant and ethereal beauty, but while some held that his beauty was echoed in the sorrow over the disappearances, others maintained that only a true heir to the Unicorn's throne could so flawlessly and viciously claim rule in such a way. The blood-spilled down the line of succession that he was born into, the legacy of his pedigree was a diabolical one. His father had poisoned the previous King and Queen with finely crafted tea made of datura, hen-bane, nightshade, mandrake, and hemlock. His grandmother, the Queen that his father dispatched, had only a mother, as her father died valiantly in the Ash War when she was a small child. That Queen's mother succumbed to starvation or asphyxiation after having been the victim of a mysterious immurement. The skeletal remnants of Prince Nyseis' Queen Great-Grandmother remain locked within whatever dark place claimed her, as her daughter never admitted to where in the vast castle the imprisoned had been hidden. There was a commonplace acceptance in the West-lands of appointment by murderous means and particularly complicated conspiracies were often the thing of legends and songs, but on occasion the thirst and ambition managed to skip a generation. Many truly believed that Prince Nyseis had too little desire to rule to have ever harmed the King and Queen whom he loved so dearly.

The people knew him well. Many more nights than not, Nyseis would travel to various villages or outposts in pursuit of pleasures. He would frequent inns, taverns, festivals, or small stage arenas where actors and musicians ply their art. He was approachable, handsome, and as liberal with his coin as he was with choice of bed-mates. The bards likened his personality to honey while simultaneously praising the choice of nature to find men unfit to carry children, as 'If Nyseis had his due, a generation from you, all of the West would call him Father-Horn.' Indeed, even the speculation of what new western baby best resembled the Prince was regular daily village gossip.

Morigan shifted and shook her head. Much of these things were known to her but she remained steadfast, "It truly is not the role of a Wanderer to serve as the eyes and ears of a crown. This Purpureus is correct," she nodded toward Reileus with a thankful smile.

"Far more important things are on the air than how well the Prince is adored, Honeios. What a waste of time!" Mytio demanded.

Nyseis shook his head, keeping a good deal of his attention locked on the clearly troubled pair: Loritia and Brasios. "Leave it off, Mytio. Poor Honeios is tired and is known to drift into the absurd when made to work so late. Brasios? Loritia? Are we all, Wanderer Morigan included, here for a purpose, or were you both just in need of a lavish welcome-home party after your arduous investigation?"

"Were it only so," sighed Loritia, also in the act of drinking more than her usual.

"You are both so troubled. And to summon one of my kind, there must be grave concerns," remarked Morigan. "How may I best help?"

The chin on broad Brasios dimpled as he drew his lips into a tight frown with a shake of his head. His eyes locked to the glimmer of the dangling lights reflected in the wine he held.

"Shall I tell this tale?" quietly, like a dirge, asked Loritia. By the pale and sick scowls, the room knew that the news could be nothing but tragedy.

Brasios, with a single shake of his head lifted his eyes to Nyseis and quietly began, "I've never liked you, Nyseis. You shirk and laze and are a shadow to the might that is your father, my friend...my friend."

The other Purpureus Councilors were clearly disturbed by the terse way in which Brasios spoke to Nyseis, but calmed and kept silent as the Prince showed no reaction beyond a nod to indicate that he was listening intently. Morigan's gaze shifted between Brasios to Nyseis and she grew quietly impressed while keenly observing.

Brasios' dismay grew, "We, Loritia and I, had gone to many villages to find word of the lost hunting party. Many. After turning up nothing more than speculations, we decided to turn our attention to the forts and question The Satyrs, as they have been on constant patrol over the matter since the disappearance. We were led to Briar Bay, where there had been a reported sighting of the royal group."

"I will do this if you wish, Brasios. There is no need for you to -" Loritia began before Brasios interrupted with a raised hand and continued with tears in his eyes, "A figure, very much like that of your father, the King, was witnessed four nights back and then again two nights later. He wandered the fields with not a stitch to cover his body. His royal crown had been discarded, or stolen, but replaced with a reed-twist crown with a long horn fashioned from the point above his forehead. He was alone, and when unaware of eyes upon him, would hum and sing what they report as the most melancholic of tunes while kneeling and stripping bush branches bare of leaves and berries to eat. One Satyr approached and got only close enough to note that his eyes were nearly full pupil before the King, with a speed that shocked The Satyr, vanished into a thicket."

"The King lives?" Honeios croaked with a hopeful tone.

"Was there truly no sign of anyone else?" questioned Mytio.

The questions swirled throughout the room while Loritia and Brasios offered little in return aside from shrugs, head shakes, and frowns. Nyseis' sparkling green eyes fixed a gaze to the tabletop as he trembled with fear and grew dark in thought.

Morigan listened to the torrent of words while she watched Nyseis who sat in some isolated den of grief and dread, as if in the eye of a hurricane. Her arms folded and with myriad deductions in play, she silently contemplated.

"You're not understanding. He was...not himself,"

33

demanded Loritia, heartsick by the optimism.

An off-comment suddenly caught Morigan's attention. Reileus happened to ask of Brasios, "What of The Satyr that saw him? The one who approached, causing the King to flee? Why did you not bring him here?" To which, Brasios quietly replied, "He's sick."

"Sick?" Quickly, over the voices of the others, and with urgency, asked Morigan. "Sick, you say?"

Brasios nodded while surprised that he had been heard or that whatever he had said mattered at all. "Sick. Yes."

"In what way is this Satyr sick?" pressed Morigan.

Brasios frowned, sighed, and indicated a request for Loritia to explain, as the weight of the whole of it finally caused him to rest his aching body against a curved wall.

"He is sick. I don't quite understand what you're asking or what it has to do with anything," Loritia remarked. "The ordeal clearly drained him of his health. To see a King like that, by a member of the royal guard, can not be a simple thing."

"Why am I here, then?" Demanded Morigan finally, annoyed that the things she found important seemed happenstance to the others.

"We have many poisons in our realm, Wanderer," began Loritia with a harsh tone in response to Morigan. "We know of none that would rob a king of his mind."

"Nonsense. You, here in the West, are masters of all manner of poisons that could rob anyone of their mind. King or cobbler. Speak truth, or I will leave."

"You would leave?" asked Mytio, ignorant of the reason for the sudden shift on the Wanderer's part.

"You know there is a connection between this sick

34

Satyr and the King," Morigan insisted. "If no connection had been detected, I see no reasonable explanation for the choice to send for me. You called me here. Why lie and obfuscate that which provoked you to summon me in the first place?"

*****

*They are dark, my son.*
*They are dark, they are dark.*
*They will find you, son.*
*With the bites and the bark.*
*They are dark, my son,*
*They are dark, they are dark.*

*They are cold, my daughter.*
*They are cold, they are cold.*
*They are ice, my daughter.*
*All the fear of the Holds.*
*They are cold, my daughter,*
*They are cold, they are cold.*

*I away, my love.*
*I away, I away.*
*To the snows, my love.*
*There I stay, there I stay.*
*One has found me alive,*
*Dead I stay, dead I stay.*

*-The Song of The Grimm. Eastern Folk Song,*
*Vivienne Oakfox*

# Chapter III
## *Of Pegasus: The First Magpie He Sees*

Marvis shoved little Otver onto The Great Stretch, the chain-and-pulley lift system which connected the majesty of GoldCloud Castle to the cliff-town dwellers below. He took a deliberately careful step on only after Otver had caught his balance, before waving to the machinery operator to lower the cage. The night sky rumbled and flashed as the storm lingered on the horizon. "Do bid the clouds farewell, boy. This may be the end of clouds for you."

"I thought you were told to outfit me?" Otver argued as his vision, like wide-winged eagles, soared across the moon-kissed and rain-drip-dropped tree-tops of the Eastern hold. A breath caught in his throat while the glimmering orange of his homeland seemed to sway for him: a dance before weeping. His eyes, the color of mud, began to flood.

"A funerary cart? Do you see room in this little box of an apparatus for a funerary cart? No, everything you'll need will be all along the shop districts and stables on the cliff. It may be possible to gather up all you need at the stables alone. We should try there first, I imagine." Marvis paused the pinching and twirling of his own tawny mustache and, with an eyebrow raised, asked curiously, "Are you crying?"

The small orphan nodded with a deep sniffle. "Why?"

Aghast, Otver's voice cracked and trembled, "Why?

Why wouldn't I be crying?"

"And why would you be?"

His shoulders slumped as he turned away and again looked to the trees as they continued the descent to the cliffs, "It doesn't matter. If you had your way, I'd be dead by now."

"This is true," Marvis admitted with a nonchalant flip of his hand. "You would be dead and Prince Edgar would have been burnt and all possible evidence of this dilemma would have been singed at the roots."

"If you would have gotten rid of the Prince, then why would I still have to die?"

"The very knowledge of the event means you would have to die, my boy. Being orderly means being tidy."

Otver sullenly grumbled, "I guess I'm lucky you're not in charge, then."

"The way in which you are fortunate is in my loyalty and obedience! Truly, I ought to throw you off The Great Stretch for all the trouble you've caused." Marvis' laugh was, in many ways, quite warm albeit rather sinister. He sighed and pulled his robes closely around his body as the wind picked up. "The body, which we will henceforth refer to as 'the cargo' for sake of keeping this whole tragedy quiet, will arrive bundled when a messenger brings down the royal missive. We'll put it straight on the cart and you and whatever unhappy Magpie Pegasus wishes to curse with your quest will be off."

"I don't think I need any help."

"What you think is immaterial. You will need help. The King and Queen, especially the Queen, are set on it," Marvis remarked before taking a few breaths and restating with a quiet severity, "You will need help,

Otver."

Slightly amazed at the show of concern, Otver moved to change the topic, "What happened to the Princess?"

"What?" Marvis was unprepared for the question. He raised a thin finger to Otver's face while his voice hushed and hissed, "You are not to speak of that."

"Well, it's only that you made it sound like she died. And the King and Queen..."

"You are not to speak on it. No one knows for good reason. Matters are being looked into and the entire thing could get complicated if it is known that she was found."

"Found? Dead?"

"Your curiosity is shifting my mind back to my first choice of shoving you to your doom." He groaned after noticing that they were nearing the end of the ride: there was not enough of a drop to cause any real damage to the boy. The slow moments that spanned between Marvis' groan and the actual end of the decline found the crotchety adviser offering forth a single hushed and dour morsel, "Princess Lavinia was found dead. She was found in a pond, just outside of Falcon's Perch. Do you know where Falcon's Perch is?"

Grieved, Otver shook his head, "I've never been."

Marvis rushed a whisper, "It's a border-town, boy. A small settlement near the border to the Ice Hold: the North. The very moment the discovery was made, the fact that she had no reason to be anywhere near Falcon's Perch told me that the Northerners had a thing or two to do with it. Lacking any true evidence, the King and Queen are unwilling to believe such a thing could have been done. But I know a thing, Otver. I know a thing: a secret entrusted to me. There may well have been cause for the

North to wish harm to the Princess." The base of the lift shook as it finally met with the ground. Marvis continued, "Speak of this to no one." He took a few quick steps before suddenly stopping and turning to Otver with open hands, "Expect that any Magpie would want to make a stop at Falcon's Perch."

"For clues?"

"For anything. Although, I don't know how wise it would be to stop at a settlement with the cargo, but once you leave the comfortable confines of the capital, what I find wise rarely translates. My preferences tend to travel poorly."

Otver followed along behind Marvis, listening to the somewhat frenzied words with a slight preoccupation. His thoughts of sudden and recent woes drifted slightly out-of-focus. He considered that the King and Queen were freshly in mourning and he thought of the pain that swallowed him when his own sister died. The breeze carried the familiar scents of drying herbs, roasting boar, and bonfire smoke, and he realized that he had already begun to think of his home in the East as a memory. His mind swam with more nostalgia than any little boy should have as his own while his thoughts grew louder and more panicked. He watched children, some slightly older than he, run and play before making wide-turning routes back to their loving families. It was as if he and the whole world that he had ever known were set on saying good-bye to each other, even those parts of the world that had eluded him: the warm meals, the family, the calm.

Marvis, who had taken to grumbling to himself about the short-sightedness and limitations of all the minds around him, abruptly stopped his progression with an urgent pallor. Ahead of them, around a linen shop and inn, stood Valé Birchbark, the Captain of The Magpies, involved in some light and courteous conversation. Birchbark was invaluable to the East's cohesion and security and, as Marvis could neither afford nor permit losing him to the menacing weight of Otver's sentence, he turned to face the boy to strike up a conversation, "You've not traveled much, have you?"

"Traveled?" Otver responded to the curious nature of the sudden concern on Marvis' part.

"Gone out? Seen the world?"

"Most time I've been away from the capital, I've been under the canopy camping and hunting."

With a squinting left eye, Marvis continued, "Poaching, more like."

"I was well away from any city, or anything."

Just as Marvis shifted a glance over his shoulder to note the location of Birchbark, a loud celebratory shriek from the stables off to their left caught both his and Otver's attention.

"What was that?" questioned Otver as he began a slow trek in the direction of the ruckus.

Relieved that the commotion drew the pair away from Birchbark, Marvis claimed an eager interest in following the noise to the source and with impatient nods, ushered the boy toward the stables.

In the dark of the evening, the only illumination beamed from a back corner of the horse stables. The bulk of the livestock were kept on a lower cliff, but the upper-stables were specific for diplomats, nobles, or Magpies and designed for the convenience of housing the horses in close proximity to their own lodgings. Horses were dearly cherished by the people in all of Four Holds as sacred animals, the reflection of their divine beings, to journey through life as close companions. Even the poorest of the people did all they could to procure a single horse for the family before that horse could breed to supply their future generations and family relations. It was a matter of tremendous importance.

Otver watched as a woman with wide sorrel colored curls knelt over a like-colored horse. Her face was saturated with tears of joy, excitement, compassion, and care. She would lay her cheek against the exhausted horse's head and whisper; Otver finally noticed there was a newborn foal just to her side. His eyes grew wide as he welcomed the happiness of the event.

The woman smiled up to Otver before noticing Marvis, who had turned to a profile to accept a rolled parchment from a royal messenger. Her joy began to melt as concern rooted itself into her mind. She could think of no reason for Adviser Marvis to be down from the clouds unless on important business. Reluctantly standing, she brushed away golden hay from her dark brown and sepia leather armor and reached to the stable gate to claim her dark green hooded cloak. Unlucky just after one of her greatest joys, she was the first Magpie that Otver's eyes met.

"Eileivia Morninglight," Marvis' voice was relieved and cold, "you have a mission, my lady."

"Is this about the find at Falcon's Perch?"

"It is not."

Eileivia shook her head in dire protest, "Forgive me Adviser, but Windwing just gave birth."

"And who is Windwing?" Haughtily, Marvis tilted his

head.

With a perplexed frown over the obviousness of the scene behind her, she opened a hand and turned to indicate to the horse and foal. "My mare."

"You'll need to prepare to travel tonight."

"She'll need at least ten days to recover, Sir. And I can't separate her from her colt."

"We'll see that she is well cared for."

Eileivia stood in silent heartache and searched the ground for words.

"Is she a Magpie?" Otver asked sadly.

"She is," Marvis nodded offhandedly while turning to the messenger with a rambling verbal list of what to bring back to the stables.

Otver interrupted Marvis somewhere between 'heavier cloak' and 'water', "I can't let her go with me."

"Go with you?" Eileivia quietly asked.

"You haven't a choice, boy. Pegasus chose her." He turned to Eileivia with annoyance, "You're to journey with this boy to the castle at Bleak Spire. They may want to kill him. The Queen would like it very much if they did not."

"What?" Eileivia demanded in shock. "Pegasus chose me?"

"The Queen remarked that Pegasus should guide his eye to the right Magpie."

"To the North? Into the North?" The Magpie stammered, in full belief that Pegasus had either been sleeping or having a joke. She looked back to her horse and the newborn and frowned, not at all pleased with the task, "What business does a little boy have with Bleak Spire, Adviser?"

Marvis, completely past any desire to stay on the cliffs longer than necessary, leaned close to Eileivia and spitefully whispered, "He killed Prince Edgar. You two will take the Prince home. In moments, all you will need will be brought along by that messenger I just sent off. This missive is to be delivered to the Queen and King." He slammed the rolled parchment into her open hand. Vexed by her sullen frown, he then demanded, "What?! The cart will have a horse!"

Otver looked to Eileivia with apology and shame. Barely could he keep his eyes anywhere near meeting hers: gold-flecked brown, like a leaf fire.

Furious and hurt, Eileivia shoved the parchment into a pocket in the lining of her cloak before turning to say good-bye to Windwing and her new baby. She wept from the sorrow of parting with Windwing and from the disturbing news of the Prince but understood duty and as such, lifted her bow and daggers which had been setting on a stool in the corner.

"I'm sorry," Otver whispered, lacking anything else to say.

The Magpie said nothing in response and clenched her teeth while watching a cart come down the path toward them. On the cart were burlap bags, pottery filled with water, and a single long thin bundle which appeared very much like an incredibly carefully rolled rug. On the bench seat were a bundle of leathers and furs. Eileivia looked to the old gelding and sighed. "What is he called?"

"Whatever you wish," Marvis remarked before dismissing himself.

"Get on," she demanded of Otver while pointing to the bench. "Those furs are for you, I suppose." She looked over her shoulder to Windwing and held a glance for a moment before speaking to her mare, "This eunuch is going to take us north. I want that colt fat and happy when I get back." She tested a smile but didn't have the heart to hold it before lifting herself into the cart and taking the reins into her gloved hands.

"I'm so sorry," Otver repeated.

Quietly, Eileivia replied, "Say that again and you'll make the trip in the back with the other lad."

# Chapter IV
## *Of Hippocamp: Siblings*

White was the land of the North Hold: cold, quiet, and white. Nearest to the borders of the Spring lands of the West and the Autumn lands of the East, the skeletons of ancient trees, long since turned to stone, loomed and sneered at the approach of any wayward traveler. A quick incline of snow drifts described that the climate was, as if divided by an invisible wall, not a thing defined by its neighboring Holds. Hot springs would glow an eerie blue and pock the white snow while the quiet of the land was like death itself: desolate, lonely, frigid. It was vicious, while soft. Dark, while illuminated. Foreboding, yet embracing. It was a place that was home to a people as equally feared as admired.

Much of the habitation in the North took place underground. Deeper to the center of the land, and the area nearest the coast, the opening of establishments and homes would be marked by the presence of grand ice statues. Where the air bit the least, to the East, West, and South-Central of the Hold, marking statues of harsh granite would stand. Unlike the Holds to either side of the North, this Hold had no graveyards. Rather, they interred the dead in memorial semi-subterranean structures as their custom when honoring the deceased. Villages were spread with outposts strategically placed between, and The Grimms would patrol the carefully worn paths which connected all of Hippocamp's followers to the capital at Bleak Spire.

It was a sunken and inverted cathedral of ice set within a fortified city. The Castle at Bleak Spire welcomed few foreigners onto her spiral stairs and long corridors. While the fiery South Hold had eons of separation from the other holds out of hostility, the West from suspicion, and the East from caution, the North Hold maintained their isolation in equal part due to the inhospitable and difficult landscape as well as the inhospitable and difficult natives. They were pleased to enjoy segregation, and as with most in the Four Holds, they had grown complacent in apathy and conceit.

There had been a time when trade and diplomacy thrived across the land. Ages ago, cross-regional cooperation found the people of Pegasus craving for spices from the West, or Northern Royals commissioning statues, weapons, and tools with the minerals and ore of Pyrois' South. People would celebrate more than their own kind, and marriages between the Holds were common. But a few misplaced choices in a few misplaced moments changed all of it and the people, injured and heartsick, went to war. For a time, mutually beneficial Holds would pair themselves against the others before tiring of the spent alliances and turning on their former confederates, like ants on a butterfly.

The last major conflict began as a thief from the East stole and distributed documents that were found in the King's Treasury in the South. The letters were allegedly written by a dignitary from the North about a concern over a conspiracy for the West to poison the water supply near the veil. From starvation, sickness, exposure, and from all the other ills of upheaval, many people died in the long struggles that followed. The end found the North isolated with the whole of the world against them. The Grimms were evolving and adapting to the new demands of a single force alone. They would strike war camps at night: icy, shadowed and terrifying. They learned to domesticate wolves and used them to herd bear into their enemies. But the most distinguishing technique developed from the disadvantage of being a surrounded and isolated force for a long duration was the newly acquired skill of a solitary Grimm to snap off from a larger unit, at any time, and wield incredible prowess and precision as a single warrior before seamlessly falling back into the weave of the greater whole. The war against the North created the terror that went on to haunt the dreams of every generation that followed while the Eastern thief that triggered it all saw his granddaughter, King Voreto's ancestor, take the throne as the bride to the blood of Pegasus. At his death, the one-time thief and father to a queen admitted that the whole scheme had been a ruse to crush the West. Relations had barely improved since.

In silence, King Alistair Aquilo sat upon his stone throne under a swooping canopy of bear skins and sheer white fabrics as long crystals dangled overhead like icicles. He watched the back of his hands, aged and wrinkled, as he gripped at the fur which draped over his legs. Of his two wolves, one sighed and one yawned. They had a lifetime of awareness: the King had always been a troubled man. His storm–gray eyes blinked and searched a blue stone on his ring, as if some deep meaning had been locked away there, in secret, in darkness. With a hushed whisper, a wind sailed down from the top of the castle, far above and away and swished past his cheek in such a way that pin-prick goose bumps raised under his ebony beard. He took a breath in and let his sorrow flood over his mind. Although usually melancholic, something set against his heavy brow with a magnitude sudden and worrisome. While obscured by mystery and uncertainty, some grave thing was afoot; some sad thing was on the air.

The King was purposeful in his loneliness. He avoided others and shied from interaction or contact of any kind. Pained and assumed mute, he served his realm well, having given the Hippocamp Queen six fine dynastic offspring: three princes and three princesses. The subjects of the North viewed him as aloof and powerful and, as Queen Isobella was so particular and beloved, if she chose him, then they unquestioningly accepted the choice. He was adrift in his own thoughts, and those thoughts, although brilliant, were rarely cheerful.

The assertive and magnificent voice of Queen Isobella grew slowly in volume as she descended the main spiral stairs in the reception atrium beyond a large set of double-doors across from the raised stage on which the thrones sat. At first, the voice was only distinguishable as being hers, but soon-there-after, the King could comprehend the matter on which she spoke. His attention fixed itself on the chime-sound of her words; both wolves raised their chins from the ground and also listened with intent. The Queen monopolized the bulk of the verbal communication while he with whom she spoke made occasional, brief responses. The heavy boots and tone of the voice settled in the King's mind that she was approaching with a son, either Edgar or Horatio from the tenor. Closely, he listened to her continue for better clarity.

"...and she said that it had been a thing found some ways near to Sorrowmore. When I asked why she even picked it up, why that would seem like a wise thing to do, she began to cry!"

"Of course she did, Mother."

"Well, what are we to tell your Father? You know I dislike it when you shrug."

"I truly have no insight, Mother."

"She insists on keeping the thing!"

"I would not think that wise."

Horatio, in the black armor of a Grimm commander, opened the door before stepping out of his mother's path with a bow to his father. "Blessings of The Gill upon you, Father. Your wife, the Queen, my Mother, is quite vexed." He was warm in his smugness.

King Alistair offered his son a slight smile with a slow blink while standing to receive the Queen to the throne stage with an open hand and a bow of his head.

While taking the King's hand with measured affection, Queen Isobella, tall, thin and covered in the customary white royal gowns of the North, remarked with disgust, "Your daughter found an ermine and wishes to keep it as a pet."

The King, with a bushy eyebrow raised, looked to Horatio for clarification while the Queen sat, smoothing her long black hair over her shoulder in exasperation.

"Eleonora," Horatio explained while folding his arms and leaning against a pillar. "Mother said she was off traipsing around Sorrowmore, found a little ermine and decided fate had reached down and chosen her for the thing's mother."

Of the Northern royal children, Horatio was the eldest at twenty-four. A couple of years his minor was the presumed alive-and-well Prince Edgar, who was four years older than the first born Princess, Eleonora. Hector had just turned sixteen and was ten years older than the twin princesses: Imogen and Isolde. Horatio was due to inherit the throne when his parents either perished or retired and as such, had been granted the role of High Commander as a Grimm. Edgar was a well-loved officer and their sister, Eleonora had threatened to run off to join The Wanderers if she were compelled to join the royal guard. Hector, having recently come of age, was eager to serve the illustrious order as soon as he could initiate.

It was on the business of collecting Hector that Horatio arrived at Bleak Spire. He had been due to arrive at the main Grimm fortification at Dark Tower days ago in the company of his brother Edgar. As Horatio lived at Dark Tower, he grew secretly concerned when neither word nor brothers turned up and, unwilling to dishonor his irresponsible brother, he decided to travel home under the guise that it had been the plan all along. He had not yet brought himself to ask after Edgar since arriving in the capital, but noticed no one acting strangely or concerned, and so continued to avoid the possibility of causing alarm.

"A filthy ermine!" Queen Isobella demanded the conversation continue.

The King, with a quiet chuckle, shook his head.

"As much as I would love to impress upon you that you may be overreacting, Mother, I am sorry to agree with you." While removing his gloves he indicated up to the King, "What say you, Father?"

King Alistair rolled his eyes and with a shrug, seemed amused, but uninterested.

"Ah! The King favors the Princess' stance! Father, I have to say: in defense of my Mothers' clear and immovable preference, those little weasels are vicious. They have been known to kill for sport!"

"This is hardly the pet for the Princess!" insisted the Queen.

"No, hardly the pet for the Princes. But, for Eleonora..." Horatio had seemed to begin to change his mind.

"What?!"

"I do not know," Prince Horatio opened his hands with a laugh, "I am not her parent, nor am I her King or Queen. This is not up to me."

"One day you shall be!"

"That day is not today, Mother."

"Were it today, what would you say to her?"

He thought for the slightest of moments before proceeding, "If she wishes to keep an ermine as a pet, then I would permit it. All creatures deserve someone to love them, even a weasel. And that weasel won the love of a Princess! Hippocamp kissed it!"

"And if it should bite your sister? Then what?"

"Then, Mother, she is bit. She would be bit and never trust another ermine again. The lesson teaches itself and she would have a lovely new pelt." Horatio, having far greater things than an orphaned ermine to occupy his mind, offered his usual charming and effortless grin while bowing as the King applauded.

Queen Isobella, under the impression that her

concerns were being mocked, applied a gelid frown and stern gaze toward her son, "How lightly you must view this inane scant thing. How absurd and foolish for me to assume to burden either of you great men with such a trivial and simple thing. Why, this must be but a seashell to the ocean of your own woes and responsibilities."

"It is but a pet, Mother," softly, Horatio nearly whined in response. While she spoke some truth to his disinterest of the ermine, he did not wish to commit to verbal conflict with the Queen and so, with a pair of extended hands, he added, "Clearly, this is a matter of deep importance to the Queen, and thus the whole of the Hold." He had not intended his words to ring quite so flippantly and as he witnessed her angered expression extend, he continued in hopes of limiting the damage, "The well-being of the Princess is a true matter, Mother. Her happiness pales to her safety. I understand."

"You think I wish her unhappy?" The Queen was unwilling to allow her son's appearance of a cavalier response to thrive unchallenged.

With a lift of his pale and angled chin, Horatio leaned his weight to his left leg and held his hands behind his back with a slight huff. He searched the face of his stoic father for any hint of assistance and when none was found there, he looked down to the pair of wolves. Having used the time of observation to contemplate, he finally murmured, "Would you like me to have a word with the Princess?"

"And inform her of what, Horatio? That her Mother wishes her misery?" She could easily identify the upper-hand when she had it and with a stern and inflexible scoff, she persisted, "Perhaps you could inform her of how the matters of the court find you bored and how little interest you hold in her safety?"

"I'll away." With petulant irritation, he bowed his head slightly and began to step back to the entrance.

"Away? To do what?" Queen Isobella demanded.

A pause and expression of surrendering annoyance preceded the reply, "Mother, I will speak with her."

Flummoxed, she reluctantly conceded with a groan and a scowl as her hand searched for the hand of the King to ease some of her rage.

King Alistair, with a preoccupied series of thoughts, donated a slight smile to the Queen before flicking his eyes to the departing Prince with the rising temper.

Horatio, worn to turbulent nerves, shoved past an attendant as he entered the corridor before sharply turning to a side incline of a wing. Out of the presence of his mother, his barely concealed anger bubbled to the forefront. It was a thing evident in his shaking hands as he forced on his gloves; it was evident in his gait and tightly drawn lips. But, in his narrowed eyes of shimmering silver, the animosity over the insignificance of an ermine, when compared to his dread over his brothers, instigated more disgust and rage. Yet, nothing seemed wrong at Bleak Spire. There was no panic and no sign of any awareness of notable troubles. A sharp anxiety began to scratch at his mind as he gathered that Edgar must have arrived as scheduled and Hector must have been collected. Otherwise, the whole of the region would be lamenting the absence of Edgar. While the path from Dark Tower to Bleak Spire replayed in his thoughts, a scullery maid taxed herself to keep her lustful eyes off of the unexpected and charming face of the Prince in passing. Quickly, he placed a hand to her chest to halt her progression, "From where did you come?"

"Prince?" in awe she stammered and blushed.

"Were you in the kitchens?" He raised a finger to the end of the hall in the direction he faced and from where she appeared.

"Oh! Yes, Prince. The kitchens, yes."

"Does Princess Eleonora linger there?"

As she wrung at her hands, her face grew rosy, "Um, I...Prince, I..."

In jeopardy of losing all patience, Horatio raised his eyebrows in anticipation of any cogent response.

She lifted her eyes to his face to steal the slightest of glances before elevating her gaze to the wave of his dark hair and beyond to the wall with a stall of an answer.

"Do you know who Princess Eleonora is?" Tersely, he questioned.

"I, yes, Prince, I do," flustered with devotion and desire, she lurched her words.

"Do you take me for Prince Edgar?" Absolutely amazed at the scullery maid's awe-struck state, he wondered if she assumed that he was the Prince who would tolerate and possibly even participate in the delay.

"Oh, No! No, Prince Horatio, Sir. I know full well who you are."

"And Princess Eleonora?" With anger, he pressed toward the point again.

"Yes, Sir, Prince, Sir. I see the Princess near daily."

The wringing of her hands had begun to fray at what little calm he had remaining, "And on this day? Is she present there – in the kitchens?"

"Oh, no, Sir. No. The Princess is in her chamber and

gave clear word that anyone...that anyone..." Again her eyes stole glances of the Prince's face before bashfully surrendering a number of awkward and flirtatious giggles.

Horatio studied her state and after giving her a window of time to better compose herself, she had not, so he questioned, "Would you like me to have you naked?"

"Sir?!" The squeal of the exclamation echoed throughout the stone and ice corridors like bats from a cave. Feeling faint, she thought better of leaning against the wall and steadied herself as best she could where she stood. Her skin grew warm, and senses sped to a lightning pace. The Prince drew closer with a darkly salacious hush to his voice. Her heart burned in her bosom before swiftly turning to frost at the sound of the words which followed.

He used the quiet tenor of a lover as he whispered to her cheek, "I will have you naked and bound to a traveler's pole at that point in the road where The Blue Shelf turns to the south and crosses with the path that leads to the Temple at Polaris. Lashed skin draws the bears but you needn't fear the pain as you'll be frozen to the bone before fully disrobed." Horatio drew away and examined the scullery maid's tear streaked face before insisting, "She 'gave clear word that anyone' what?"

"If anyone disturbs her, she will kill them, she said." The maid's fearful weeping made the words painful to utter.

"Fantastic," he growled while turning to storm back toward the chamber level. He shoved out a harsh sigh and yanked at the hood of his armor which had been lowered and felt as if it was strangling him. Agitated and perturbed, his gloved hands rubbed at his eyes as a turn of the corner forced his cloak to plume out and strike a servant which triggered a glance of rage from the Prince as if the servant had been the cause. Saying nothing, he dismissed the trembling and apologetic worker with a nod before continuing to his sister's chamber. Desperate to find some way to calm himself, he let his mind wander to the thoughts of how long it had been since he slept.

It had been three days since he left Dark Tower, and Edgar was expected with Hector three days before that. Nearing a week of restlessness and the exhausting facade of maintaining that all was as well as planned, he stopped to breathe, and nearly could not. Again he pulled at the unused hood of his armor and collar as if madly wishing to escape their grip. He wondered when he had last eaten, and with an unfamiliar suffocation of fear digging through his skin, he frantically searched his mind for the memory of what meal had been his most recent. Awash in too many possible answers and with no true recollection of the facts at all, he surmised that the thought of the meal did little to help him regain a focus. He glanced in both directions once he neared Princess Eleonora's room and once convinced of being alone in the corridor, he slowly began to count to himself while timing his breaths. To calm and not alarm, to control and to embody strength, slowly he let his breath in and out while holding his Grimm armor as distantly from the skin of his chest as possible. He steadied, and just before opening the door, opted to lean close for a listen after curiously hearing nothing at all.

With a new nervousness he waited and listened and the silence mocked his attempts to relax enough to play his role. After a few quick blinks, he placed his hand on the door latch and raised it with a loud, purposeful jerk to announce presence, not yet opening the door at all. No sound followed and after sliding his booted foot to the door to block it from opening too far, he pulled the door toward him with a hard motion. In response, a quick and sharp Flick, Thud against the door on the inside greeted the movement.

With a groan of finally knowing what was afoot, Prince Horatio moved his foot and let the door swing open. He glanced at the dagger which had been the cause of the sound: it was lodged very deeply. "You do only have the one blade, yes?"

Princess Eleonora's bright eyes lit up with joy as she realized it was her brother come to visit. Having been sitting on the floor near the window, she leaped up and bounded over a chair and table with the little white ermine in her arms. "Horatio!" She embraced him while he tried to keep the small white rodent away from his black garb. "Why are you home? When did you get here?"

"Long enough to have heard that the Queen-Mother finds this thing of yours vile, Sister," he nodded toward the ermine with a flip of his hand. She was disheveled. It was the first thing he noticed as he watched his sister cradle the animal. "Are you alright?"

She nodded in the emphatic way that people do when they truly believe they are, but are not.

"Why were you at Sorrowmore, Sister?" softly he questioned while taking a seat on her bed with an unintentional frown.

"In passing."

"From where, to where?"

She shrugged and stroked the ermine's fuzzy head. "Maregill Temple? Little else is near Sorrowmore."

Eleonora did not answer and frowned before tapping the animal's head, "He is with me now!"

"I see that he is." Horatio's sadness over the state of his sister drenched his words, "Does he have a name?"

Eleonora, who had always seemed unusual to everyone but her Mother, nodded and admitted, "It is Douglas!"

"You named your snow-rat Douglas?" Horatio frowned. Douglas was the name of a Priest of Hippocamp at Maregill Temple. The rumors surrounding the relationship between the young Princess and the holy-man were numerous and varied. Some claimed that the connection was romantic while others claimed scholarly. The Prince, very displeased with the name of the creature, continued, "Why would you give the thing such a name? That name is already taken, Sister."

"No, Horatio! This is Douglas." Her voice left little possibility of a joke.

"...is Douglas..." Horatio's head had begun to quake with pain.

"He has a curse on him! Horatio, make the Grimms fix it!"

"Make the Grimms fix what?"

"The curse! He was cursed to look like this!"

"You ask me to involve The Grimms? To make them act on your..."

"You can bring him back, Horatio!"

"I truly can't..."

Eleonora began to cry and fell into a frenzy as her words quickened, "Please! You are the Prince of the

North! He is a Priest to your blood!"

"Your blood too, Eleono-"

"Yours is stronger! Yours is older! You have to!"

Prince Horatio stood with a roar, "Silence! Enough of this! Sit you down and cease speaking for moments, just a few precious...You do know that the very instant that creature is found out by a house-wolf, it will be the end of it? You know this? Do you know of the injury that an ermine can cause when fighting for its life? Do you know the injury they can cause when simply bored? That thing will be a meal and a wolf will be harmed...all over what... your disturbed belief that a Priest is magically a...I truly... I do not..." Although furious, he tried to collect his temper. He loathed whatever had his sister's mind locked in fits, and slightly less, he loathed to see her cry, "Edgar?"

"What about him?" She sniffled, holding the ermine close.

He raised his eyebrows and extended both arms in a shrug, "Collected Hector?"

"Yes, of course."

"When?"

"Days ago now. Why?"

He shook his head, "It is nothing, Eleonora. I was confused about when to expect their arrival to the tower. I think I must have missed them by a day. I will return in the morning." It was a false calm to set her mind at ease.

"Everything is alright, then?"

"Yes, Sister." He stood and kissed her forehead before stopping at the door. "Tell Mother and Father that I have gone back to Dark Tower. They must have anticipated my visit: no one asked after Edgar and Hector when I

60

arrived. Tell no one of what we spoke."

"I will be quiet. You will look into it, won't you, Horatio? If anyone can do anything, it would be you. Please?"

Silently and with apprehension, he offered a single nod before leaving.

# Chapter V
## *Of Pyrois: Conscription*

Etched by the flame of lava, the South Hold was a labyrinth of cliff passes, gaps, notches, and contours so complex that navigation without the aid of a native would prove far too treacherous to venture. Over generations nearly too numerous to count, those of Pyrois cultivated a society born of fire and ore. The refined Serpentronum, once fiercely sought as the finest material in any Hold, could be found nowhere but in the South, and by only the skillful hand of a master blacksmith taught in the old ways could it be worked. Their cultural skill with metallurgy, craftsmanship and stone artistry were unsurpassed in all of the land. Even with trade routes having been dismantled ages ago, the wealth acquired from the age of war served particular families with the comfort of luxurious livelihoods, even now.

Rock-cut villages, governed by clans of kinship, dotted the spider web-like arteries of the region. A traveler would have to pass through multiple townships en route to anywhere at all as the sheer volcanic cliff-facings from which the architecture was carved were far too high and promised nothing beyond but harsh wastelands above. Villages would often feature a massive, singular living structure wherein the clan would live in separate apartments, while partaking in communal kitchens, eating spaces, and gathering halls. A dome arching over a sulfur spring, medicinal spring or hot spring would mark a large and luxurious bathhouse while near-to that, an amphitheater, utilized for a range of entertainment to public notice addresses, would be common. Most settlements featured a link in the Hold's aqueduct system and a water-processing center, which punctuated the society's inter-connectivity as it flowed before rushing along, over the black sands of the South, into the hot sea. The entire Hold was viewed by her people as a singular palace of many halls and homes while the seat of the Crown, Tephra Keep, was the heart of the land.

Each village would include a treasury attached to, and often beside, a clan tomb wherein urns containing the cremated remains of ancestors managed to deter even the most ambitious of family thieves. Inscriptions and pictographs on the facings of all the structures, carved from the very place the stone resided, would clearly indicate and define the family of rule, and the main clan chief could be either patriarchal or matriarchal, but never both at once as control and representation was viewed as an individual's responsibility to both kin and crown.

The arrangement of marriage would be a bond between two villages with the decision of which clan the couple joined being based on pure function. The family which supplied the less wealthy spouse would claim the new union while the wealthier family supplied the dowry. Although seemingly a machine fueled by the appearance of balance, the system was, in itself, a powerful political tool. A murdered or missing bride or groom over a family's view of a poor match was not uncommon, nor was the overemphasis on courting the richest of available suitors. Hearts were broken, clan houses were shunned, orphans were made.

In the wake of the way in which society clamored in the South, the rightful heir to the throne of Pyrois, Gabija, spent many lost years in the pursuit of a worthy king to her people. Unlike the other clan houses in the Hold, the Royal House, House of Pyrois, always claimed the marriage union that involved the King, Queen, and their children. When the royal offspring married, the children born from those unions, being the grandchildren of the King and Queen, were not eligible to remain with House of Pyrois in their own marriages: they joined their spouses' clans. The only exception occurred with the children of the King and Queen's first-born, who brought their spouses into the House of Pyrois. To Gabija's mind, the branches were vast and luck found her in the position of sibling-less to a long dead King and Queen. After earnest attempts spanning two decades, she abandoned any wish to play the games of match-making and with little opposition, she took the crown of the fire steed as hers alone. While some hopeful clans harbored hurt feelings over a son of theirs not filling the throne to her right, many more were thankful that the throne had not been filled with an adversary's son.

Those who, at the onset of the coronation, groaned at the choice made to retain the whole of House of Pyrois as her own quickly silenced their complaints when she revealed her plans for dynastic succession. She would, with the guidance of the temples, select children to adopt from the orphans of the South. So plentiful had been the cousins of her ancestors that she claimed to see the divine in the eyes of clan-less children so often that her heart set itself to it.

The orphans were under the care of the temples in

the South and every five years, by using methods kept secret from all but the most senior priests and priestesses, a group of five would pass a series of examinations to be presented to the Queen as candidates. Queen Gabija would meet with the five and select one to join her home while simultaneously offering the other four the option to join the royal guard, The Red Spines, once they would come of age. It was a tremendous honor and despite the great chance at play, the poorest of families would surrender infants to the temples in hopes that one day their child could rise above the poverty and shunning that they endured. It was a deeply meaningful and emotional gesture: a grand act of faith. The people, either the tear-stained or heavy pocketed, had largely grown to adore her.

Queen Gabija adopted her first child, a son: Mugdi, when she claimed the throne by inheritance in her twenty-fifth year. Her forty-fifth birthday was approaching, and soon she would welcome her fifth child into the House of Pyrois. It had been written into House Law that the rule of succession for Gabija's children would not hinge on birth-order, but rather by merit and election. The Houses would vote and the Queen would be granted a single veto if she so desired. It was a system with little opposition.

Queen Gabija quietly listened to the court musicians play while awaiting the Congress of the Houses, a regular meeting of the clans at Tephra Keep, to begin. She calmly watched while various men and women, great leaders of their families, socialized, laughed, and in some pockets, whispered and frowned. Drummers offered a heart-beat tempo, hands against goat or lizard skin surfaces while wide-bodied stringed instruments of various sizes, pitches, and tones were plucked with bone picks with great mastery and care. Long and thin with a bell at the base, woodwinds with double-reed mouthpieces rang a smooth hiss through the air. Again, she took note of those who would whisper and frown while her calm began to slowly suffocate under the concern of a problem. She lifted a lean cut of lizard meat from the plate which sat on the grand meeting table and took a bite to quietly hush any threat to comfortable happiness. Something hung in the air, a sort of suspicion that the sweat on the brow of some was an indication of news most dire. Quietly, she began to dread the start of the session.

Mugdi, now a capable and quiet man of thirty was recently engaged, by arrangement, to marry Zillah of House of Itzal, whose patriarch was among those drawing the Queen's attention over a spattering of unusual and hushed discontentment. Whereas tradition demanded only the first-born attend, both Mugdi and his sister Creo were compelled by their Queen-Mother to sit in attendance for the Congress of the Houses. Their age, and possibility of ascension, demanded an understanding of the deep and ancient systems of governing at work in the South and so their presence offered an invaluable education by exposure.

For the Queen, the matter of accepting an arrangement of marriage seemed like a softer affair for affable, but shy, Mugdi than it was for charismatic and beautiful Creo, who had just turned twenty-three. For reasons unknown, she acknowledged every proposal, sign of attention, or even glance with suspicion and apprehension. Those parts of the process which were amusing or even enjoyable when dealing with Mugdi had turned to ash and defense when Creo became the fulcrum. The Queen always believed that she viewed all of her children equally but the strange fracture of equal, but opposite emotions forced her to internalize a host of doubt. It ate at the roots of all other thoughts. She worried she was too quick to choose and smile on the path for Mugdi, or too slow to choose and smile on a path for Creo. On either side of that crevice, she found sheer cliffs and she feared having to travel along in their shadow for her other children: her son, the spirited thirteen-year old Fazil, her ten-year old daughter, the brilliant and serious Yuma, and this fifth child, which would be her last child.

The drummers began to play the ceremonial beat, which signified the opening song to start the Congress. All in attendance stood while the Queen, lost in preoccupation, noticed that she remained seated during the initial heart-swells of tempo thuds. She sighed in a way to ensure that all would notice it: it was annoyance on display. Her linen dress, little more than a single length of dark red fabric laid narrowly over a shoulder and widely cinched at the waist with a gird-wrap of orange, reacted to her standing as the bottom hem flowed to dance at the sandal straps over her toes. The small, decorative coins pinned to the large, graying curls piled atop her head jingled, while her eyes, black and bubbling with strength and authority, cut across the room to Tibon, the patriarch of House of Itzal with silent accusations of wonder over what he could possibly have to mutter about in shadows.

Tibon I'Itzal held an unwavering gaze of urgency with

67

Queen Gabija as he, with his compatriots: House of Raquour's matriarch Mirza, and the patriarch of House of Bahasin, Duman, felt their grievances strengthened by the others' seemingly similar woes. The three had an eerie eagerness to the anxiety that they were responsible for projecting onto the otherwise ordinary gathering. The song which marked the start of session had barely concluded, and the offering of tithe began, before Tibon I'Itzal marked his notice of the Queen's dissatisfied stare with a remark, "One could see that the Queen wears worry on her face."

The other Heads of Houses were going about the usual tasks of contributing their sacred tax collections and praising the fire-steed, Pyrois, when the terse interruption caused an interested, albeit fairly offended reaction to the comment. Attention flowed down to the sitting Queen as all searched for a thing not present: worry.

"Worry should be worn when a clan is represented by a man who would suspend all offerings to our sacred Pyrois to voice his own observations. Especially when incorrect," Queen Gabija countered with a slow overturn of her hand.

"Forgive the impudence. The eyes of the Queen seemed interested in something upon my face, perhaps?" Tibon I'Itzal, who, as the likely future father-in-law to Prince Mugdi, had less than no reason to speak with such combative words, shocked all in the room but Mirza I'Raquour and Duman I'Bahasin.

The Queen held up a finger of silence before pointing to the large and ancient pottery in which the three whisperers had yet to offer their sacred due. Mirza

I'Raquour donated without delay while Duman I'Bahasin hesitated slightly. After Duman I'Bahasin finally offered up the taxes from his clan house, Tibon I'Itzal begrudgingly followed suit.

"While the ears of the Queen are shocked by your belligerence, the eyes of the Queen are most interested in why tithing was such a task, Tibon," Queen Gabija remarked while interlocking her fingers.

"A task? Did not call it such," Tibon scoffed and shrugged. "Other concerns, my Queen, we have." He waved an emphatic hand of gesticulation to his own chest before indicating to Mirza and Duman, "We three have other concerns."

"You have concerns other than the concern for what Tephra Keep is owed?" Questioned Cyrus I'Demai, equidistant neighbor to both Tibon and Mirza. He resented the notion that something unknown had been shared between House of Itzal and House of Raquour, and a house clear across the Hold from their territory, House of Bahasin, and himself being so completely in the dark to any of it. "What cause has any of you three to frown and whine?"

"Careful now, Cyrus I'Demai, my brother. This is a thing you want to have no part of," Duman I'Bahasin demanded as softly as possible with a hand outstretched, palm-out and warning.

"The Queen's birthday festival is on the horizon! Our last sibling will join the family of Pyrois! Whatever authority your little houses believe they have to extend treaties is a waste of conversation for all of us here," Princess Creo, suspicious chiefly of Cyrus over rumors of his involvement with border villages of the West, demanded while utterly unaware that her accusation had nothing to do with the state of Tibon, Mirza, and Duman. The Queen, without looking back to her daughter, reached to and calmly gripped the Princess' arm to cease her words.

Cyrus I'Demai rubbed at the sweat on his scruffy cheek while watching Tibon with a scowl of betrayal. "So? Speak of this thing! What is this thing that finds you so shaken? Share it with us all. Here, now."

Mirza, frail from age and quiet by nature, again stood and raised both hands, "Love and affection for the Queen, her children, for the Houses and the children of those houses. To offend, we did not intend. A thing has attacked us, we three. Thought to be separate, before how related it was, was known."

Tibon folded his arms with a rage barely contained as Duman nodded along with Mirza's sullen and severe words. The other heads of house, Durriken I'Wuaz, Nusair I'Na'if, Pia I'Salido, and Ahanu I'Magomed, listened closely with the Queen, Prince and Princess while Cyrus, with venom in his mind, glanced to Princess Creo after her comment.

"Until moments ago, it was thought that what happened to my House of Raquour was isolated. It is not isolated," Mirza continued. "It comes in the night."

"What comes in the night?" the Queen quickly asked.

"Its face, we do not know. Its name, we do not know," Mirza replied. "We thought it to be a sickness. Death came to more than usual, suddenly. Then, before we put those we lost to the flame, some would vanish: thieves, we thought it to be. Then, an illness to those closest to the dead ones. A cycle. A cycle. Those who had death come to

70

them, but disappeared before sent to Pyrois, some have been heard. Some have been seen. It is not the work of thieves."

"You say some who have died have been heard? Seen?" Queen Gabija demanded while looking from Mirza to Duman I'Bahasin.

Duman nodded somberly, "This is the same. All the way to our home at the eastern border."

"This is not a known event to us," offered Ahanu I'Magomed, the matriarch of the closest settlement to Duman's.

"No, nor to us," Cyrus remarked in the direction of Tibon and Mirza, his colleagues at the western border.

"Keep it from your knowledge," demanded Tibon before turning his enraged gaze to the Queen, "The sluice gates must be closed."

Taken slightly aback, Queen Gabija raised an eyebrow and awaited further comment from Tibon. The sluice gates were a carefully crafted system of Serpentronum doors which slammed shut certain ravine paths to coerce the flow of lava from various volcanoes away from the great houses and to the sea. "All of them, Tibon?"

Tibon, in a frenzy, nodded.

"And in the event of an eruption?"

"There will be no eruption," he swiftly responded with a disconcerting slur which caused several in attendance to narrow eyes of wonder.

"What assurance?" the Queen, still willing to hear out any plan, questioned.

"There will be no eruption!" again he demanded. His voice boomed as a shout as he stood. His dark skin began to pale.

Prince Mugdi lifted from his own seat at the same rate as Tibon while Cyrus I'Demai slipped away to fetch whatever Red Spines he could find. Tibon I'Itzal did not seem like himself. As the room fell into a worrisome panic, Princess Creo stood and blocked any approach to the Queen which afforded Queen Gabija an opportunity for an unusually timed hiss of secretive guidance to her daughter. While she watched I'Demai, the subject of her advice, depart, she quietly growled, "Never again single out one among the many. Never do this!"

"The sickness has him!" demanded Mirza, slicing through any tangential interest or attention. "Away, stay away," she specifically shouted at the Prince as she, swiftly, and without warning slipped a curved blade into Tibon's back, severing his spine. Crimson spilled and pooled.

*****

*Shaped of dirt and flame,*
*of water and wind,*
*Comprised completely,*
*of words to tend.*

*To be clouds, to be moon,*
*to be stars, like the sun,*
*As welcomed as fortune,*
*to be strangers to none.*

*Shall kneel to no throne,*
*nor bend to uprising,*
*No honor is greater*
*than completely comprising,*

*O migration of knowledge,*
*grand archivists of Holds,*
*That, by collecting our histories,*
*they preserve our souls.*

*-The Wanderers. Traditional*

# Chapter VI
## *Of Wanderers: Morigan's Path*

On foot, Morigan traveled. She had left The Sepal some time before and filled those moments which passed on her journey with voracious interest. A strange thing punctuated her thirst for learning the root of the Western mystery, and while a king gone mad was a common tale, something gnawed on the threads of her inquisitive mind, suggesting shadows at play. She whispered fragments of thoughts aloud as her pace quickened. Tightly, she pocketed herself into the gray Wanderer's cloak. There had been something glowing on the faces of the Purpureus Council members when the dire news had been expressed. Something glimmered in the jade eyes of the Prince Regent, too, who, while so delightfully unprepared for the sudden weight and value of his own life, begged for answers which she did not have.

There was a story, she thought, a myth of a flood which quickly slid aside for the memory of a fable regarding a key before a thought of a cloud, said to spread and rain down sickness caught her attention. Nearly tripping over an exposed root, she turned and took two steps back and found herself standing at the edge of a bog basin, with the fiddle-heads of ferns tickling against her shins. Her boots sunk slightly into the rich mud and with all her might, she quieted her mind and took inventory of her surroundings as the act of losing one's way would likely prove deadlier than usual. It was an affliction that The Wanderers often joked of as being the primary way in which one of their own would meet an untimely demise: strolling off a cliff, or into a bog, or hole in the ice, or a volcano, all in the name of being lost in the land of thought. It was spoken of as amusing until it actually claimed lives, which had been known to happen with some uncomfortable regularity. Morigan's gray eyes shouted to her mind to silence itself.

She looked to the east and observed a soft whisper of the promise of dawn behind the Veil Mountains: black-smoke fog swirling and rippling in an eternal dance of incline radiated a soft and slight blue as the sun would rise behind it in due time. The crickets had begun to calm their songs and the frogs with the higher chirps had given way for the toads of the lower croaks. The scent on the air was minty and, with a turn of her head, she found a subtle note of salt which marked her direction with enough satisfaction to set her back on her way. A rustling in a blackberry patch was low enough to the ground to indicate little more than a hare or other-such rodent. She walked on and aimed herself to return to the village of Thorn Bush, where her Wanderer brethren camped under the hospitality of the family of the young Satyr initiate, Caradis. She had much to report and, in her estimation, even more to request.

Then, with little accompaniment of sound or disturbance, a young man appeared, standing a small distance away, to the right of her path, swaying slightly, facing north. He was disheveled, caked with mud and blood, which Morigan's limited sight failed to distinguish in the mess of his form. He did not appear distressed, and, curiously, Morigan watched as he did little else than stare into the sky and lurch from one side to the next, effectively wedging his legs deeper and deeper into the hungry mud of the swamp. He was alone and before she could lift her voice to call after him, he began to hum a sullen, haunted tune. As quietly as possible, she knelt and removed herself from the glowing beams of moonlight while observing the strange behavior.

The figure lingered on dull flat notes in awkward places and hissed when he drew his breath in, as if taking his air through a reed. He seemed uninterested in his own state and his clothing appeared to have been yanked or pulled to tatters in a self-inflicted fashion. Each time Morigan came close to calling after the young man, he would moan and teeter. Each time she let the opportunity to offer assistance pass, her anxiety mounted. As time passed, the figure had an agitation brewing and Morigan suffered with her silent watch, ashamed of her fear.

Wanderers were the physical representations of calm, knowledge, history, and hope. Ever ready to assist with an injured child, or sick villager, they had earned an honored reputation of steadfast kindness and courage. Yet, Morigan could muster none of these things. She was frustrated with panic and distraught over her trepidation. She should have offered him assistance, but something held her quiet, in the shadow of a cherry blossom: vigilant to keep her eyes on the man for lack of power to bring herself to offer much else. As she grew more disgusted with her own shortcomings, he, ignorant of her presence and completely independently, grew more frenzied.

The distant sound of approaching horses caught the notice of both. His jarringly hummed tune and long rasp breaths gave way to guttural howls and throaty growling. Morigan, aghast and fearful of the possibility of being

76

trampled while deliberately in a shadow on the path, stood and with stealth, tried to judge from which way the horses would approach. Unfortunately, the figure also turned his attention to the path in wonder and, once aware of the presence of Morigan, conjured an incredibly horrible shriek. With a multitude of tonal layers, it was a sound so unusual and horrifying, Morigan's only response was to shutter and weep. She and terror became sudden and unexpected acquaintances.

His face had been bitten by something, half ripped and hanging to whatever framework his mother once cherished. The golden, Western hair was only hinted at as the gore had, in layers unknown, saturated the crown of the boy. And he was a boy: this became clearer as his frame fought and struggled against the mire. He could have been no more than in his late teens to Morigan's eye. He had been a boy, for what he was, as he threatened and snarled at her trembling form, from the distance of a few closely rooted trees, was a thing awful and unknown. Finally, out of either bravery or lack of options, she opened her sobbing mouth and called, "Have you been attacked?"

Shrieks again, littering the air with shards of scorn: the shrieks demanded in a manner more severe than a bear's roar.

"You...can't understand. This is plain," ardently, she tried to bide time on the hopeful eventuality that the riders were coming down the path. Shaken, she did all she could to convince herself that she ought to speak to the young man as she would any young man, unaware to what extent his behavior was caused by viciousness and what was caused by pain. "You are stuck? You are stuck, yes? Please be stuck." Whimpering, she quickly looked down the path in both directions. Drawing herself deeper into the cloak, she considered trying to flee just before noticing that his howling had seemed to attract a number of shadowy figures which crept from over a hill behind him. As despair, dread, and hopelessness began to crash into her consciousness, she badly wished it was not customary for Wanderers to travel unarmed.

A trio of steeds, guided by three Satyr riders, galloped around the bend and drew to a sudden stop dangerously close to where Morigan stood in cowering fright. Adorned in the uniform armor, the rich colors of purple, sapphire, roseate and pomegranate, one of the three riders dismounted in close purposeful proximity to Morigan, while the other two turned their attention to the figure whose screams drew their pursuit. He removed his helmet as the traditional Western, golden face mask glinted in the moonlight, and shook Morigan from her trembling as she suddenly marked that the Satyr helmets were far more intimidating than she had ever before noticed.

"Have you been harmed, Wanderer?" the attending Satyr's voice softly vied for Morigan's complete attention. He would slide a bit to block her gaze when she would lift notice to the other two royal guards and the figure they approached before again speaking, "Wanderer? Have you been harmed?"

Morigan, in shock, shook her head slightly spilling black waves of hair from her cloak hood.

The Satyr nodded once, "Are you traveling alone?"

She nodded, mouth still agape.

"Do you know where you are?"

With a slight pause, she shook her head once, finding the question unnerving, "I am...I am in the Hold of the West."

"Good. And?"

"And I travel from The Sepal to Thorn Bush, down at Briar Bay."

He placed his maroon leather gloves on her arms in hopes of blocking her view of his colleagues completely while muttering, "You have veered badly, I am afraid."

Cognizant of his alarming calm, Morigan turned suspicious when suddenly one of the others, a female, sadly spoke, "It is young Euclid, General. The hound handler."

The man addressed as General did not break his gaze from Morigan's face as he replied, "Does he seem willing to accompany us, Sulaelia?"

The figure, reacting to the proximity of the encroaching pair, thrashed and screeched.

Sulaelia responded, "I do not find him terribly willing, Sir."

"There were more," Morigan offered with quaking words.

With disbelief and sudden obvious concern, the General tilted his head and adjusted his helmet under his arm, "Pardon, Wanderer?"

"Did she just say there are more?" the other guard, a male to Sulaelia's left sharply asked for swift clarification.

Morigan nodded, feeling only slightly less afraid than she had been in the light of the apparent comprehension and control the Satyrs seemed to hold, "On the hill. They moved very erratically and lingered back, as if watching."

"Should I give a look?" the male asked.

"Manage the one before you," the General had begun to wince from the constant and unrelenting howls from the figure that had at one time been the hound handler, Euclid.

"You won't harm him, will you? He didn't attack me." Morigan, madly needing to make sense of the encounter, again wept.

The General, with a narrowing of his eyes in consternation, smiled slightly while quietly explaining, "He would have, Wanderer. He is too far ill." The silence shared between them punctuated to the General that the kind-hearted Wanderer had no idea of the seriousness of the condition. He was not overly surprised: the information regarding the sick was new and constantly changing. As she claimed to have just come from The Sepal, he knew that the capital was likely less aware than The Satyrs from having being hidden safely within the grand tree, even with a Purpureus Councilor or two roaming from secure fort to village to fort to village. Irritated by the swelling surge of sound emanating from the figure, he raised his voice and extended a hand, "Come. I will take you to Thorn Bush, lost Wanderer. I am Lysander Barro."

"General Lysander Barro," Morigan stated to indicate that she noticed that he failed to mention the part most would celebrate.

He shrugged in a good-natured way, "My rank means little to a Wanderer." Soon-there-after, his tolerance for the delay in silencing the swamp-locked figure began to fade. He snapped a terse comment over his shoulder to the pair with an authoritarian bark, "What delays you?"

Knee-deep in bog mud, Sulaelia, who lingered back

only slightly from the other Satyr, turned and remarked, "Markos is watching the hills, Sir."

Markos turned slightly to indicate that Sulaelia was correct, when suddenly he lost the deep foundation that held his foot. He slipped and had his arm instantly gripped by the creature that had been Euclid. Letting out an injured shout, he could not free himself from the grasp.

Sulaelia lunged forward and grabbed at Markos' torso as he wailed in pain, "General!"

General Lysander Barro pointed at Morigan and demanded, "Get on my horse. Do not leave unless all is lost." He shoved his helmet against her chest before turning away.

"What?" Again, the fear paralyzed her courage.

"Do not steal my horse, Wanderer." He drew his sword and rushed toward his officers, passing their panicked steeds, stopping short of where the actual swamp began to survey the extent of the damage.

Markos was lost, ripped to fatal tatters, so much more severely than should have been possible. Sulaelia was in hysterics, screaming apologies to the parts of Markos she still held: all but his arm and head, which the creature removed once it lodged its fingers under Markos' chin. She had gotten too close, and knew that if the General approached he too would die.

"Sulaelia!" Lysander shouted, placing a hand against the body of a tree to steady himself. Finally Morigan witnessed an appropriate emotional response. He was not calm or aloof, but rather, deeply, he felt sorrow and failure, "Sulaelia! Look at me!" Morigan saw it: he was afraid.

"I'm so sorry! General, General, I'm so sorry!" Sulaelia grieved with a clamor of such intense sadness and torment, that Lysander, too, began to weep.

"Sulaelia. Listen to me. You have to destroy that creature that took Markos."

Stranded past her hips in the thick mud, she grunted while making every effort to move closer to the creature. She began to howl mourning songs of the West as she used parts of Markos to climb along to the best of her physical ability. The strain was incredible. "I can't!"

"You can!" The General demanded, "You can! Nikias told me that his mother was a great hero of the West. I told him that you would be... He told me you were. He told me you were a hero, already, Sulaelia. Please."

Her body stopped moving at the sound of her son's name as if suddenly she realized she would never again see his face.

"You can. Sulaelia, you can."

A sorrow of a different sort filled her heart and, rather than weaken her already hindered form, it gave her strength. Further she waded and with the suction of the mud ripping her boots from her feet, she produced a small blade that had been holstered behind her shoulder.

With his complete attention on Sulaelia's plight, Lysander reached to the reigns of the two frightened horses. The small metal forehead plates, a fashioned horn, glimmered as they jerked their heads in nervousness.

Morigan, from atop General Lysander's horse, held her hand over her mouth at the sight of the catastrophe. There had been no way for her to have been prepared for such a thing: the tragedy and terror were far thicker than she had ever expected to encounter.

Quietly, Lysander watched as he re-sheathed his own blade with the hand not holding the reigns.

The figure latched onto Sulaelia as soon as she had come close enough to touch. He squeezed and tore, yet she kept her right arm free enough to swing the blade into the ear of the beast, silencing the screeching. Standing between the remains of Markos and Euclid, she cried and sunk back a bit. "Tell him I love him."

Lysander nodded, unable to use his voice.

"Tell him I did my best to be a hero."

"What is she talking about?" demanded Morigan. "Even if her arm is shattered from that thing, we can get her out!"

Lysander shook his head at Morigan's words while still looking across the bog to Sulaelia with an absence of all things but grief.

Morigan, utterly insistent that something be done to help Sulaelia, again demanded, "What are you doing, General? Help her!"

Sulaelia, wishing for more moments but accepting the limit of things, again let the heaviness of sadness surge like the tide within her. She saw the anguish on Lysander's face and rather than tell a Wanderer information that would best come from a General, she chose to silence the Wanderer's remarks rather than letting her press Lysander further. With no words, she swiped the blade in her hand across her throat and, like melting, slumped into the saturated earth just as the sun's rays began to bake away the misty, shining fog of dawn.

# Chapter VII
## *Of Pegasus: Back Roads and Baldachin*

The gale breeze caught small mounds of ruby-gold
leaves and wildly threw them into dances so perfect and
cyclonical that the pace of the old nameless gelding
seemed almost at ease with recreation, as if taking in a
spectacle of autumnal leisure. Morning dew shimmered
as delicate and precious beads on careening threads of
gossamer; the spider silk flicked and hovered before
diving and gliding. A cold and clear mountain stream
slithered on to their right as springs of goldenrod sailed
over the glittery ripples on their long journey to the sea.
The dark of the night found little more than silence
shared between young Otver and The Magpie, Eileivia
Morninglight and the morning was proving just as
uncomfortable.

Finally, as the cool air began to warm, The Magpie
quietly spoke, "How we are to endure an entire journey
like this is truly beyond the limits of my imagination."

Otver blinked his dark eyes while moving hair from
his forehead with the back of his hand. He was relieved to
hear her voice, yet knew not to what she referred: the
slow horse, escorting a valuable body, the choice to stay
off the main roads, or the incessant squeak of the back
wheel on her side. At a loss of which complaint to
address, he used the opportunity to reply with the thing
that had been hounding him since King Voreto and
Queen Etvera demanded that he have a chaperone, "I am
sorry, Magpie. It wouldn't much matter which Magpie sat

next to me; it is a thing I should say."

Eileivia exhaled and let her top teeth grind against her lower while hearing his words. She felt terrible to have been caught up in any of it, but even more-so terrible to have treated him so coldly. While she was angry at the crime which found her aiding in such a task, she couldn't help but pity the boy. She scraped her thumbnails over the reins and squeezed before responding, "Would you?"

"Would I what?"

"Would it be a thing you would say? Would you say it if I seemed happy to join you on this trip?"

Otver gave it a thought and shook his head, "I don't think the question makes much sense."

"It does."

"How? Why would anyone be happy, Magpie?"

"You fancy yourself the thief of joy, do you?" Eileivia smiled a bit and nudged him, "You don't have to keep calling me that, you know? You can call me Eile."

The name was so simple, Otver thought to himself. So childlike and sweet in a way he never experienced in his few, short years. It had the playful ring of a name in a storybook. Sullen from the weight of the undertaking and skeptical as to why she, of all people, would show him any kindness, he shook his head. "I should call you Magpie. You earned the title."

"Earned?" She laughed in soft mockery, "I earned it? You place much value on earnings?"

"What you earn is what you are."

"Horse-piss."

Otver, sincerely shocked by the combative chat, friendly or not, folded his arms and mumbled, "Whatever you say."

Eile furrowed her brow at his capitulation and noticed his reaction as far more surly than she had anticipated. Again, she sighed and added a roll of her eyes and a shake of her head. "I didn't think about it like that. I apologize."

"What? Like what?"

"I said I'm sorry for not thinking of how hard you must have lived. It was unfair of me." She had a lag in her words and, with pursed lip, looked down to a tear at the knee of his trousers: he was filthy and bones. "Do you have parents?"

"No."

"Who feeds you?"

"I feed myself."

"Not well," she grumbled in judgment of his skinny frame. "How many years?"

"How many years what?"

"Have you been breathing? How old are you?"

He fumed a bit as if having been asked was an offense too far, "What does it matter?"

"Every year matters. Every minute matters, little boy..."

"Otver," he quickly corrected with a snap of a demand.

Eile smiled again and nodded at his reaction, "Good, Otver. You haven't gloomed the pride out of your heart. You'll need that, and I'm happy to see it present."

"It was a little more agreeable when I thought you didn't like me."

"Here, I'll give you two points to mark. We're lucky to have a nice uneventful ride and plenty more ahead of us, so here you go. First: The poor are angry people," she felt an opening for interruption and so sped her words, "No, hear me out."

Flatly, Otver watched the leaves fly past while listening. He had no intention to interrupt.

"There is an anger that brews when you are told that all you are worth is what you earn. It's a kind of illness that latches itself on the brightest spots of the soul and sucks away the light. The poor work so hard because they need to earn, so they work and they earn and they never seem to earn enough. And then, because of the complex tricks people play on people, they begin to feel guilty for all that they didn't earn. All the ways they should have worked harder, even when they really could not have. All the ways they failed casts shadows over all the ways they didn't. They grow angry because reflection on achievement is not a luxury they know. They grow angry because they build and create and have all they produce taken from them for the price of a pat on the back. They starve so that the wheat makes it to market. It is a thing that bothers me."

"I can see that," Otver quietly replied.

"The wealthy do better, live better, when the poor work harder and live worse. Children are not only not taught to read, they're taught to not read. It keeps them locked into a pit of servitude. It's systematic, little boy."

He reacted as if he had been slapped, "My name is Otver."

"Can you read?" she asked, oblivious to his continued annoyance.

"A little."

Happily, Eile smiled and nodded, "Good! That's

good! A little is always better than none. A little can grow into more."

Otver took her words in and frowned, "Nothing can grow from cursed soil."

"How do you mean?"

"I mean I'm going to die."

"We all die, little boy."

"I'm going to die for the death I caused."

Eile chewed at her lower lip and watched the gelding's back bob while walking. The tone of his response gnawed at her and no matter how she tried, she could not find the right words for what she wanted to say. Eventually, she swallowed and added, "I'm not going to let you die."

In disbelief, Otver's young voice squeaked a whine of persistence, "I do deserve to die for killing him."

"Death is not deserved, it is earned. It is the one thing worth earning."

He sat in a silent stupor.

"You haven't done enough to earn death, yet. Stop rushing toward it. It isn't for you." She gave a stoic glance around to the left of the slowly moving cart. The trees seemed to snicker at their comically lumbering cadence.

"Was that the first thing? The first of 'two points to mark'? Was that it?"

"Wasn't that good?"

"I don't even know what the point was, Magpie."

"The point was: you don't have to be what you're told you are. You don't have to be miserable and sad just because you're expected to be nothing more."

"You mean because I'm poor?"

"I mean because you're alive." She offered a curt nod

before pressing on, "My mother works hard. She is in her seventieth year and works so hard." With a smile she looked to Otver, "She would have died years ago if she wasn't happy."

"Happy?"

"Yes! Feathers-and-flight, you are a gloomy one, little boy! Happy! She is happy!"

"How is she happy if she works so hard? Or, why does she work so hard, if she is happy?"

Eile nodded emphatically, "Now you're beginning to understand! I grew up in a house that had been in my family for generations. On the land, there is a granary and fields of gold as far as you like. She wakes with the sun and sleeps when it sleeps and loves every second of her life there on that farm. If she had been forced to be a laborer on another farm, or maybe even bake and sell cakes, I think she would have lost her life years ago. She would have earned death with the currency of her joy. My father died when I was about your age. He had been a Wanderer that stopped wandering: set roots with my mom. He earned his rest. Died of sorrow or boredom or both, I think."

"So, you say the word 'earned' as if it is a bad thing?"

"I link it with mercy, I think."

"You don't think that your mother working all day, every day isn't earning?"

"Cock-of-Pegasus, no! Not in any way I mean, anyhow. She plays around all day like a child."

"But, she does work? You said she works hard?"

"Yea, like I said: like a child." Eile yawned. "Forget it. You missed my grand point completely. My point was: life is there, unless it gets sucked out of you. The end."

Otver placed both of his dirty hands against his face and shook his head. "What was the second thing you wanted to say?"

"What do you know about magpies?"

"I know they guard the Hold and the..."

"No, no, no. Not The Magpies. Magpies, like the birds."

He dropped his hands from his face and folded his arms again, "I have heard that they're very chatty crows."

"Was that to be an insult?" With a put-on seriousness, Eile looked hard at Otver until he finally turned his face to lock eyes with hers. Once he had, she smiled and caused a small ripple of a smile in response, "Yes, they are. But, there's more." She resumed watching the complete lack of a path while continuing, "If you draw your sword and set it before a dove, a crow, a sparrow, a falcon, and a magpie, all but the magpie would peck at the reflection, thinking that the bird they saw was some strange foreign threat."

"Why would a dove, a crow, a sparrow, a falcon, and a magpie all be in a line together? Where in nature would you ever expect to see that group all just calmly sat in a row?"

"That's beside the point."

"It really isn't. That's a silly thing to say: 'a dove, a crow, a sparrow, a falcon, and a magpie...'"

"The magpie would know it was looking at itself."

"What? How? Why?"

"They just do, I don't know how they do."

"Why a sword?"

"Huh?"

"Why would you lay a sword...? Why would these

birds just line up to have a sword laid out at their feet?"

"Well, it's reflective, isn't it?"

"Yes, but why do you think that set of birds would put themselves in that position?"

Eile scratched the side of her nose with an impressed chuckle, "You know, most children would just take the damn story and be grateful for it."

He nodded and offered a shrug, "Right then, tell me more about magpies."

"They're very proud. Haughty. Territorial."

"Are you still on about the birds or is this about the guards now?"

"Both. It's all been about both the birds and guards. Look, if you line up a Satyr, a Red Spine, A Grimm, and a Magpie, all in front of a sword, The Magpie would be the only one to not peck at the reflection."

Otver laughed and scrunched his nose. He was unaware that he would welcome the comfort of humor, but did and was deeply thankful for it.

Eile pulled back at the reins and stopped the cart while still chuckling, "I'm hungry. We should catch a few fish and get a scope of where we are."

"You don't know where we are? How is that possible?"

"I see no signs, do you?"

"You're a Magpie! You should know where we are no matter where we are in the Hold."

"Well, yes, I'm a Magpie. I'm not a damned Wanderer or anything. What do you expect from me?" She stood and set her dark green cloak over a stack of fur goods sent to protect Otver from the coming cold.

"I think we might be near Plum Pond," he offered

while looking around.

"We'll see." she hopped down from the bench and stretched before approaching a tree near the river bank, "Can you climb?"

Otver nodded.

"Properly? In a way that you probably won't fall to your death?" She pulled out a small pair of spiked palm gloves and rolled her eyes as Otver seemed confused. "Right. Watch me. I mean, keep a look-out, but watch me." With a quick movement, she began to scale the large round tree.

Amazed by her agility, Otver tilted his head and watched the careful precision of Eile's movements. Little time passed before she pierced the canopy and shuffled out of sight. To the north, a good distance yet, she observed that which she had secretly hoped: the border settlement of Falcon's Perch, the place where Princess Lavinia's body had been found afloat and snagged against the small rock dam which fed the stream they followed. She had set her mind to the visit to investigate and justified the choice by reminding herself that they were to travel north anyway. While following the winding path leading west out of Falcon's Perch, the path they opted to avoid, she looked to an equidistant point to the east, not far from the coast, and noticed a small, secluded cottage. It had chickens, a goat barn, and a vegetable garden only large enough to support a small family, and with very little deliberation, she decided that the cottage would serve nicely as a base from which to rest. While silently reminding herself to keep the brief detour to investigate a covert plan, she turned to descend the tree when suddenly she glanced, with wide-eyes, at the horizon far to the south. Smoke billowed. The whole of the South Hold looked to be afire.

*****

-That I breathe,
oh lust,
that I feel more than one should trust.
All indulgence,
shower me,
all sumptuous petals and scents sweet as song.
Of all desires and filled gratifications,
of all wishes, all satisfactions,
that I breathe
all lust.

-That I survive,
ever moving,
never trusting what they're doing.
All suspicions,
flower me,
all trickery, whispers, teasing tensions of time.
Of all mutations and evolved adaptations,
of all deceptions, all masked affections,
that I survive,
ever moving.

-That I end,
so clever,
punctuated by what would sever.
All expectations,
out-dance me,
all luring of lavish and luscious, oh, limitations,

*of cunning and fulfilled,*
*That I end,*
*by one cleverer,*
*or never end at all.*

*-Brio – Western Mourning Song, Traditional*

# Chapter VIII
## *Of Unicorn: Rake's Rest*

Well to the southern border of the Western Hold, around a crooked bend and sunken slightly in a low point was the shanty hut Rake's Rest. For years the structure, now abandoned and dilapidated, had been a handy resting stop for the difficult task of gathering herbs, molds, and fungus from the near-by system of grottoes. Newer structures had been built closer to the individual caves and featured rafts for high tide, and clear, connecting paths for low tide. Thus, Rake's Rest had become a relic: a constantly damp, half-roofless, half-swallowed shell of a place that was once Rose's Rest and sheltered the adventurous.

The sinking interior angle was severe and to stand-in-wait within meant a fairly constant pull and strain at the ankles. The cypress knees had begun to break through the lowest corner of the hut while palmetto fronds extended their wide open hands through the unobstructed, circular windows. Unlike most shelters in the West, Rake's Rest had not been built into a tree, but rather, was a cottage built onto a platform attached to the base of four trees, indicative of the structure serving as a temporary travel refuge. Bull alligators growled in deep rumbling croaks while songbirds jokingly chided the cicadas and tree frogs. In vain, mosquitoes laid their long thin proboscises against the shimmering sweat of Reileus' caramel skin. The Purpureus Councilor, with folded arms, propped his weight against a sharp angled support beam, waiting. No sooner did a mosquito sink itself into his flesh to dine, than it fell away in death.

Reileus, in a place he should not have been, wore a light linen tunic in a deep shade of blue over dark trousers and completely average traveler's boots coupled with an equally unspectacular, wide-brimmed hat. He wore no jewelry and brought a plain satchel, which had been hung on a high tack to place it somewhere up off of the ground, away from water and also out of his hands. Silently, he stood awaiting the arrival of a co-conspirator and pensively, he watched the midday sun fleck off of the surface of a ripple pool just beyond the destroyed wall before him.

"To meet so late, it is not what was planned." The trill of the Southern accent alerted Reileus to Cyrus I'Demai's approach and once a friendly grin had been exchanged, Cyrus continued, "Much has occupied my time on this day. No, this set of days. The last few days: no good has come of it." Wearing deep browns and white, the Clan Head of House Demai lifted himself from a small flat raft into the shack of Rake's Rest. Having finally situated himself for a conversation, he remarked, "You do not look so good, my friend."

"No?" Reileus remarked in a cool and calculated manner.

"No. Have you what we spoke of?"

"I do. And you?"

"Plenty." Cyrus I'Demai waved a hand back to the raft on which a rather large bag sat.

Reileus, with an interested eyebrow glanced past Cyrus before offering an approving nod. Without words, he unfolded his arms and pointed to the satchel dangling from the beam.

"So little?" Cyrus questioned, nearly losing his balance to observe the goods high above.

"It won't take much." He pointed to the raft, "It that quite heavy?"

"Heavy. Very, I apologize." He slightly bowed his head.

Reileus nodded and drew in a breath, "Pity to come all this way for little more than a smuggling run."

"The things I could tell you! It is unbelievable, my friend." The Southerner looked around and began to tap at his throat, "Have you any drink?"

"Should I have offered? I had no idea our friendship had evolved so." Reileus removed his hat and offered it to Cyrus.

"Hair so golden, I could sell it." Cyrus smirked while grabbing the hat, "What is this for?"

"Look to the water. There are spots where the mud is cleared to the side and light gray sand surrounds a small hole. Do you see?"

Peering with dark and narrowed eyes, Cyrus leaned out over the wooden shack side and spied a few spots like the ones described, "Ah! Yes, Here!"

"Fold the hat brim into a small canal and sink it to direct that water into the bowl." He looked his nails over with an arrogant, yet kindly tone.

"What? What if snakes live in those?"

"Snakes?" Disbelief peppered Reileus' scoff. "Why would you expect to find a snake in a hole through which water constantly, and frankly, quite powerfully moves?" He paused and indicated with a turn of his hand, "It's a spring source, I'Demai."

Cyrus, skeptical and hesitant, searched Reileus' face

for trickery.

"It is perfectly safe, I assure you."

"These are not words we are taught to trust from Westerners!" With a loud belly-laugh and a point before a shrug, he lowered himself to fetch some of the spring water.

"I mean, well, do watch for snakes. But none dwell in those little holes."

Cyrus, suddenly pleased with whatever amount of water he managed to scoop up, leaped out of the water in fright. He watched a smirk roll over the lips of Reileus before surrendering himself to jovial laughter. "You! Frightened me!"

"Of course I did."

"Come, let us trade stories so that this meeting between you and I could have some conversation to it," Cyrus asked before gulping the fresh water.

"Stories?"

"Have your Royals been found?"

Reileus sighed and leveled a cautionary glare in Cyrus' direction.

Taken comically aback, Cyrus insisted, "What? This is an interesting thing, no? Would you not want to know if the Hold below had such...I do not know...um, sadness?"

"Uncertainty?"

"Sorrow."

"Instability."

"Instability," he nodded with a shrug.

"A million dark skinned lava lizards would die before even reaching this point, I'Demai. An invasion is ill-advised." With venom and a deeply serious scorn, Reileus shook his head. "A million more would bleed on the black

99

sands of your lands when the West reacts to having been entered. An invasion is ill-advised."

"Easy, my friend," Cyrus laughed disarmingly. "Be easy. This thing which I am to tell you...this thing will set you softly. There will be no such invasion."

The Purpureus Councilor refolded his arms and leaned against the support beam again with an interested nod for I'Demai to continue.

"A head of one house, slain a head of another. This, I can not make this up. I tell you, this is just for you, there is something very dark in the South."

"What?" Reileus' shock was apparent. "When?"

"Since this time yesterday."

"Are the Houses warring?"

Cyrus offered an incredibly dramatic shrug and with the down-turned frown of a jester, tilted his head, "It would seem, no?"

"Who was slain?"

He shook his head and raised a finger, unwilling to admit that the headless house was the only other border-town to the West, "This I will not say."

With a single nod, Reileus surmised that it was either the Queen herself or I'Itzal. Otherwise, Cyrus, who rarely misses the opportunity to ramble on about all he knows, would have spoken a name. "Of course, I'Demai," assented Reileus.

I'Demai was eager to shift the topic and so shook his head and questioned, "How is your cousin?"

"Overwhelmed," Reileus remarked with an authentic tinge of exhaustion. "Much is asked of him."

"Fortunate is he to have such loving family in times like these."

In a quiet dark thought, Reileus nodded, "He is."

"I imagine those other Purpureus intend to...how do you say...cause influence?"

Hushed behind a chuckle, he replied, "They will try. They will die for it."

"So loyal to your own blood!"

"What a simplistic outlook, I'Demai." He cleared his throat and ran his fingers over his head and through his hair, "In the hat, where the water was, there are likely small grains of sand?"

Cyrus opened the wide-brimmed hat and peered in, somewhat concerned that he had been poisoned, "Ah, yes, my friend. I see this sand here."

He held up two fingers, "Two grains," before pointing to the dangling satchel. "I have given you a fairly large vial. All it would take to kill a man my size could be held in two grains of sand."

"What manner of delight did you manage to procure?"

"It is a milky liquid secreted from the flesh of very particular blue and yellow tree-frogs when they are frightened: Shiverotoxin. It is a sure and horrid death."

With impressed gratitude, Cyrus nodded and rubbed his hands together, "Very painful, yes?"

Reileus lifted an eyebrow and professed, "Yes..." with a leery hang on his voice. "So, I was correct to assume you wished to cause suffering, and not just death?"

Emphatically, Cyrus nodded and began to ramble, "There are things...to know that one is facing the end... fear, I want for this."

"You're either incredibly angry or so blindingly an amateur that I can barely stand much more of this."

"Why would you say such a thing? You harm me."

"A poisoner should never leave a hint that he was there. This that you're doing: this is a show."

"It is. You are correct."

"With clearly Western poison," he grinned.

"Will it be known?"

"Oh, I do hope so. Your temples are home to wise thinkers. Surely someone will figure it out. The death is quite unique and spectacular."

"And you want this?"

"And I do," Reileus smirked while in an impersonation of a Southerner.

"Your cousin will not like this, should he find it out."

With a raise of his hand, Reileus snapped and down from a hole in the roof came a masked henchman clad in mud tones with leaves draped around his body. "The Prince Regent will not find out," he remarked with confidence before hushing Cyrus' sudden panic at the presence of the unexpected spy by speaking to the interloper, "Fetch the satchel and deliver it to I'Demai's raft."

Obediently, the henchman bowed and began to effortlessly scale a minor incline of a fallen wall to reach the parcel.

"What is this?" Cyrus demanded, unnerved by the addition of the once hidden lackey.

Reileus furrowed his brow while dusting away dried mud from the hat before placing it back onto his head, "A man who wants a statement made of poison dares to question me on the matter of discretion?" He laughed, "Come now, I'Demai." With a shake of his head, he glanced past Cyrus to the spy on the raft, "The bag from the South?"

The henchman knelt and made an effort to lift the clearly weighty sack.

"Sink it," Reileus demanded. "Beneath Rake's Rest, near-to a stilt."

Again, the spy did as told as quickly as possible.

Chuckling at Cyrus' nervousness, Reileus asked, "Oh, what is it?"

"In that bag, my friend: do you know how much wealth is...?"

"I do."

"And yet, you would drown it?"

"Can ore and gems drown?"

"Well, they can degrade, surely."

With a nod of obviously false concern, Reileus nodded while rubbing his chin for emphasis. On and on he nodded until the spy returned to his side. "There is little to worry about, I'Demai."

Confused, Cyrus clutched the bag of poison close to his chest and began to take steps back to his raft. He kept his eyes on Reileus and watched as the Purpureus Councilor offered the spy a small weighted payment bag. Upon opening the leather pouch, scores of tiny spiders emerged and ran along the henchman's arm, up his sleeve and across his throat, injecting venom all the while. Reacting to the poisons, the spy stiffened and fell in death like a boulder against the water-rot floorboards. Reileus stepped aside as the plume of spiders scampered to bore into the dead flesh, while nonchalantly, with a hand raised, he smiled to the Southerner.

"Safe travels, my friend. May your Steed-Lord watch over all endeavors, now and always. Do be in contact if any concerns arise."

"This I will," Cyrus responded with a shake to his voice. Quickly, he stepped onto his raft and began to disembark with a frantic lack of delay. "May yours do the same for you, my friend." He avoided eye-contact and trembled as his hands gripped the oars.

"Health to your crown."

"And to yours."

# Chapter IX
## *Of Hippocamp: On Durability*

"The next person to walk through that door with complaints about supply shortages will have their ribs divided by my boot!" Roaring, the second-in-command of The Grimms, Lord Banquo, Thayn of Lockfrost, slammed his hands down against the top of a table in a third floor assembly arena at Dark Tower. A cue had formed out into the corridor as a number of disgruntled officers had come to make a scheduled report on the status of those under their watch, be it their troops, their fort staff, or neighboring villages. Recently, the reports had turned more dire than usual: food shortages, animal attacks, sickness. Very few brought news that they were pleased to share.

"Lord, I did think it wise to, at absolute least, mention it...," a snide officer, the oldest son of a noble family whined and groaned before Banquo interrupted.

"What did you just say?" The burly, bearded man leaned forward to display disbelief. His pale and aged skin whispered behind sheets of coal black hair along his face and worn long on his head, down his back. His eyes, blue and strong, were daggers of ice.

"I said it needed to be mentioned, Lord."

"Did you? Somehow 'the absolute least' is the same in your mind as a 'need'?"

"Commander Banquo,...."

"What?" Banquo snarled his response quickly while shoving everything that sat on the table to the side in an effort to portray that his undivided attention had been achieved.

"It was..."

"It was what?"

"I thought..."

"What did you think?"

"I thought you should know."

"Get out!" His shouts served to peel away a few layers of petitioners who lingered in the corridor. Yet, some remained and were relieved to notice the face of the Prince, Lord Commander Horatio Aquilo, arrive at the top of the stair to the back of the mob. "What else? If I am to be hounded the VERY MOMENT I separate from my saddle the absolute least one should expect would be a damn warm ale. And, by the by: that would be an appropriate place to use such a proclamation of standards. 'Absolute least'? What kind of shit speaks like that?" He turned his attention to a trio of pages, and narrowed his eyes, "If there be three of you, why is there no fire yet built, nor drink to warm?" They scattered to build a fire and fetch ale while the next officer in the cue stepped through the door.

Prince Horatio moved to the wall to allow a lane for one of the pages to scamper past and down the stairs while noticing even more petitioners ascending. Secretly, he leaned to the nearest officer, an aged woman and an administrative sergeant, and whispered, "Has this been all day?"

"The doors just opened, Lord Commander."

Horatio narrowed his eyes and looked to a port window in confusion. Assemblies were to conclude by midday, just before dining. It was night and the ribbons of light that were so often a part of the black, twinkling sky had turned from a usual green to a rippling purple. It was a rare sight and added to the burdens on his mind. As the page returned with a bottle of heated brew, Horatio stopped the boy and took it into his own possession before turning to pass the others who impatiently waited to be heard. The boiling conversation hushed in waves as Grimms stood aside with salutes, bows, and reverent silence to honor the Lord Commander.

The man standing before Banquo was hesitant to speak and his face bore apologetic and fearful eyes.

"Is this about supplies? This isn't about supplies, is it?" Banquo groaned as the pair of pages behind him stoked the fresh fire.

"Commander, the good stores are woefully low across the Hold. It is not just a problem here at Dark Tower."

With a slight laugh of madness, Banquo rubbed at his big black eyebrows and took his time with a response, which came as a thunderclap, "I do not wish to hear anything further on the matter of supplies! Find a quartermaster and have this talk there. Then let the quartermaster know that it is their job to acquire goods from the temples! We have done this for hundreds-upon-hundreds-upon-hundreds of years!" His demeanor shifted dramatically when he noticed Horatio, his friend and Prince, standing in the doorway. "Finally! Is that something to drink?"

"It is," Horatio nodded while crossing the room to the table. Quietly, he spoke to the petitioner who was in the act of a low bow, "These supply issues have worsened from your last report? Please don't bow." He was exhausted from his journey from Bleak Spire and his voice reflected the lethargy created from not only the travel, but also his silent worry for his siblings and a generally quick aggravation in response to much of anything at all. He was well-known for being of even temper, so the worn appearance triggered notice from Banquo who sighed heavily at the sound of Horatio's inquiry.

"Ah, shit's-sake! Here we go," he muttered in soft protest while accepting the bottle from Horatio. He did not say much else and knew the line between what Horatio would accept as a level of friendly heckling and what would be considered disrespect may have been thinned due to the Prince's curious condition.

"Yes, Lord Commander," the man's words were nervous as he did not want to annoy his Prince in the same way he had Banquo. "Grains are very low and herbs are nonexistent, which would be fine if the herbs were solely for seasoning, but the temples have been unable to supply many with medicines. It has grown so severe that any not within walking distance to a temple stay in their homes knowing that they would be turned away for treatment due to shortage."

Horatio earnestly listened and nodded his fatigued head for emphasis while the man spoke. With the pursed lips of contemplation, he cut his gaze from the complainant to the drinking Banquo before looking back, "This is not the first time you've been here with this matter in hand?"

"No, Lord. I came at the last wide-moon with the same concerns. Those concerns were less than those I have now here."

"What name is yours, Grimm?"

"Corin, Lord. Corin of Sorrowmore."

"Sorrowmore, you say?" His drooping eyes read clear intrigue. "What family?"

"No family of consequence, Lord."

Banquo let out a slip of a chuckle, knowing him well enough to know the sort of response to come from Horatio.

It was just as the older Grimm, his friend, expected as softly and in a rehearsed cadence, Horatio remarked, "There are no families devoid of consequence." It was not truly a thing he felt, but was a thing said in opposition to the view of his mother, regardless of what the people had been led to believe about how she felt for them. He smiled, and Banquo, with a frown, observed it as something of a chore. "So, Sorrowmore is starving," he sullenly muttered with a rub of his eye. "This obviously won't do. They are fortunate to have such a dutiful Grimm as their representative."

"You honor me deeply, Lord."

Banquo rolled his eyes and turned to expose his palms to the warmth of the fire. He listened with calculation, aware that some preoccupation had a grip on Horatio.

"The honor is the Hold's, sir." Again Horatio supplied a faint smile before continuing, "One must surmise that the inadequacy of vital goods has been addressed with the priests at Maregill Temple?"

"Yes, Lord Commander. Maregill claims that their stores are emptied and that the conservatories of all the temples are bare."

Nutrition was more of battle for the North and South Holds than for the other, more fertile pair. Climate and terrain forced the societies to create clever alternatives to conventional agriculture and great care and esteem was given to the profession. In the land of Hippocamp, a particular class of priest, whose job and purpose it was to protect and cultivate the food stocks, had been developed ages ago. The conservatories were always present at the temples and built nearby, beneath the surface snow, as a bubble of a dome with a grand system of ventilation and piped skylights. Utilizing much of the same style of architectural engineering that the residential structures enjoyed, heat could be effectively trapped and, with carefully treated layers of enchanted soil smuggled from the West, The Bearing Shrines, as they were called, produced enough goods for the temple and the nearby villages they served. Until recently, it had been assumed that the tilling and flipping of the Unicorn-soil would be enough to maintain viability, but after eons of use, the vibrancy faded. The yields lessened and the lack of abundance had hit a low enough point that people had begun to steal, horde, or starve.

The North had never seen crime so violent and desperate before the shortages. Murders for theft had become common-place and The Grimms were situated to act on the word of law as agents of the Crown. The most decorated royal guard officer in a village would be appointed as sheriff and they would be responsible for installing a liaison, like Corin of Sorrowmore, for the task of reporting to Dark Tower. None of the process involved an election and a cold and hungry populace fostered resentment over the silencing. Many commoners would remark that one would never find a thin priest or Grimm while few could recall more than a week's worth of days to pass without the death of a friend or family member from sickness, starvation, or exposure.

Horatio understood the civil unrest that was brewing. He knew that the delicate boundary that kept his princely head on his neck needed to be preciously guarded at all times and he felt a burning frustration at the Crown's ignorance of this matter. Always, he was expelling tremendous effort in maintaining his roles as Prince, as Lord Commander, and as a Northerner: three masks that were often in opposition.

As Prince Horatio Aquilo of Bleak Spire, heir apparent to the Crown of Hippocamp, he was mysterious, aloof, charming, and desirable. He had not settled on a marital courtship as his availability provided protection. Very few noble families risked offending him for hopes that their daughter could become the next queen. It was a possibility made to seem all the more realistic by the ruse that he reacted very affectionately towards many noble daughters: a manner of behavior that Horatio wished Edgar, his younger brother, did not emulate quite as closely, and without half the comprehension of purpose, as he did. However, as handsome as he was physically, he could never tolerate extended stretches of being particularly pleasant. He was unfortunate to excel in haughty irritation at the slightest of provoking.

As Lord Commander of The Grimms, protector of all the North Hold, his performance was two-fold. Firstly, to the other Grimms, he did all he could to be honored, respected, and cherished. For any who would wish to not encounter a Grimm, he wanted fear. He was vicious in his execution of criminals and the occasional lost traveler. His methods of punishment earned him a ferocious reputation. Again, his brother, who he truly loved very much, failed miserably at compartmentalizing the need for varying images. Prince Edgar was beloved as a gregarious man that never really had to work very hard at anything. It was infuriating for Horatio, even while his soul was consumed with growing dread over Edgar's absence and the absence of their youngest brother, Hector.

As a Northerner, he was the very image of a child of Hippocamp. His hair was as black as the deepest shadow with occasional waves that rolled across his crown like drifts of snow saturated in ink. His eyes were the storm-gray of the North, and his skin was as fair as a calm wintry day. He was suspicious of foreigners and as insulated and mistrustful as any child of the North: a trait on which he and Edgar were also at odds over, as his younger brother would often comment on the chief quality of The Wanderers being their diversity.

"In your dealings with Maregill, Corin of Sorrowmore, have you ever come in contact with a conservation priest by the name of Douglas?" Finally Horatio spoke, finding it increasingly difficult to filter his focus on much else than his brothers. Luck had been on his side to ask after the man that plagued his sister's thoughts.

Corin took a moment to formulate a response, as he shifted and creaked in his black officer armor, "I had brought the matter to the attention of Dark Tower at my last visit, Lord Commander. I regret to offer the follow-up that he has yet to be located."

"Pardon?" Horatio was barely able to disguise his intrigue and amazement. "Missing? The conservation priest by the name of Douglas of Maregill: missing? And you reported as much?"

"Yes, Lord Commander," there was a bashfulness in the admission. The delivery of Corin's words suggested that he did not wish to imply that Dark Tower had failed in any respect, or that his own investigation had made no ground.

Horatio turned to his brawny colleague who drank by the fire, "Knew you of this, Banquo?" His expression formed a steady glare; he knew Banquo, as his friend, was aware of a link between Douglas and Princess Eleonora, so his resentment grew quickly over having been kept in the dark regarding the report.

Banquo nodded while glancing over his shoulder to spy the glare, "It had been mentioned."

"And?"

"And an investigation is ongoing, Lord Aquilo. Young Corin here has his best Grimms on the matter, do you not Corin?"

It hadn't truly been up to Corin. He, and a small group of others, had been assigned the task of unraveling the mystery and finding the conservation priest by the commander of The Grimms at Sorrowmore. And aside from his own efforts, little else had been done. "Yes, Lords. The matter is being closely scrutinized."

"Alright?" Banquo leaned back with another glance to Horatio, who began to succumb to temper.

"Yes. Fine. Of course. Inform Maregill Temple to expect a visit from her Prince. I should like to inspect and ask after why my people, in her care, are starving. Also, on the related issue of the wayward priest: you are to report your findings directly to me, Corin of Sorrowmore. Let us see if we can't make a name for an inconsequential family. Results would please me greatly."

"Directly to you?" Banquo barked in disbelief. "Haven't you enough to do without..."

"That will be all, Corin." Horatio remarked to the young Grimm who had painted himself in all the colors of promise and gratitude as he bowed to leave. "Hold the next petitioner, if you would."

Again, Corin offered several bows and nods and left giving the message to the cluster beyond the door.

"Never do that again, Banquo," Horatio's cold voice spoke at a low volume.

"Pardoning my manners, Lord, but never do what again?"

Horatio responded with a frown as he poured a drink. "You're overstretched as it is, lad."

"You know I would want to know about this Douglas!"

"I know that the filthy little gill-scum probably wandered out into the night to stick his shaft somewhere it didn't belong and froze for it. I didn't see fit to trouble you with it until a body was found."

"You let your familiarity with me undermine me again and I shall be very cross."

"You are already very cross," he grumbled before taking a drink. "Besides," he continued with a disapproving whine, "Why would you promise the boy a title?"

"Incentive."

"Do you really believe he isn't doing all he can already? Wouldn't reporting to you, his Prince, his Lord Commander, directly, be enough incentive to not knave about with it?"

"Threats and rewards provoke differently. I don't want him worried about disappointing me as much as I want him lunging for treasures. It's the balance between the promise of lack verses the promise of gain."

"And what will you give him? Build him a town, will you?"

"Did he not say - perhaps I am ignorant of what he said - did he not claim to be Corin of Sorrowmore?" Horatio, flipping over a few parchments, clearly tired of the conversation.

"Sorrowmore is a slum, Horatio. A slum governed by Lord Polonius."

"Governed into a slum."

"He is a Grimm Commander."

"That stands to reason as he is the governor, of course he is a Grimm Commander, Banquo! Why are you vexing me so?"

"You intend to strip one to clothe the other?" Banquo made notice of a loud ruckus that had begun to rumble from a corridor that connected to a lesser keep.

"For what, of merit, is Polonius responsible?" Horatio growled and huffed, annoyed by being second-guessed, if even by a friend.

"Polonius is the Queen's uncle, Horatio."

"Yet again you regale me with that which I already possess in my comprehension. Should I cower, Banquo?"

"It seems to be an unnecessary insult."

"I insult my mother daily. My hesitation to breed is deeper a wound than a sword slash to the throat."

"But, the instability his removal would cause?"

"That I would remove the ineffectual? Even if the incompetence came from my own family? No, I think it would reflect very well. Besides, old Polonius has the luxury of seeking residence at Bleak Spire. Retirement will suit him. It is an advantageous possibility that this Corin presents."

"How sad for Douglas that the best thing he ever did was vanish."

A chuckle escaped from Horatio before subsiding as a young female Grimm burst into the room in distress. "Lord Commander," she begged with a lack of breath.

"The Lord Commander specifically demanded that all petitioners wait! Damn you, is patience and obedience so impossible?" Banquo demanded with a furious point to the door. "By the gills, if this is about food, I'll be sending the lot of you back to whatever snowdrift you came from – roasted to feed the throng!"

Instantly, Horatio recognized her where Banquo had not. She was not a representative from a village, she was an officer stationed at Dark Tower. Having been born a noble, she and Horatio had a relationship which featured many sexual encounters. But in time, she grew precious enough to the then young Prince that he finally admitted that while he valued her, she and he would never pair due to his aversion. Amicably, they parted, and she chose to become a Grimm for the betterment of the Hold. She quickly developed into an excellent Grimm and brought great honor to her already high name. "Anne?" the way he questioned marked deep concern as he held up an outstretched arm to Banquo for silence. "Anne, what has happened? Are you harmed?"

"Your brother, Lord..."

"My brother?" Panic shot though Horatio's heart as he crossed the room and handed her his drink to dampen

116

her throat.

"Your brother was found, bound, in the company of thieves, dear Horatio. I am so sorry. By the sea-steed, I am so sorry." She waved away the drink and, although wished against it, wept.

"Bound?"

"He is in a very poor state."

"Is he alive?"

"He will not wake. Poor little Hector."

His breath caught in his chest and held refuge, refusing to exit his body. A sound, high and sharp screeched in his ears and his balance shook. Hector, his youngest brother, should have been in the company of Edgar.

"Where is the boy?" Banquo demanded with a fury burning.

"Here at Dark Tower. A group of Grimms stopped a cart manned by a collection of thieves and a known highwayman. In the back, bleeding and restrained, they found the little Prince, unconscious. The abductors have been placed in the cells. I believe they have been badly beaten."

"They'll be beaten worse!" Banquo shouted as he began to cross to exit.

"Wait," Horatio cried. "I need them alive."

"Alive? They absconded with your brother! Did who-knows-what to him!" replied Banquo. "You can't be serious?"

"He was with Edgar," Horatio admitted with dire hopelessness. "Hector was collected by Edgar from Bleak Spire. They traveled together. He would have put up a fight. He would have defended Hector."

"Who thought that to be wise!?" Banquo shouted, forcing Anne to flinch. "Two of the three princes? Alone? Did he go alone, Horatio?"

"I imagine he did, although, I do not know."

"Certainly he did! Untouchable, damn Edgar! Damn him, what has he done?"

"Please, don't," Anne begged as the bluntness of Banquo's words, although accurate, clearly harmed Horatio further.

"A small murder of Grimms would have prevented any of this! I'm off to get answers from these worms!"

"Do not touch them, Banquo," Horatio insisted as he gathered his strength to make for the door. "Anne, take me to my brother so that I may see the extent of this damage."

"He is being cleaned of grime, Lord. Give it small time and we will go together," Anne offered softly.

"I will go now. Banquo, ask, only ask. Do not harm these criminals. Feed them and see that they are warm. They will need their durability for when my attention shifts to them." With a nod, he motioned to Anne to lead.

*Sing of tides and fire-brides,*
*(sing of sea and snow).*
*Find ye lad, a fire-bride,*
*(sing of sea and snow).*
*Never feel the chill again,*
*never going home again,*
*For mother'd surely turn ye out,*
*than hear that bride go scream and shout,*
*(sing of sea and snow).*

*For Grimmlan was a pious man,*
*(sing of sea and snow).*
*Til flames did lick his glovèd hand,*
*(sing of sea and snow).*
*Lost the black and took the red,*
*lost his soul and lost his head,*
*Ice around him cracked so flim,*
*Til melted lakes did suck him in,*
*(sing of sea and snow)*

*Sing a song of hot regret,*
*(sing of sea and snow).*
*Sing to never once forget,*
*(sing of sea and snow).*
*Under the tides and curse your name,*
*those fire-brides are all the same,*

*Best to sleep under the snows,*
*than ever let your father know,*
*(sing of sea and snow)*

*-Fire Shanty, Northern Sea Song*

# Chapter X
## *Of Pyrois: Immolation*

The grand dining hall of Tephra Keep was a wide circular place outfitted for use for banquets and balls. Twice daily, its most usual fare found the Queen-Mother Gabija orchestrating a time for privacy with her children over meals. She cherished the closeness that the ritual provided and often took advantage of the refreshments to hold conversations and council with her young. This particular feast, however, held little joyous laughter or light talk.

A pair of Red Spines stood post at each of the three doors to the dining hall. Their presence, which would often provide a comfort to the Royal children, set Yuma, the ten year old Princess, on edge. There had been no discussion yet as to why, and with such furious quickness, The Queen, Prince Mugdi, and Princess Creo, had been rushed into that place where they commonly met for this, their evening supper. She watched as Mugdi stared, with wide and fearful eyes, into a stone cup of water. Silent with the pallor of a man who had done wrong or seen a thing so gruesome that words were meaningless to describe his twisting mind, he barely moved as he breathed. Yuma was frightened by what could have transpired.

Princess Creo paced and toiled with a bound rage that sizzled and cooked just behind her dark eyes. She was raging like the belly of a volcano, churning and brewing and threatening with every accidental glance. Yuma watched her sister with trepidation and took into her young hand a palm's width of crimson hair, flipping it over. She was granted the ability to do so by her hair being left down: a custom in the South until young girls and boys come of age. She adored her hair and retreated to the grooming of it when seeking comfort or facing unsure circumstances. 'It was the red of the Fire Steed,' her mother would remark while soothing the restless child when she was very young.

Red was known as a hair color for the Southerners, but it was uncommon. Even more uncommon was the vibrant depth of Yuma's locks: nearly a wildfire or a storming tornado of blaze. More often, children were born with deep brown tresses that suggested whispers of ruby in particular lights, before growing out of the hue with age. A vast majority of those under Pyrois' care, as adults, featured dark brown hair with a shade somewhere between the stark, cold black of the North and the airy, waving auburn of the East. Their skin was the darkest of all the Holds and displayed a larger range of variation than those of the other regions. Unlike the ice-white of the North, the pink-blush of the East, or the golden-sun tan of the West, the Southerners could be either as dark as night or a simple few degrees lighter than a Westerner: a comparison so close that one would need to stand next to the other to even notice. It was a visceral and poignant example of the harshness of several generations of boundaries and insulation. To some it was a source of pride and strength, but to others, it was a rally-cry for revolution: a thing that had become of secret interest to the young Princess Yuma.

While the Queen, like a majestic statue, sat at the head of the table in unreadable reticence, Prince Fazil swooped around the room with skips, laughter, and taunts to the Red Spines, who knew well enough to stand silently and offer the boy no eye-contact. At ten years younger than Creo, he was only three years older than Yuma and his antics often served to polarize the siblings. Anything he seemed to get himself into was always viewed as the innocent stupidity of adolescence and as such, a low level of expectation had been set for Yuma. If she ever dared to excel, or if she seemed to form a contrast between her actual abilities and the abilities assumed of her by the recklessness of her brother, the other two would accuse her of instigation or cruelty. She was not cruel, and despised having her own worth attached to someone outside of herself. She observed him for some time because watching her mother, eldest brother, and sister, and their reaction to whatever had happened, only frightened her. Finally, Fazil's behavior triggered words to be spoken. Having received no reaction to his jeering and bullying of the dutiful Red Spines, he decided to extend a hand and poke at the chest of one with some derisive comment.

"Fazil! Stop it!" Yuma demanded in all the strength of her young voice.

The Queen's attention snapped her gaze to spy what Fazil had been doing while Mugdi continued to stare into the stone cup.

"You would tell him what to do?!" remarked Creo, who truly was priming for a conflict.

"Why should he be so mean?!" Yuma replied to Creo before pointing to her brother, "Fazil! Sit down!"

"Why would you treat your brother so?" asked Creo, bending at the waist with an indication back to Fazil. Her noble curls, pinned high and tight, threatened to come flailing out with every word. "Do not treat him in this way!"

"You say while yelling at me? He is mean! I have done nothing to be yelled at!"

"You pick at him!" Creo offered with a scream. "Why would you pick at him?"

"I think he should sit down! I think he should sit so that we may eat!" Yuma waved fiercely at the untouched food that sat upon the table. Hard flat breads, roasted lizard, and grapes gave testament that while volcanic soil is very fertile, there had not been enough time between eruptions to cultivate much in many years. The sluice gates, which had to rotate to avoid buildup, offered some protection in some areas and enough had been harvested that most people in the South enjoyed at least one good meal a day.

"I think what you think matters not so much. Eha, Yuma?" sneered Fazil with an obnoxious laugh. "I think these belong to the Crown as much as these walls or those lizards, no?" Again he poked at the same Red Spine who grunted at the gesture.

"Sit, Fazil." Queen Gabija had seen enough of the display to not allow Yuma to take any more of the brunt, from either Fazil or Creo. As much as Yuma's reaction to Fazil's treatment of the Red Spine filled Gabija with a great sense of pride and justice, she did not comment on it and waited for her pouting young son to take his seat. Once he had, which took a good deal of time, Gabija continued, "On the matter of your new brother, we must speak."

"A brother, then?" Yuma brightly questioned. She

was overjoyed to have any conversation at all to break the silence and was fairly aware that the alternating pattern of Gabija's adoptions would result in her final being a male. "Have you met with him, mama? Is he very kind and sweet? Does he smile often? The little smiles! I do love little smiles!" She was very anxious to have a sibling younger than she was.

Gabija smiled, warmed by the delight which the topic brought to an otherwise chaotic and bloodied day. The excitement seemed to extend to only one child, though, as Creo continued to pace, Mugdi stared and Fazil yawned, leaning back. "Yes, my Yuma. I am glad for your zeal. With two possible, I have met."

"Still between two?" Yuma asked, taking her hair into hand again.

"Both boys?" Creo unexpectedly asked.

Gabija nodded after taking a sip of her water. As she set the cup down, she stated, "And I am sorry, little Yuma. Neither boy is a baby."

At a loss for words, Yuma shook her head. She knew that a child younger than her did not need to be an infant, and so asked, "No, mama. But littler than me, yes?"

"I wish I could have given you a little one to care for, Yuma. I do. This would have been a thing you would do well. You have a heart, like a mother's heart," she nodded and watched the disappointment drip from the chin of her little girl. She took a deep breath in and wistfully began to speak, "Many nights have I had the dream. The dream I wake from with such a joy. Many nights I have dreamed of you, playing with, and caring for a little thing. You would protect it. See that it is fed and happy. And you would smile. Oh, Yuma, this smile is unlike any other. This dream, this dream makes me so very proud of you. And then I wake. I dress. I sit for hair, and I sit for face and I think on it. I can not escape that smile and the hope that smile gives me. And then on days like today, that smile is all I have. It is the most precious of my thoughts. But now, you frown. And I hurt, and I beg of you, please do not frown."

"No, mama! I am happy!" Yuma claimed while noticing how tired and worn her mother seemed. "I am happy! Any brother – please, don't be sad, mama!" Her chin and lower lip trembled, suggesting the possibility of tears.

Creo scoffed and demanded of her little sister, "Why do you cry?" The information that the boy would not be small sent concern into Creo's mind for a host of different reasons. "Tell us of the two, Mother."

Gabija smiled and reached to hold Yuma's small hand at the sound of her other daughter's scolding as if to offer comfort and calm. While still in the act of wordless affection to her youngest child, the Queen continued at the request of Creo, "There are two. This, I have said. It is an unusual case that the temples have set out for me. As you know, often when the children reach an age, they are sent off to make their way in our Hold. Some join Houses, some find apprenticeships, some become goat drovers, and then some join the temple – help with the other little ones. If they wish to join the temple, when the festival nears, a test is offered to those orphans who are grown. It is part of their joining, you see. In case someone had been overlooked, this is a thing I agreed to when it all began."

"One must be twenty of years to join the temple, mother." Creo's voice was a thin, worried thing. She was barely twenty-three and with a sudden sense of peril to her own ambitions, protested, "This is not a child, mother! This is not the point of what you do! You save children, no?"

"I am growing old, Creo," Gabija remarked.

"But, this is not what the ceremony is for!"

"Would a twenty-year-old not be as a son to me? Are you, at your age, not a daughter? Is Mugdi, at thirty, not a son?"

"I can not agree with this, mother!"

"It is not for you to agree!" Gabija shouted and with a slam of her hand, stood. "It is not for me to agree! Great Pyrois gives us the options. For you, I chose you! For Mugdi, for Fazil, for little Yuma – Pyrois gives me the options! And I chose you! How dare you, with all that you have burning in your mind, come with bitterness to me?"

"What have I done now?" Creo screeched in offense.

"What have you done? You divide. You always divide. You think it wise to cut lines in everything."

"Divide? When have I divided? How have I angered you so?"

"Your treatment of Cyrus I'Demai was uncalled for." The Queen interlaced her fingers and shook her head, referring to the passing accusation of rumors suggesting I'Demai had been involved in contact with the West. "You can not treat people in such a way. This I have said, and you know that is what we talk of."

"He is a traitor, mother!" Creo challenged. "Many talk of his journeys to the West Hold!"

"Many should not be you. It should never be you with no evidence of such a thing. And, it should never be you in a room filled with his colleagues!"

"But you, with your combative words for poor Tibon I'Itzal? This is acceptable?" the furious Princess asked.

"I am the Queen, girl."

"He had worry on his mind, and you made him to be...to be...What Mirza I'Raquour did..."

"That I did that? This is what you think? That I held the blade?" the Queen roared.

Yuma's eyes widened as she sunk deeply into her seat.

Creo drew further from the table and situated herself near-to a Red Spine as she pressed, "Mugdi was betrothed to his daughter!"

"And he still is," Gabija remarked, which finally drew Mugdi's dark eyes from his cup.

"How could this be?" Mugdi, with a shaken voice, asked while tilting his head. "All is in ruins, mother. The House of Itzal and the House of Raquour, they will clearly war with each other over this crime."

"Mirza I'Raquour is in custody, my son. Answer for her crimes, she will, although she has begged solitude and suicide."

"How will this satisfy House of Itzal? Tibon I'Itzal was a good man and a much loved clan head." Mugdi protested with a tone of impudence.

"She will not be granted suicide," the Queen offered while breaking a piece of flat bread before offering Yuma half.

"That is not the point!" Creo added.

"Will there be battles, mother?" Fazil, finally interested in the conversation, questioned.

"Would you like there to be battles, little Fazil?" asked Gabija. "Do you find them exciting?"

128

Fazil nodded before adding, "I do not like to be called 'little' anymore."

"Well, my little one," she set the bread on a plate, "a mind that thirsts for battles for little more than the opportunity to fight, is a little mind. This is fine. Perhaps you will grow." She was corrective and even in her words before looking over to her grousing older son, "You will marry the I'Itzal girl, Mugdi. And as a sign of faith in her ability to fill the void left by her father's murder – and yes, it was murder – you will forsake the fire throne and support her rule over the House of Itzal."

Creo attempted to hide a grin, but was indelibly pleased with the outcome. Fazil laughed and clapped and Yuma, wide-mouthed at the severity of the proclamation, looked from her mother to her brother. Mugdi, who had assumed his entire life at Tephra Keep to eventually be the one to inherit the crown, swallowed dryly, "Why should I be imprisoned, mother? What have I done to injure you so that you could discard me, like this?"

"Discard?" Gabija, with annoyance asked. "You would see the potential to save thousands of lives as a discarding of your own?"

"House of Raquour will still want revenge!"

"The murderer will face trial. It will be a dispute between two people, not two houses. You will unify, Mugdi. Is this not honorable?"

"They will kill me!"

"For what?" the Queen demanded, "You have no value to kill! You give up possibility to ascend to show that this matter is meaningful! You would not be a target! You will heal people."

"And now, I am interested in the matter of this new

son of yours, mother," Mugdi coldly proclaimed with a growl.

"What of it interests you, hm? You think this is a thing related to this murder? This thing that happened just hours ago, hm? This thing which surprised and made fearful me just as much as you, boy! You think months of testing and filtering and refining for just the right candidates is somehow related to what – to getting rid of you? Is this it?"

Mugdi shrugged and scowled.

"These are unrelated things. And to assume, Mugdi, to assume, as you have: that a son would have some leverage to my crown, where a daughter would not: you shame me. You shame yourself. Also, to assume that being placed in a position to heal a hurt people is, in actuality, you being discarded? This is shameful."

Creo smirked smugly while Fazil again yawned.

Yuma placed eight of her finger-tips, four from each hand on the table to ask, "Mirza I'Raquour murdered Tibon I'Itzal?" The curious news hit Yuma very hard. The oldest person she ever knew, even with temple priests considered, was Mirza I'Raquour, who would commonly sneak small stone toys, sweets, and even history scrolls to the young Princess when none were watching. She was kind to Yuma and the thought of her as a killer made a hot, wet gurgle erupt in her stomach. Feeling very unwell suddenly, she asked, "What happened? Why should she have done such a thing? To Tibon I'Itzal, no less? The Houses are friends! Neighbors!"

"There was a sickness in Tibon, Mirza said, my sweet girl," Gabija calmed her voice to explain to Yuma.

"Was he sick?"

"He did seem unwell, Yuma. Like another person in his skin," the Queen replied with a tilt of her head.

"He was fine. He was upset, with Mirza, and Duman I'Bahasin about a sickness. They were all very frustrated and perhaps, may have felt provoked by the Queen's treatment," Mugdi remarked with a scowl. "The old woman, Mirza I'Raquour, she may have gotten too worked up. Maybe, it could be, maybe she did not feel heard and so made a scene? Who could say?"

"She would not do that, Mugdi," Yuma flatly stated. "And mama would never have one feel unheard."

"You were not there, little Yuma. You have no way of knowing, now do you?" Mugdi, vexed by the turn of events, steamed and fumed.

"What are their names?" Fazil asked of the Queen, completely changing the topic as if all that had transpired was a small and meaningless affair. "Those two who may be my brother. What are their names?"

The Queen surrendered a sigh and was relieved to have something to speak on that was not rooted in chaos and killing, "Basem and Daim, Fazil."

"And they are older than me?"

"Yes, my son. They are seven years older."

"Both are?"

Growing swiftly impatient with the prying, Queen Gabija leveled a silencing glare to young Fazil before remarking, "Yes, my son. Both are."

"What are they like, mama?" Yuma asked in an attempt to coax the talk back into a place of calm. Having never been a part of an adoption of a sibling, she was eager with anticipation, even if the brother was not to be a baby.

Longing for slumber, the Queen arched her hand over her brow and caressed her aching head while succumbing to the interest of Yuma, "They are young men. They are, ..." her words trailed as effort was made to formulate words. "I met them together twice. Where there were three candidates when I selected you, little Yuma, for them, it is only them. For your group of three, I only met you as three once, because I knew when I saw you that you were my daughter."

Yuma smiled and inched closer, engulfed in the melody of her mother's voice.

"They are hard to describe. Very quiet, observant, almost too much so," she softly laughed. "They were both surprised with having been selected after all of this time with the temple. I imagine that all of you may have met them, except Mugdi. Mugdi was ten when he came to live here at Tephra Keep. Both Basem and Daim were found as babies in separate parts of the Hold. Abandoned. One at a mine near to the West border, one near a sluice gate, an open sluice gate, to the south-east. One has eyes that are suspicious with wisdom, the other is bigger and a stronger man. Together, they are comfortable and quiet. When separated, they grow agitated, physically. It is not an offensive thing, or something meant to be purposeful. Always together, they have been always together."

"You would separate two who need each other, so?" Creo asked, finding an opening to voice opposition.

"These are the two that great Pyrois has presented me, Creo."

Creo exhaled a dismissive chuckle, "You speak of my divisiveness? How could you, knowing what you know of these two, how could you accuse me of dividing everything? Of anything?"

"What happens if they die?" Fazil offhandedly asked while taking a bite of his fifth roasted lizard.

"Idiot! Why would they die?" Yuma barked.

Mugdi, anguished about the conversation detailing what he regarded as his replacement, stood and forced a bow, "I have a duty placed to me by the Queen. Excuse me, I have much to do before my journey."

"The Queen is still your mother, Mugdi. This will never change." Gabija, in all possible sincerity claimed with a glance of deep sadness.

"While it is a thing I question, I have learned that what the Queen says is law." Hatefully, he bowed. "So, thank you, my mother."

Creo grinned and stepped aside as Prince Mugdi stormed away with a single, attentive Red Spine following. "He is displeased," she remarked in the direction of the table and the three who still sat at it.

"He is. Yes. I expected as much, but did not know how poorly he would react. He will see the sedation that his presence will bring and temper his outrage. He views thirty years of misspent life where I wish he would see the luxury and opportunity. He is a kind man going off to marry a beautiful and smart woman – whom he preferred above all others! His frustrations will subside." The Queen grumbled and groaned as if she had been thinking aloud in the privacy of solitude. With a slow motion, she stood and offered apologies, "I grow tired, my children. I am in need of rest. Please eat your fill and sleep well. You will find a Red Spine to guard each of you on this night. Please, do not be alarmed. It is the wish of an overprotective mother to have them linger, such."

133

"Good night, my mama," Yuma softly said while standing to embrace the Queen, who held her tighter than usual.

"Good night, my little one." Gabija kissed the young Princess' head before releasing her and crossing to Fazil, who sat and ate uninterrupted. "Good night, my son," she said while placing a hand on his shoulder.

Fazil nodded and, without thought, lifted a free hand to tap, in recognition, the hand that the Queen extended in affection.

Yuma glared at Fazil's disregard and comprised a series of things she would like to say to him once left unchaperoned.

"Creo, walk with me a moment," she said, finally reaching the spot which Creo occupied once all of her pacing stopped. "You ate nothing?" she lightly asked while still in the presence of the younger children.

"I was not hungry, mother," Creo claimed while turning to follow the Queen into the hall. A pair of Red Spines, as if choreographed, turned from their post to follow.

The Queen, hounded by a lame knee which ached whenever she sat too long, began to limp slightly and reached to steady herself on her daughter's arm. Quietly, she confided her words, "You are pleased with Mugdi and House of Itzal?"

"It was his pick of women, as you said."

"You are too pleased, Creo." Her voice was stern and for the second time that day, she felt the need to lecture her daughter. "You harm him with your grins."

"Happiness is what I feel, mother. Why should I not smile? It was no grin."

"Happiness, I would welcome. I give your brother a gift that he does not want, and you gloat."

"Mother, please," Creo laughed contemptuously, as if lessening the offense.

"You say you were not hungry? This is a lie. You hunger for all things, my Creo. This ambition, you must dampen it or it will engulf."

"Mother, calm. I wish for what is best for the Hold. This is all. I am pleased for Mugdi to get this – gift, as you say. I am pleased to root out the truth of the talk about Cyrus I'Demai. And, I am pleased for your new son, although I do question the worth of saving adults from the toils of a child. That is not for me, as you say. It is the unflinching will of Pyrois." Her placation was evident as the Queen, frowning and aware, finally arrived to the door to her private chamber.

"Get you a lover tonight to sate this hunger. Your temperament is a thing I do not welcome. Find a body to set aflame and let me keep the fires of the Hold at bay without your constant kindling."

Creo's faux smiles faded as she heard the words.

"Good night, my daughter."

# Chapter XI
## *Of Wanderers: Entreaty*

The encampment of The Wanderers, on the family farmland of the Satyr initiate, Caradis, was a typical dawn-drenched Western field, filled with scores of sleepy canvas and skin tents. The bonfires smouldered from hours of neglect, morning birds and seagulls swooped low to pick up any remnants from the prior night's feast, and the latrine pits featured mostly fresh coverings from vigorous use throughout the night.

Rainfall was most frequent and fierce in the West, and as such, the majority of the Hold was comprised of lush wetlands. Where settlements had been developed, in and among the thickest of trees, the extreme fertility of the soil found areas often cleared to facilitate expansive cropland. The farm owned by Caradis' family at Thorn Bush was much like any other average farm in the region: set just outside the gates to a town. As most of the family homesteads were generational and cherished as ancestral, few new farms were built anymore, yet the land cleared and developed by Caradis' family was quite different.

It was an eccentric and welcoming place, precious in every aspect to the hands that lovingly established it: Ljudot, which meant 'anyone, everything' in an ancient Northern dialect. Caradis was born there to parents who retired from wandering fourteen years before she had been conceived. Her mother, born to unknown parents, was of the East and named Volati. Caradis' Father, Sadiz had once been known as Sadiz I'Salido before he left his homeland in the far south to travel with the roaming scholars and, per custom as a Wanderer, disown all surname and regional loyalty. With free choice to settle where they pleased upon retirement, they considered their options carefully and, having decided that they would like a life apart from their own respective heritages, narrowed the consideration to either the North or the West. Knowing that they were wishing to start a family, the cool days and warm nights of the West easily won out over the harsh and vicious Northern climate. Yet, still longing to pay their respects to the Hold unrepresented by their family, they discovered the word Ljudot in an old scroll of myths, and felt it expressed, most completely, the kind and loving philosophy they held for their family.

The family home at Ljudot was a standard tree-house design. Six large cedar trees had been chosen and utilized as the stilts to the home. The windows were dressed in vibrant and mismatched silk drapery while bells and chimes tossed their song through the breeze. Bottles, of every color hung from twine off the side lip of the roof to catch rain water and herb pots, in the artistic shapes of heads with smiling faces and flowing green aromatic hair, seemed to nearly burst from overcapacity. The weather, as Thorn Bush was fairly close to the border to the North, yet still near the coast, was often some of the coolest in the Hold. It supplied excellent growing conditions for berries of all kinds and exquisite leafy green vegetables like coriander, chard, kale, and cabbage. The homestead was a place of loving sanctuary for occupants as well as weary travelers.

The sun rise, gold and pink, trickled over the dew as

Morigan, on the back of General Lysander Barro's horse, approached, looking bedraggled. Barro, glum faced, followed closely on his departed colleague Sulaelia's horse, which moved with a depressed cadence. In his red gloved hand was a let out lead with the steed of Markos, who had been the first of his troop to die the previous night, straggling behind in sorrow.

"This is the place, General," Morigan remarked, nearly falling of the horse with her dismount.

Lysander nodded and ran a gaze across the multitude of yurts placed in a dormant field. While offering a hand to receive the reins of his own horse, he commented, "I will linger."

"Why? You've delivered me. And I appreciate it. I don't need a guardian."

His breath was slow and deep while he quietly considered a plan, "You said this Caradis is a Satyr?"

"A child."

"But a Satyr?"

Morigan nodded and pointed up to the family house that stood in the six cedar trees.

"I should hitch the horses and have them watered and rested. I would like to fill that time with knowing what you Wanderers make of what we saw. Also, I'd like to meet this child Satyr." After coming off the horse of Sulaelia's he signed and patted the gentle animal's forehead, "Besides, they deserve their time to weep."

Morigan stood with little to say and nodded with a heaviness in her chest. She did not gather that she had just been asked to collect Caradis for the General and as such, received a slightly irked frown, "What is it?" she asked.

"The Satyr?"

"Caradis."

"Yes. That one."

"What of her?" Again a strange expression from Lysander met Morigan's words, "What? She's up there!" She pointed to the high house with a pale hand covered in inky swirls.

"And you would have me knock at the door?"

"Why not?"

Sarcastically, Lysander nodded and shrugged, "Yes, let us alarm the locals when the highest ranking Satyr arrives at their doorstep before breakfast. Let's do that. Shall we do that?"

"Shall I fetch her for you?"

"Yes! Please!" In exasperation, he noticed that a few Wanderers had begun to stir from their tents. "Rather, second thought...I'll do it." As much as he did not wish to alarm the parents of a young royal guard, he wished even less to be surrounded by curious Wanderers who had no way of knowing why he had come around.

"Suit yourself," she scoffed with a wave of her hand before turning to beat a quick pace to the largest teat which sat at the perimeter.

Lysander waffled between making his approach to Caradis' house and following Morigan. With an unsatisfied grunt, he decided to participate in whatever Morigan had to say to her superiors, and so accompanied her with a skip to catch up.

With surprise, Morigan stopped and stared at Lysander.

"I think I should be involved."

"With what? In what? Why are you following me? I

said thank you, didn't I?"

"No, I don't think you did," he remarked while removing his gloves. "To whom do we speak?"

"About what?"

Flustered, Lysander shook his head a single time, "Are you being purposefully obstinate? Why are you doing this?" With a quick flick of a glance around it became evident that he was growing uncomfortable with the encroaching Wanderers who were interested in his presence.

Morigan didn't answer immediately and considered how much Lysander had lost in the few hours they had known each other while scanning the whispering faces of her scholarly brothers and sisters. They would mumble behind cupped hands into the ears of the person standing to their side and it served to ease her approach to what he seemed to need. "Alright. You come with me, then." She reached to the sleeve of his ornate armor while calling over to a Wanderer who appeared to be a honey-haired native son of the West, "Eusebios! Run up to the house and see if Volati's daughter is available, would you? When she is ready, bring her to the tent of Mother and Father, please."

Eusebios nodded cooperatively and raised a hand with a smile before immediately heading over to the family house, calling back, "Right, Morigan!"

Lysander raised an eyebrow with an impressed tilt of his head.

"Family works together, General. The Wanderers are a family. There is nothing extraordinary in what you just saw."

"He was very eager to assist."

Morigan continued her trail to the large tent, "It is nothing extraordinary."

He nodded and followed while commenting, "I don't feel particularly welcome here."

She stopped again and turned to spy the grins and giggles. "They know who you are. At least some of them knew beforehand. But now, everyone does."

"What do you mean?"

"General Lysander Barro is a man of legend, sir," she regained her pace and nodded. "Though I admit, I expected something else."

"What?" he demanded as they arrived at the large shelter. Although the entrance flaps were down, plumes of smoke slithered out from the small cracks at the hem of the fabric. Lysander quickly pointed with one hand and rested the other on the hilt of the blade on his hip, "What is this?"

"What is what?" curiously Morigan replied while following his gaze from eye to tent flap. "What, the smoke?" she asked with absolutely no hint of worry.

"Is this normal?"

She laughed, "Is it morning?" She waited a few breaths to see if he would calm his concern, and when he did not, she added, "You have to relax, General. No one is up to anything here." She pointed in a circle to the Wanderers around their immediate area, "These people are just interested in you. They mean no harm. There is no danger." She shook her head. "I'm sure if you stood around long enough a line would form of women asking you for a reason for their retirement." Again she chuckled but was met with a flat glance of consternation from Lysander: he had no idea what she meant.

Finally, and with a hushed voice, he asked, "How are you so calm? How could you be relaxed? You and I, we saw the same thing, didn't we? We saw what happened to Sulaelia and Markos. And yet you would smile and make excuses for the leering?"

"Well, I wouldn't really call it leering, General."

"You do know there is something deeply wrong with what we saw, right?"

Before speaking, she sighed and turned to face the tent to best conceal her words from onlookers, "I know that all things under the sun come with an explanation – no matter how hard to locate, an explanation always exists. I know that the Prince Regent just got word that his father had been found in a mindless state and I know that both The Sepal and Purpureus Council want me to stay behind to help with whatever is afoot in your Hold. I know that the King and that hound handler may have had the same sickness, and I know that they may not have had the same sickness. And I also know that an interest in a handsome stranger is not always a case of leering, and really, that was a very mean thing to say."

"You've been asked to stay?" His sympathy for the position that the request put Morigan in was clear.

"They asked me to stay on, yes."

"Stay on? You were offered a position? By The Sepal and The Council?"

She nodded with the first hint of a frown since their arrival to Ljudot. "We should speak with the Mother and Father. I'll just have to repeat all of this anyway." With a lift of a shoulder she eased an entrance flap to the side and awaited notice.

The Wanderers were led by the single-most senior

male and woman among them. They set the pace at which travel progressed, made all the major decisions if the group as a whole could not find common-ground, and oversaw the blessing of dismissal: the rite of retirement from the tribe. Information as severe as something concerning a possible sickness running rampant through a Hold would be of great interest and concern for the Mother and Father. Kind, patient, and often holding their post until death, the Mother and Father were revered as almost mystical in their vast knowledge.

"Come, sweet Morigan. Sing us a song of The Sepal. How are things at the capital?" an old woman, Mother, asked while greeting Morigan and her guest at the entrance. She took Morigan's hand into both of her own and led her to a sitting pillow which was arranged atop a large circular rug in the center of the tent interior.

"I suppose you're happy no one else wanted to go, now?" Father, a skinny little old man of bones and ligaments, laughed through a plume of smoke which he exhaled as he removed the mouthpiece of the smoking device from his lips. He scratched at his loincloth, which was all he wore, when noticing Lysander, "By the Veil! You brought The Fox to visit?"

"The Fox?" Lysander questioned while offering a nod of gratitude for the repeated motion from Mother to sit next to Morigan.

"Wanderers give all the generals nicknames. The rulers, too. Makes it easier to speak freely while we travel," Morigan explained in an almost apologetic way.

"Well, not all the generals," Mother expressed while pouring steaming mint tea into a set of four cups, "Just the important ones."

"Ah, I see," Lysander remarked with a courteous smile.

"Just the handsome ones," Mother flirted unabashedly which caused a grand guffaw from Father.

Morigan covered her face and rubbed her temples, embarrassed and dreading having to deliver the news.

Lysander uncomfortably shifted and offered the faintest of chuckles.

"So, what happened at The Sepal, Morigan? Anything of interest? It was nothing, yes? Just asking when we would be on our way?" Father asked before leaning to Lysander with an aside while pointing to Morigan, "Poor thing. No one wanted to go, so she volunteered. Such a good one, this one is."

"We really have been here for a little longer than usual," Mother added as if thinking aloud. She shrugged, "The rains have been so heavy. Breaking a camp this size is no small matter."

Thunder softly rolled in the distance which triggered a gripe from Father, "Ah! There it is again! These damn rains, they never stop here, excuse me for saying so, General Fox."

"You may call me General Barro if you wish. Or, Lysander: that is my name."

"The Sepal received a report that the King had been seen by Satyr scouts close to here. At Briar Bay. Caradis was asked by a pair of Purpureus Councilors to come and collect a Wanderer, and she only told me some of what awaited me when she walked me to the edge of the farm. And not even all of that as she had no way of knowing what would happen: just that the King had been seen in a bad enough state that the Prince Regent may have

144

questions that only a Wanderer could answer." Morigan, in a flurry of words, worked to get out all she could. "I went. I heard what they had to say: that the King lumbered around in the nude, and that his pupils were very large. A Satyr scout saw him and called to him but he dashed off."

"Hm. Chewing on a bit of plant to get a buzz, sounds like," Father muttered drawing the sudden, yet silent ire of Lysander, whose attention shifted as Caradis entered the tent.

She was a young woman with the clear build of a sprinter, and, as she was at home with her family, she was dressed in a casual tunic and trousers. She had hair of a dark chocolate color and seemed to appear exactly as the child of a Southerner and Easterner should: rosy, yet dark. The polite smile dropped from Caradis' lips as she noticed that the General sat in attendance and she grabbed and clutched her hands together, star-struck and swooning, somewhat.

"Ah! Little Caradis! Come, sit. Have some tea!" Mother demanded while motioning with a wide swoop of her arm.

"I'll share words with you when this business concludes, initiate," Lysander nodded and spoke in a quiet confidence while waving away a salute with a friendly shake of his head, "Sit."

"Yes, sir." She sat, accepted the tea and blinked in Morigan's direction.

After Morigan bowed her head at Caradis, she continued while turning back toward Mother and Father, "It was not plants. I thought it may have been. And then I thought it was poisoning, an assassination attempt, but then, I don't think that was it either. They had a large group to go missing. Sixteen, it would seem."

"Sixteen? All together the group was sixteen?" Father asked leaning further back. "I thought it had only been the King, Queen, and a few others."

"There were sixteen in the royal hunting party," Lysander confirmed.

"Right, okay, so, sixteen gone. They think they saw the King. Or, at least whatever was left of the King. The Prince Regent seemed at a loss. The Purpureus Councilors seemed seconds from consuming each other over – I don't know, worry, or fear, or whatever it is that drives politicians. And all of a sudden, all at once, they all...well, they all asked me to stay," Morigan admitted with a cornered frown. "And I didn't know what to do – and I still don't know what to do, but I didn't know what to do then, specifically, and I was thinking about it on the way back here, and something happened."

Lysander nodded and set the cup of tea down with an arched hand and lowered eyes.

Mother and Father leaned closer to hear the tale while Caradis watched the subtle and poetic curves and angles on the back of Lysander's hand and wrist.

Morigan glanced to Lysander, noticing Caradis with a squint of surprise before turning back to both Mother and Father, "I was walking, and not paying attention. I was thinking on their request and the King – and what could be wrong with the King, when I noticed suddenly that I was lost. Quite horribly, terribly lost. I then saw a figure in the bog,"

"She had veered into the edge of The Peat Wastes, near the temple of Mossglen. Had she not stopped she may have crossed into the North Hold if she had managed to stay on the path between the two and not into the depths of the mud."

"My, that's a bit to the east," Father scolded. "That's very dangerous territory up there." The only area that one could pass from the West Hold to the North, or back again, was a lane of land that started at the coast, near-to Briar Bay and stretched to the east to the temple of Mossglen, with the center point as Thorn Bush and Ljudot. The Sepal itself was situated more-or-less south of Thorn Bush. Morigan had traveled far too easterly and truly may have met her end if she had kept on and strayed into The Peat Wastes.

"I stopped because I – I knew I was lost," Morigan remarked with a shameful shake of her head. "I stopped and tried to get an idea of where I was when I saw, I don't know. I thought he was hurt, or sick. I don't know."

Lysander frowned but let her continue at her own pace. He was unwilling to add comment on the matter unless asked.

"What did you see, my child?" Mother asked while placing a hand on Morigan's back.

"A thing. A thing that had once been a man. A young man! The General said he knew the fellow and that he was the hound handler for the King and Queen's hunt. His name was Euclid. But he was not who he had been." Morigan covered her mouth and searched for the words to explain, or even express what she had seen.

"How do you mean that he was not as he had been? What does that mean? Do you mean that you feel as if whatever had the King had this hound handler as well?"

"I can't be certain as I did not see the King in his

condition. But, it is of value that both men were part of the same entourage," Morigan offered while looking to Lysander. "You are being very quiet on this."

The General gave a half shake of his head by way of turning his cheek only slightly, "I don't know what you'd like me to add."

"You were there."

"We were. Three of us."

"Three of you?" asked Mother sullenly. From the expression on Lysander's face, the fate of the other two was an obvious and sad event.

Lysander was hesitant but glanced at the pleading eyes of Morigan and conceded, "Yes. Three of us. For a few days we have had some knowledge of a sickness spreading out from the part of the Hold nearest the Veil. Those that fall ill are prone to a particular cry, a shriek, really. They degenerate quickly. The information is so recent, in fact, that a report has not yet been made to the capital. Two Satyrs and I left from consulting with Mossglen, on our way to The Sepal, when we heard the shouts from the one Morigan found."

Both Mother and Father were quiet with thoughts and fear.

Morigan quickly looked from one to the other, insisting, "Well? What could be the cause?"

Neither had an answer and unsure glances were shared. Finally, Mother broke the silence and remarked, "Fox. Thank you for saving our Morigan, although clearly, that cost was great."

Lysander nodded and said nothing.

"We can not compel your mind on this, Morigan," Father remarked. "But, were I in your position, I would stay where I was so badly needed. Even if that meant parting with the family that loves you. I have rarely heard so sound a reason to retire from the wandering."

Mother sadly nodded.

Lysander looked from both Mother and Father to Morigan, quietly awaiting whatever she would say as her face clearly described a deep pattern of calculated thoughts.

Slowly she nodded and muttered, "I haven't much choice, really."

"You always have a choice, child," Mother maintained.

"I really don't, Mother. I can't possibly leave this Hold to fend without whatever help I could offer."

"You would have my support," Lysander offered. "I swear you would."

Morigan nodded quietly, "I'll take my retirement and accept the appointment offered by The Sepal."

"Then, may I present your personal guard, Lady," Lysander nodded from Morigan to Caradis.

Caradis recoiled in tremendous shock and honor, "Sir?"

"The part you've played has already been so vital to where we are now. I'm sure Briar Bay has some paperwork laying around regarding some reward for service. That could take years. Or – I could overwrite it all and give you the role of a court Satyr. Very prestigious, I assure you," he smiled.

"She is child, Lysander," remarked Morigan with a shake of her head.

"She is no child. She is a Satyr, and now you are a court noble! Unicorn works magically." Lysander, in every effort to conclude with some pleasantry clapped and bowed as he stood. He turned to face Mother, smiling past her to Father as he spoke to both, "It would give the West great comfort, and great honor, if you would allow me to escort The Wanderers to the border of the South Hold, when you're ready to depart."

"That's hardly a usual request, Fox," groaned Father, who held the need to keep allegiance to none high on his list of tenants. "Wouldn't look right to be protected by the royal guards of the West, would it?"

"It isn't usual, because this is an unusual situation. There is no telling how this illness moves or when you may come in contact with a carrier. Please," Lysander, in his soft coo requested. He placed a hand to his chest before speaking further, "I would personally be present."

"Please take his offer," Morigan unexpectedly asked, dour with a sudden goalless nostomania.

With sympathy mixed into gratitude, Lysander glanced at the sorrow that radiated from Morigan before continuing with his offer to the leaders of The Wanderers, "We would benefit from it. It would do my soldiers good to do something of worth."

Slowly, and with great reservation, both Father and Mother agreed.

Relieved, Lysander Barro bowed and clapped once, "Excellent! I'll seek out a messenger at Thorn Bush to send word along to The Sepal detailing the arrangement as well as assignment orders to gather up as many idle Satyr as can be found." He bowed deeply to Father and Mother, remarking, "Please expect my return shortly." With a smile and a shrug, he turned to Morigan, "The West is truly fortunate on this day."

150

# Chapter XII
## *Of Pegasus: A Place Hidden for Good Reason*

It had been decided the moment Eileivia's eyes detected it: they would travel to, and post up at that small cottage obscured in the forest. The gelding was as slow as expected while the Magpie rambled for some time on the merits of her plan. She was ardent to sell the idea as a thing without ulterior motive.

"It seemed quite cozy! Quite a nice little spot, really. There was smoke billowing from the chimney and some livestock and crops. Surely they'll welcome us in for a nice little bowl of soup," she urged as the congestion of the trees grew in around their cart.

"There wasn't a path?" Otver complained. The terrain had quickly become difficult, with broken branches and logs strewn as if victims of a recent flood. "It doesn't seem like we'll be able to even find it, Eile."

She smiled at the use of the name she requested while jostling and bouncing uncomfortably, "We'll find it. I understand you to be an excellent tracker."

Otver coughed and shook his head, "Obviously. I tracked a deer and killed a divine-blood. I'm obviously very good at tracking." His sarcasm faded slightly as he continued with a more dissenting tone of voice, "Really, I don't know about this. This doesn't seem very smart."

"What isn't smart about it? We'll need to rest. And even if we didn't need the rest, this sad horse will. Just a short stop. An overnight break. We're close to the border and should take security where we can find it. We won't have many opportunities like this once we cross into the North Hold."

"Is the North Hold really so terrible?"

"I've never been, myself. But, of the few I know that have so much as set foot across the line, only a handful of them ever came back. And the stories they would tell: awful."

Otver winced at a particularly jarring bump but begged, "Like what?"

Eile lifted a shoulder. "The sound really. It was the sound, or the lack of sound that was the most frightening."

"How could there possibly be a lack of sound?"

"Something about the snow and ice. The ears go funny, like 'reaching for ropes to not fall' I've heard it said."

"That does sound awful."

"And you can't sing! The natural, normal thing for an Easterner is to sing when, you know, we're a song lot, but you can't."

"Why not?"

"You'll be found."

Otver nodded cautiously and noticed just in time a large, low hanging branch. Lowering his head to not face an impact, he again voiced his dislike of the idea of trying to find the cottage, "This seems like a place put where it is to avoid visitors."

"Have you really never come across such a place in your poaching adventures?"

"I don't poach. Will you please not say it like that?"

Eile laughed and swayed out of the way of a few branches herself. "Alright, easy. I'm sorry. It wasn't poaching. It was survival. Still, my dear ole mother would shoot you on the spot if she saw you sniffing around her land. Like a fox or some nasty little raccoon."

"Lucky for me I never roamed onto your mother's land. Like the nasty little raccoon I am."

"Why are you so salty again? You are such a glum little boy!"

"This is a stupid thing we're doing. We are currently in the act of something so dumb."

Eile yanked up on the reins to stop the cart before turning to Otver, "Listen. I am doing the best I can here. This is a good possibility for us. Have you had a decent meal?"

Otver shook his head in slow shame.

"Nor have I. I had just come in from my detail because Windwing had gone into labor. We had been riding, hard riding, for three days over the missing, and then found, dead, Princess Lavinia. And we had no answers and it was frustrating."

Otver nodded, listening carefully.

"I'm hungry, Otver. I'm cold. And all that damn Western rain is blowing in and it isn't going to get any better. When we hit the North Hold, we will be more hungry, and more cold. And we'll wish for the Western rains as they would be a refreshing warmth to the ice that falls from the sky up there."

"Ice? Ice falls from the sky?"

"It does," Eile nodded with a professorial frown. "And it doesn't care much for who it hits or when. It's horrible, horrible, awful."

Otver chewed at his lip and began to realize how cold he was. With a shiver, he nodded, "Alright. I'll stop complaining."

"Yea? A good warm bowl of soup sounds nice, doesn't it?"

Otver nodded before asking, "Are you sure, though, that we're going the right way?"

"Took a straight line from the tree I climbed. Well, as straight as we could with all of these old trees in the way." She urged the gelding to start on again and professed, "I don't know, though. You may be partly right about this. I've never seen such a dark and hidden place."

The birds were silent as the gargantuan trees, hemlock, pine, yew, and red cedar, groaned at the touch of the ferocious wind at their heads. The ground, due to the density of the canopy, knew no grasses. It was naked earth littered with the debris and bones of the tress that gathered there and it whispered a sense of eerie warning. Otver glanced around in observation before he finally remarked, "I don't even see rabbit warrens, Eile."

Eile, with a turned expression of new-found foreboding, looked to Otver, instigating him to elaborate.

"There should always be rabbit warrens. It's a sign of safety."

"Maybe...maybe there are too many raptors?" She raised her eyes to the tall and clustered trees, instantly feeling dizzy.

Otver scooted down a bit off the bench of the cart and, once his small body was nearly horizontal, looked up with squinted eyes to study the under-belly of the canopy, "No. I see no nests." Sitting back upright, he studied the trunks of the tress just ahead of their progress, "No falcon hole-nests neither." As he gave a glance to the dirt of the treacherous ground, Eile, impressed, submitted a question.

"Do you find that helps?"

"What helps?" he asked while in sharp study for any sign of birds on the ground below: feathers, droppings, nest twigs.

"Laying back like you did. Do you find that helps when looking up?"

"I've always done it. I don't know. I think so. Look, I don't see any birds either."

"Maybe it's nothing," Eile shrugged.

Otver, in disbelief shook his head as he spoke, "Nothing? What do they teach Magpies? How is it nothing? No rabbits: alright, so, too many natural predators. No birds? In the East? What?"

The back wheel that had been squeaking since they left GoldCloud offered a sound similar to a snapping board. The cargo, body included, which had begun to emit the odor of death, jumped and slid.

"If we stop, it may fall off," Eile quietly commented in defeat.

"What if it falls off because we're moving?"

"It may have been a branch. I was having trouble paying attention while you were tutoring me on how to be a nasty little raccoon tracker."

The trees had begun to part in their placement slightly, and finally they caught sight of the cottage. It was not at all as Eileivia witnessed it from high above in the treetop. There was no smoke billowing from the chimney, no livestock, save a few skeletal remains in the pens, and no crops in that dark and horrible cold dirt. The clearing was a small one, only large enough to accommodate a thin, circular bald set of land that held the house, gray and broken, at its center. The door, ancient and weathered, hung low on the iron hinges and the slat-boards of the side of the home had begun to slough toward the dirt.

"Is this what you saw?" with words less accusatory and more worried, Otver asked in fearful amazement.

"No. Unless I looked a hundred years back in time, this is not what I saw." Crushed with disappointed bewilderment, Eile guided the gelding and cart up near the cottage. "How could this be?" she whispered with perplexed sadness. "It was not like this just hours ago."

The wind, having never truly stopped, whipped up into a gale. The chimes which dangled from the porch, all hollow bird bones tethered to twine, clamored and thrashed together in an argument of sound. The door, having been shoved by an erstwhile breeze, creaked open and the mouth of the house looked back in wide shouts to the pair of travelers. The air had the distinct bite of frost as it lingered so near to the North and with admonishing signs of oppressive despair, the place suggested, by its very existence, that no good could ever come from finding it.

The two sat on the cart for some time in silent reverence for the scale of the horror. The gelding became uneasy and exhibited more spirit in his clear protest of the place than he had at any other point. He shivered and puffed with whinnies and whines. Stomping his hooves, he bucked slightly, catching the attention of Eile who quickly lowered from the cart in a natural effort to comfort him.

Otver stayed stark still, staring into the abyss that the recently opened door offered. With a quiet voice, he interrupted Eile's whispering to the gelding with unexpected words, "We should stay the night, at least."

"Why? This place is terrible," Eile demanded as quietly as possible so as to not upset the gelding further. "I made a mistake, Otver. I'm sorry."

"It's alright," he offered while lowering himself onto the dirt. With a glance around and a shutter, he continued, "It's late. You were right about that and needing to find somewhere safe to pass the night."

"You call this safe?"

"I don't know. There's certainly no one around to worry about with the cargo. That's something at least." He grabbed one of the furs provided to him for the journey and wrapped it around his shoulders, "I can find some firewood and I think I hear a stream nearby."

"You hear the wind."

"I know the difference, Magpie. It's water, and close. Something caused all that flood damage that we had to cross." He sounded older than he was and his words demanded that Eile trust his instinct. "Besides, people don't build houses far from water. Even ones as lonely as this one. We can't really set back out until dawn anyway. We shouldn't try to travel through all of that mess in the dark."

While carefully stroking the gelding's mane, Eile admitted, "You're right. You're completely right, Otver."

He nodded and smiled slightly at her respect for him before walking to the back of the cart to retrieve his bow and quiver.

"Oh, we have kindling, young archer," a crone, hunched and lurching, crowed as she, in the company of three others who were huddled tightly, appeared from the back of the cottage to the side. "How thoughtful of you to offer." Her voice was like the death screams of a hawk. The four old women wore cloaks of feathers with high and wide shoulders, like opportunistic vultures.

"Who are you?" demanded Eileivia in a strong voice. "By the Crown of Pegasus, I would ask your names!" She kept a steady hand to the cheek of the gelding while her other hand extended as if shielding Otver, who stood a good distance away.

"Oh, by the Crown, you say? How very fortunate are we, dear sisters, to enjoy such illustrious guests!" said the one who appeared to be the only that possessed the power of speech. Of the others, unusual characteristics became noticeable to both Eile and Otver: one had extraordinarily large ears, one had huge round eyes like an owl, and the third had a long, hooked nose, like the beak of a falcon. The one who spoke to them smiled and her abnormally large mouth presented a curl at the ends, as if her lips extended far beyond the norm.

"Please, ma'am. We're not any type of trouble," Otver offered, terrified, but wishing to take a route contrary to the Magpie's trained force. "We thought we saw a family home from high in the canopy."

"Did you, indeed?" Her words scraped their way from her throat while she stepped away from the cluster of the other three. She slowly hobbled near-to Otver, completely by-passing the alert and vigilant Eileivia. "You saw our home, did you? With those little almond eyes of yours?"

"N-no, ma'am," he trembled. "M-my chaperone. My chaperone saw it, ma'am."

In swift and patterned unison, the silent three shot from their position with a blinding speed and situated themselves around Eileivia in a suffocating closeness. They stared into her and were unmoved by her scream of alarm.

"What are you doing?" Otver whimpered.

"They wanted to have a look, little archer," the speaker answered Otver while looking back to the terror-stricken Magpie, still having words for him, "Why do you travel under the protection of the Crown, little archer?"

The beak-nosed crone opened her decaying mouth, huffing the scent of Eileivia's fear, while the wide-eyed sister blinked at a lopsided rate. Their faces nearly touched her panicked chin.

Otver, completely invested in the sight of the assault on Eile, shook his head, not knowing what to say. She stood very still in her fright, and had tears on her cheeks.

"My sisters and I, we would like to know, little archer, why do you travel under the wing of Pegasus?"

"We, we...w-w-we, we do a thing for Pegasus."

"A thing?"

Otver nodded nervously.

"You do a thing for Pegasus?"

Again, he nodded while shivering.

"This is good," she relented, turning to her sisters with a raised hand. "Pegasus sends these."

While the three slowly stepped away from a nearly fainting Eileivia, the beak-nosed assailant snapped a quick turn of attention in Otver's direction, specifically, the cart and cargo.

"What is this you find, Podarge?"

Podarge extended her arms far from her bony body; the feathered cloak was a wingspan as she hobbled an odd and unnerving crow hop toward the back of the cart.

"Oh? Has my sister found some treasure? Some gift from the Lord Pegasus? Are you here with gifts, little archer?"

Desperate to protect the remains of Prince Edgar, Otver threw his little body between the cargo and the approach of the horrifying crone.

"Otver, no!" Eile cried just as Podarge, with a swing of her cloaked arm, knocked the child from her path. Without thought, Eile removed herself from the presence of the two lingering crones, the wide-eyed and large-eared sisters, and ran to lift him from the dirt, looking him over for injury.

"Is the feather for the Crown your mama, little archer?" The speaker laughed and stood aside while her sister, Podarge, began to rifle though the contents of the cart's haul.

Neither Eileivia nor Otver, bruised and winded, answered. Once Podarge's beaked nose began to shove and thrust into the rolled rug that held Prince Edgar, Eileivia's protective embrace around Otver's small frame grew tighter, while Otver struggled and begged, "No, please..."

The corner of Edgar's face, alabaster and lifeless, became visible by the relentless flipping of the edge of the loosened rug. With a gasp and screech, Podarge was repelled and quickly sought refuge behind her sister that spoke. The large-eared sister tilted her head and approached the disgusted and shaken Podarge while the sister with the wide-eyes drew near to the corpse for inspection. She peered closely at the face of the Prince and dragged her osseous finger across his forehead, sliding aside wisps of ebony hair.

"It is Hippocamp?" the mouth asked in astonishment. "Ocypete? This is Hippocamp?"

A delayed blink of the two massive eyes on the sister, Ocypete, indicated an affirmative and with a nod as she pulled away, wrapping herself tightly within her feathered cloak.

"Why did Pegasus send you here with Hippocamp, little archer?" With grave concern, the speaker of the sisters pulled her three kinswomen close, again becoming a unified heap of feathers. She offered a wary sidelong glance to both the Magpie and Otver, who were still on the ground, one in the arms of the other. "Answer us!" a caw of a boom was her demand.

"We're to take him home, ma'am," Otver explained. Aware of their sudden fear for what they saw, he suited his words to their superstitious reactions, "We're traveling to take him to his Hold."

"Pegasus offers us a challenge. We see this, now. Pegasus wishes to test our love."

Eileivia, having never encountered anyone so deep in the forest, was unprepared for the folk-faith she witnessed with the sisters. She had no way of making sense of the women and felt fear winning out over any attempts at reason. Pulling Otver closer, she whispered into his ear, "Please stop talking." Her eyes remained locked on the unusual physical characteristics of the four sisters.

The speaker crone extended her head and neck to an unnatural length before swooping any exposed piece of her body down into her cloak with rumbling whispers to her sisters. The mound of feathers that covered the four pulsed and shook with hissing and spit. There was anger

161

in the confusion and veneration for the divine.

The gelding repeatedly turned his face toward the commotion with an anxious and scared eye as he began to gnaw at the bit in his mouth. And, despite whatever had been said to him by the Magpie, he could not stay still or calm himself. He stomped, snorted, and squealed. He flicked his ears nervously and when not flicking, his ears shifted back and were close to his head. Eileivia noticed his growing agitation and grew more tense at the sight of it.

"You should help him," whispered Otver. "I'm okay."

With a dry throat, she swallowed and espied the huddled mass of feathers that she would have to pass to get to the gelding. "I think we should call him Raccoon. It's what I called him to calm him earlier. I named him after you." Timidly, she stood while still holding Otver's hand in hers. After helping him to his feet, she released his hand and carefully began to sneak toward the gelding, Raccoon.

Otver wrung his hands, and looked to the dead face of Edgar, before deciding to be braver than he thought he could be. Once Eileivia reached the trembling horse, she placed her hands gently on him and began to whisper, when Otver saw his opening to do his part, "Sister Crones!"

The feathered heap stopped moving as they slowly began to unfurl at Otver's hail. One folded out from the next until finally the speaker appeared. "Yes, little archer?"

"It was very rude, what you did," he trembled a great deal, but held fast with courage. "We, of Pegasus, have to return this...Prince of Hippocamp to his land. And...you,

162

sister Podarge, you shoved me to the ground. And you have frightened us. And...our horse. And Pegasus would want to know why."

"Frightened you? Have we frightened you, little archer?"

"You have...ma'am, yes," he clenched his fists in fear.

The four crones quickly encroached on Otver, encircling him as they had with Eileivia, who quickly shouted in reaction, "Hey! Stop it!"

"Be still, feather of Pegasus. We will not harm this boy. Nor you. And perhaps not the beast," the speaker of the sisters remarked. "We will have you stay for a night."

Eileivia could not see past the rippling wall of feathers to Otver, and as such, said nothing.

"You will stay and we will give a gift, yes? This is good. We give something good from our love of Pegasus." The four unfurled and took an individual position in a line as the speaker, hunched and crooked, turned to Eileivia, "There is no way to say no, my dear."

Otver, nearly as pale as poor Edgar, began to breathe rapidly as if he had held his breath when they were upon him. He looked to Eile for guidance and was surprised to find her looking to him with the same expression. "Isn't there always a way to say no?"

"Clever little archer. Not with us. We have seen into your heart and we see our Lord Pegasus there. So too, have we seen into the heart of your champion, the feather, and so too is her heart true now - now that you've become more important than the Princess."

Eileivia shook her head in denial and began to badly unravel at how they could have known anything about her actual intentions in the choice to camp where they had. Her mind swirled at the facts of their words: Otver, for either urgency or duty, had been made more important than her quest to investigate the death of the Princess, from the instant that no rabbit warrens were witnessed. Silently, she promised to herself to see the ordeal with Otver to its end, to protect him, and keep him from as much harm as she could. It had been a promise made mere moments before the crisis in which they presently stood. Her head shaking slowed and she looked to the mud on the verge of admitting her scheme. Suddenly, though, she lifted a glance and nearly questioned in what way they saw Pegasus in Otver, but decided against it, not wanting to cause any more ripples than necessary.

"We would have had you eaten by now," groaned the speaker as she walked, "but as things are, we will not provoke the gods. Let us have a bland potato soup and share in some bread. Come inside, the storm draws near. Your Raccoon may sleep in the barn: not the boy, but the four-leg."

Dumbstruck, Otver held perfectly still as the four crones, who had just exhibited multiple feats of supernatural physical ability, hobbled past Eileivia and Raccoon before grunting into the cottage.

"Come in, little archer, and help with the fire. Let the feather mind the cart," the speaker called out through the door.

Otver shrugged toward Eileivia. They had both wished to communicate in the privacy of the barn but at the terse tone of the demand, he began walking toward the cottage. "Please don't be long," he begged.

Eile shook her head and swiftly started to guide

Raccoon and the cart toward the barn. "Quick as I can." She shoved out a suddenly hissed whisper to Otver as if in near after-thought, "Walk slowly."

He slowed his pace and felt his body shiver with chill and fear.

The large-eared sister stood waiting on the dank porch and twisted her head with jerked attention from Otver to Eileivia and back again. Once Otver arrived on the porch, he offered her an unsure smile before the wide-eyed Ocypete lunged into view. With a blink of her yellow right eye, eventually followed by a blink of her left, she nodded down to the bundle of fire-wood in her arms and again blinked to Otver.

"A fire?" he asked, looking past the apparently frail old woman to the room: it was tattered and seemingly abandoned. "Do you four sisters live here?" he asked toward the speaker as she diligently peeled vegetables with the beak-nosed Podarge.

"Oh, yes, little archer of Pegasus. Our whole lives."

With a snapped glance toward the barn, Otver witnessed Eile emerging with a number of the packed fur pelts in her arms. She looked to Otver and began a jog to catch up so he wouldn't have to enter the questionable cottage on his own.

"I brought these from the cart for you," she muttered with a nod to proceed inside.

They stepped in, Eile after Otver, with the large-eared sister in the rear, shutting the door. The cottage was little more than a square room with no clear space for sleeping. It had at one end a fireplace, across from which was a side-table where the vegetable peeling took place. Over the side table, herbs were hung from a rafter and large jugs of water sat on the parts of the broken floor stable enough to still feature floorboards. In the middle of the room was a rectangular table around which eight shabby chairs sat. There was a bundle of clothing of all kinds heaped in the corner, and nearby, a child's rattle, covered in dust and seemingly attached to the falling wall by way of a spider's web. There was a horrible darkness in the place: the sort of sadness that causes otherwise healthy bodies to ache and minds to wander to far-off people and places never again to be seen.

A sorrow hit Eile immediately after entering the home as she lowered herself to sit for worry that she would fall. Every guilt or pain that she had ever known seemed to charge from her heart to mind and a hopelessness woke to wrap her in its dark arms. She was unprepared for the onslaught and, with a propped elbow on the table, she covered her mouth and let tears drip while watching Otver's efforts at the fireplace.

Otver had been considerably less affected, and actually issued a small smile to the wide-eyed Ocypete, who seemed quite keen to linger near him in a doting manner. She, with hands like twigs, would reach to a log, one at a time, and offer to help as the fire sparked up. Once the fire was built, she seemed to have trouble with standing, causing Otver to assist by offering his hands. The gesture was not overlooked by any in the cottage.

"Sister Ocypete sees much, little archer. Nothing escapes her sight," the speaker remarked while filling a cauldron with the vegetables: carrots, potatoes, and onions. "Are you very fond of the little archer, sister?" she asked.

Ocypete gave her head a hard tilt, blinked, and

nodded.

The speaker shook her head to Otver, "This is not good, little archer."

"How could it not be good?" Otver asked, finding that he was shoved down before the fire to warm himself by the suddenly strong arms of Ocypete.

The speaker chuckled while stirring the pot until a boil began to churn, "She would keep you for a pet as your kind keep puppies. Which, if you think about it, makes you two lucky twice: you haven't been put in a stew and you won't be kept as a pet. What a fortunate night you're having!"

Ocypete blinked and withdrew to the table to dust it off. While she used the sleeve of her long earth-toned rag-dress to wipe, she slammed her wrist and fist into Eile's elbow and scowled until she moved.

"Will the...Hippocamp...be alright out there all night?" Otver asked, not really knowing what caused the distant expression on Eile's face or how to talk to the women.

"He may not be out there all night. It would be rude to leave Hippocamp out in a cold storm while we feast by a warm fire."

"I think he likes the cold," muttered Otver who received a sporting laugh from the speaker in return.

"Clever boy, little archer." She tapped the wooden spoon on the cauldron and turned to face him for the rest of what she had to say, "Do you know who we are?"

"I have no clue, really," Otver admitted while glancing over to the unresponsive Eile with worry. "Eile? ...Eileivia?...Magpie!"

With a jump, Eileivia shook her head and looked to

Otver. "What?" she asked, unaware that there had been anything awry or that she had fallen into a fugue. "Are you alright?"

Otver nodded once but maintained a curious expression.

The speaker continued, "There are mean songs that children sing. Mean stories, too. These are not the tales of truth. Well, some truth, but mostly – no." She lifted an arm with a shrug before overturning a hand to point to Otver, "You were scared?"

"I apologize, but I am scared, ma'am."

"But you are of Pegasus. What have you to ever fear? Were you not who you are, you would be gone from this world. We would have done that."

Otver frowned and lifted his chin, not truly understanding the incoherence.

The speaker snapped to the beak-nosed sister which triggered the delivery of a jug of goat's milk. She took the jug and poured it into the cauldron while returning to stirring, "If you wish, we could bring Hippocamp back to you."

To that statement, both Otver and Eile snapped to attention. "What? You could?" Otver quickly asked. "How?"

"The how is not important. Shot him, did you? Through the heart?"

"I think so," Otver eagerly admitted with a nod of his head. That she spoke on a thing which she had no way of knowing was of serious interest to Eile, who folded her arms and silently listened.

"Would this be a thing you would wish? You of Pegasus? Would this offering please you?"

"Careful, Otver," Eile warned.

Viciously, a raging hiss swarmed from the speaker, "Do not speak in such a way to this child of Pegasus!"

Otver looked from the crone to Eile with trepidation and impotence.

"If that is the child of Pegasus, and he is my ward, what does that make me?" Eileivia demanded, having less fear than anger finally. "If you wish to feed us, then feed us. If you wish to shelter us, then shelter us. If you wish to kill us, I welcome your attempt. But you will not promise that which you can not dispense, and break the child's heart for a second time. I will not have it."

"We could bring him back."

"You could offer a length of a thing where repayment would outweigh the result!"

"Ah – repayment. To the cut, we see."

Otver looked from the Magpie to the crone and back with confused fear, "What would be this repayment to give his life back?"

"We would need her life." In unison, the four sisters lifted an arm and pointed to Eileivia. "Is that not why you brought her here?"

Feverishly shaking his head, Otver demanded, "No! No, that is not a thing I would do."

Relieved beyond measure, Eile exhaled and looked to the sisters, "No deal, then."

"Are you not sworn to do your duty to the death, feather?" the speaker asked.

Eile nodded before saying, "It would not be doing my duty to sacrifice myself and leave the boy in the care of the man he slayed. That would be idiocy. Dangerous idiocy." She leveled her eyes toward Otver, "Say it works and he is right as rain come morning: he would kill you. He would wake in a Hold not his own, with who-knows-what on the mind and he would kill you. That's if it works. You can not welcome life back into a shell it vacated. It can not be done."

"It can," demanded the speaker.

"It won't be done. Can or can't be damned, I won't have it," Otver declared. "You would offer me a way to excuse what has happened? I can't run from what I did."

"We have displeased Pegasus?"

Otver shook his head and raised his hand, still not clear on how to address the perceived connection to the Hold-God.

The winds roared and slipped into the small cottage as rain and thunder began to quake the structure.

The sisters, in a near state of rage, all stood and connected hands as the speaker voiced, "If we can not win the affection of Pegasus, little archer, then we will win the praise of Hippocamp." With a flash of lightning co-current to a thunderclap, the fire blazed into an inferno before the room fell dim. The fire burnt very low; the sisters were gone.

A single second was given to the shock of the scene before both Eileivia and Otver dashed out of the door and to the barn. Through the windstorm and cloudburst they rushed, drenched, to the cart. Raccoon had been disconnected from the cart by Eile, and where he was resting, on a mound of old hay, he had been cut at the throat. Utterly appalled, Otver looked from the carnage to the open and emptied rug: Prince Edgar was gone.

"Otver, on the underside of the rug, there is a linen."

He nodded in something of a daze.

"Rip it from the rug. Hand it to me and quickly, very quickly, collect a jug of the water from the cottage. Do it now, Raccoon isn't yet dead. Go."

Awoken to a path to save the innocent gelding, Otver tore at the rug that once cradled the body of the Prince before braving the torrential rains with a run back into the house.

\*\*\*\*\*

*The four of curse,*
*The birds of dread,*
*the four what lure and trap.*

*No one can find a way outside,*
*You're never coming back.*

*The first, they say,*
*Calaeno may*
*speak of sweet reward.*

*The second rose,*
*Podarge's nose*
*can smell a family line.*

*The third's no treat,*
*for Ocypete*
*can see into your soul, son.*

*And fourth, all fears,*
*to Aello's ears*
*even whispers are as yells.*

*Run!*

*-The Snatcher Sisters – Eastern Children's song,*
*ancient*

# Chapter XIII
## *Of Hippocamp: Bleed*

The torches on the wall hissed and ripped their flame at the whirlwind of frost blown into the gray chamber in which Hector, youngest Prince to the Northern Crown of Hippocamp, softly wheezed in slumber: a long heave before a stabilizing exhale. The pattern seemed to repeat endlessly and, although Horatio did not notice, Dark Tower had never been so silent. From the servants to the highest officer, few could do more than sit in thought and dread. The windows were all sealed, yet the draft could convince a dark chamber that a damp and horrible snowfall had whipped up within the rooms, halls, and passages. It was a degree of ominousness uncharacteristic to an already somber place.

Hours had passed while Horatio watched the rise and fall of the chest of his brother, such a small thing under the bulk of a large white bear skin, in a bed near the fireplace. He sat with a slouch at Hector's side, frowning, watching, and thinking. He could imagine no way in which Edgar still lived, as he would have fought to the death to protect the little one. Had he somehow managed to survive whatever assault found the two Princes, he would have reported the event immediately. This is what Horatio penned to the King and Queen at Bleak Spire moments after entering the room where his brother was laying. There was no hope in the tone of the missive as he coldly dictated to a page the words: '...with one brother dead and the other as good as..." The phrase haunted him still, so many hours after the fact. He, with pity and mourning, watched little Hector and saw, for the first time in years, a child. That was not a soldier or a young warrior to train, those sentiments on which he, the eager older brother, led the charge: he was a little boy.

The anguish in his failure to protect his family, and further the realm, as reflected by Hector's lifeless skin, became too great a pain to endure. He stood and turned to the priest of Hippocamp that had been periodically monitoring the young Prince for signs of improvement. No improvement had yet come, and as such, Horatio, in a hushed voice as to not disturb the sleeping brother, requested of the priest, "Notify me of any changes."

With his sleeves covering his clasped hands, the robed old man bowed his tonsured head, "Yes, Lord Commander. At once."

Anne, having given Horatio a distance of respect, had been waiting in the corridor the full length of time. Surprised by the door suddenly opening, she leapt to attention and was anxious for news regarding Hector's condition.

Horatio, almost aggravated by her optimistic eyes, shook his head and muttered quietly, "Wheresoever he is, he is deeply there."

Anne nodded and reserved any idealistic words of encouragement; Horatio had never been particularly grateful or graceful in the reaping of such talk. She waited for him to speak, and when he did not, she offered, "Shall I sit watch, Lord Commander?"

After a thought, he gave a single nod, "I think that wise. The temple is supplying a representative, but should he wake, I think he would be much pleased to see you. You're not a bald ghoul at least," he tried a smile and it was faint and forced.

"No, not yet," she smiled in return. "I'll sit with him happily. I am honored to do so. I hope to have to wake you with good news...Horatio."

As much as he felt the urge to correct her use of his familiar name, they were alone and so he relented, choosing to answer instead, "I will not be sleeping. I will be below in the cells."

Her shock was difficult to conceal, "Should you not rest before confronting the criminals? They will not go anywhere."

Horatio had no words to respond so well as the expression of anathema for the way she continued to speak to him. He knew she truly cared for both him and little Hector, but her kindness was doing very little to soothe the rage and fury he had built against those who had harmed his brother. Every soft attempt that Anne made forced him into a darker state-of-mind and the blurring of the boundaries of their relationship, for whatever reason it occurred, caused him grave discomfort. "I will be below. In the cells," he repeated with a stern pause for distinct emphasis.

Wise to his mood, she bowed her head, withheld the apology that would serve to only irritate him further, and replied, "Yes, Lord Commander." She heard his boots turn and storm away down the corridor before finally lifting her sad eyes.

As he wound down the stone-slab halls, all but his vengeful pace remained silent in the keep of Dark Tower. None wished to speak and even held a sense that the whispers of thought could threaten the fragile and tragic circumstances under which all felt buried. It was tension frozen in an ice-block of despair, and nervously, in the privacy of the bunk-halls and chambers, wordless pleas to the great Hippocamp became all that made sense.

The wide double-doors of the bastille groaned open like the sleepy jaws of an ancient dragon. And like that dragon, puffs of steam exited Prince Horatio's flared nostrils as he entered, observed the accused and began a slow and menacing walk: from one end of the cell-faces to the other, before repeating.

Intentionally far colder than the rest of the fortress, the ancient prison was torture in its very design. Much like a long, rectangular stone of the darkest gray, the architecture was a simple one. Divided by solid stone walls on both the left and right sides, the ten cells themselves had nothing but steel bars as walls at the front and back. On the front, where each had an imposing gate locked by a series of three keys each, Grimm guardsmen held post. The turnkey, an officer, was rarely in the room with the cells unless needed, except on this occasion: he stood with his arms folded in the far corner near-to the seated Lord Banquo, who simmered in effort to contain his violent anger. The back wall of the cells, beyond a set of long frigid beams of steel, was nothing more than the elements. There was no wall to protect from the wind and snow and drifts had begun to build up hills of white within each.

The highwayman and his criminal troupe shivered with lips of purple as Horatio slowly studied each in passing. He said not a word and again went back and forth. With a glance to the floor near the gates of each, it was evident by the presence of plates: they had been fed as ordered. They wore the clothes they had on when apprehended: enough to commit crimes against the Crown, enough to stand and wait, so far as Lord Banquo was concerned. So, while the command to see that they were kept warm was interpreted quite liberally, Horatio was not bothered enough by the questionable implementation of the directive to mention it. Again, he watched the inmates while moving back and forth, holding his gloved hands behind his back.

The highwayman, a broad fellow with wide shoulders and a large head full of matted black hair and beard looked familiar to Horatio. Recognized as a cut-purse that prowled the path between Bleak Spire and the Hold's treasury city, Alberich, he felt that charges had been filed fairly recently against the man, and silently wondered why he was not serving a sentence somewhere horrible. However, it was the other four that attracted Horatio's sudden predatory interest. They were each a thing extraordinary unto themselves. The implication of their differences was an incredible offense to fathom.

"One has to wonder," Horatio began to speak in a firm and rich voice while continuing to walk, "how rare a thing it is to find an incompetent Northern cut-purse in the company of four unfortunate thieves, so very far from home." He glared to the other four in passing: a Southerner, an Easterner, and a pair of Westerners, all in individual cells, unable to see the others due to the thick walls between them. Once he arrived again to the front of the Northerner's cell, he remarked while pointing, "You I know, do I not?"

In a gruff yet ashamed voice, the man muttered, "Yea."

"Yes?" Horatio asked.

The man, with absolutely no hint of courage, nodded fearfully.

"Did you mean to say, 'Yes, Prince'? Or, 'Yes, Lord Commander'? Or, perhaps even, 'Yes, Grimm'? I would have even settled for 'Yes, sir'. But here you cower so, and I have to wonder at why? Do you know me well enough to cower but not so well as to address me in some way that might win you clemency? For, well, let us see...for the second time? Did I not save you from being beaten to death by a murder of Grimms just outside of the capitol gates?"

"Yes, sir. Yea, that was me," he shuttered and offered meekly.

"And out of all of the options I presented, you decided on yes, sir."

The freezing man looked to the floor and began to beg, "N-n-none of this is how it seems, Prince Grimm, sir."

"Is it not?" He flatly intoned his question like a statement. "Truly, it does seem very bad. It does seem very, very bad." He slid his attention down the line to the others before stepping closer to the cell of the Northerner. "Your name? I do not recall."

"Mowbray."

"Mowbray. Why are you not at a work-camp, Mowbray? Did you stand before a judge at Forseti?"

Forseti was the judicial capitol of the North. A city comprised completely as a court setting, it crawled with lawyers, the occasional thayn, and the accused. It was an unusual circumstance that the cells at Dark Tower were being used to house anyone but Grimms who had been implicated in the commission of crimes. Mowbray had

178

never even seen Forseti: he had eluded his transport guards and scrambled off with the assistance of the colleagues that presently occupied the other cells. Horatio tilted his head awaiting an answer.

Mowbray, painfully cold, shrugged and shook.

"No?" Horatio asked. "No, nothing? You have nothing to say? So, I spared your life so that you could kill my brother?"

"This is not what happened, King of North," the dark man, a Southerner, protested while kneeling in a ball against the gate of his cell.

Raising his chin, Horatio shifted his attention to the cell at the opposite end of the line from Mowbray's. Slowly he approached, and growled with a quiet voice, "I am not the King, fire-born."

"Apologies."

"I understand your kind would have trouble knowing a king when one is seen. It is expected and not something for which you could apologize."

The Southerner grabbed at his own shins trying madly to find some heat.

"Have you a name, fire-born?" Horatio's hatred was evident in the slight drag in his words.

"Aslan, although 'fire-born': this is okay too."

"You traveled very far from your home to find the end of your life, did you not, Aslan?"

"The end comes for us all, Grimm," he shivered as Horatio stepped away and looked to the man in the cell next to Aslan's

With light brown eyes, the man, an Easterner, was the youngest of the group: about Edgar's age. He trembled and quaked: he had far too small a frame to

179

endure much more of the exposure.

"Do you know who I am, young man?" Horatio asked with a voice slightly more kind.

The Easterner nodded and struggled to speak, "Prince."

Horatio knelt while nodding, situating himself on a level plane to the small man, "That's right. Of all other outsiders, I have always found the East the least distasteful. So, in honoring your winged-steed god, I will ask you: what is your name, and what is your part in this?"

"Valerian," he trembled, seemingly unable to say much else.

The Lord Commander waited a few moments for the rest of the answer. When it became apparent that the Easterner Valerian could not, or would not answer, he turned his attention to the Westerner in the cell to Valerian's right.

"And Unicorn, the trickster, sends two of her best and brightest all the way to the empire of the white wastes... for what?" He asked the first of the two golden Westerners.

"We are friends, sire," defiantly and with a shivering smirk, the man remarked.

"The five of you?" Horatio asked with a wave of his finger, indicating to the other cells.

The honey haired man nodded with some undeniable pain from the cold. Yet still, he maintained a grin.

"What is your name?"

"Dimitrios, sire. And Mowbray is not lying. None of this is what it seems."

"Convince me."

"We found the boy-Prince. We were bringing him back to his home," Dimitrios, with a vexing amount of playfulness remarked while Horatio noticed that the other Westerner, in the cell next to Dimitrios, seemed suddenly more uneasy than the others.

"Name?" the Prince demanded.

"Iairos, Grimm, sir."

Horatio nodded, stepped back, and addressed the five imprisoned, "Some leniency may come to he who gives me the answers I seek." He had grown impatient and his anger would not thaw. "However, all but one of you will die."

Iairos placed his face between his knees and began to rock.

Mowbray was the first to offer comment, "These others, they threatened me! They made me their victim as much as that poor child, the Prince!"

Denials and protests erupted from all but Iairos, who continued to rock and sway, keeping silent and detached. Even little Valerian sprang to his feet and screamed at the obvious lie.

Horatio observed with some interest the remarkable quickness of the turning of the thieves. He raised an eyebrow at the suddenly spirited little Valerian and asked, "Does he lie, wind-born?"

Valerian, emphatically nodded, "Sir! This man promised us that it would be a simple thing!"

"And what would that be?" questioned Horatio.

"That little damn monster! Mowbray told us that little Hippocamp killed my Princess!"

"Lavinia?" With an even and knowing voice, Horatio questioned.

"Yes!"

"Impossible." He shifted back to the sniveling Mowbray and asked, "Did you tell the wind-born that Prince Hector killed Princess Lavinia?"

Aghast, Mowbray attempted a reaction of offense, but was very poor at acting, "Why would I ever even suggest that good Prince Hector would ever so much as think of that wind-wench?!"

"Is she dead, Mowbray?"

"Oh, yes. Yes, sir."

Prince Horatio, having heard absolutely nothing on the matter of Princess Lavinia's demise, looked over his shoulder to his officers first, and then the turn-key, before Lord Banquo, with a curious expression.

"I'll have it looked into," remarked Banquo, who was finding it an easier task to stay calm while Horatio interrogated the imprisoned, rather than just sitting around and watching them in silence.

"How do you know this?" Horatio turned his questioning back onto Mowbray.

"Begging your pardon, Grace, but it is a known thing among travelers."

"Do you cross the border into Pegasus' lands often, Mowbray?"

Stunned at the incriminating conversation, Mowbray just shook his head and began to babble.

"Does your Crown believe that the North is responsible for the death of their only child?" Horatio asked Valerian.

"Who knows what they think? They haven't even said anything!"

"Haven't they?" He turned to make eye-contact with

Banquo with an inquiring furrow of his brow. "In what condition was Prince Hector found?"

"As you found him with us," shouted Aslan.

"And where was he found?" Horatio asked as a frown began to indicate that he was not pleased with the lack of response. "Where!?" his body shook as he shouted. Yet again, no answer came. His breathing became hard and deep and with a few scans of the five men from a vantage that no motion was truly required for the task, he, with a calm and dark voice again, commanded the guards behind him, "Bring the barrels."

Four Grimm guardsmen swiftly exited and returned moments later with large sealed barrels rolled in on a flat cart.

"Answers. Simple answers. I will ask again, where was Prince Hector found in that condition?"

"This is a story I have heard," began Aslan of the South. "It is said that the Queen of this North had a baby born with no life. This baby, she held and cradled and tried to nurse, believing that this god of yours, Hippocamp, would restore the spirit to the baby."

"Shut-up, Aslan!" roared Mowbray. Out of either adoration for his Queen or some wish of solidarity through silence, the reason for his forceful demand was unclear. Most likely, the silence was requested as the look on the face of the closely listening Prince terrified him.

Prince Horatio drew closer to Aslan, listening to the well-known tale.

"Hippocamp forsook her. And a midwife, innocent and kind, came to take the baby from the weeping mother. Only, this Queen of yours is made of evil things and is a monster hidden from the world of good in a palace of ice and hatred. When midwife came back to see the Queen's health, this creature of a Queen had made a stew of the midwife's two small children. And they dined together. And most viciously, the Queen let the midwife live knowing what she had eaten."

Horatio had little visual reaction to the story as he snapped to a pair of Grimms to roll barrels over.

"This tale: is it truth? The children are told this in my homeland to better cherish their younger siblings. To better know how well Pyrois loves us when compared to others."

"It is," Horatio remarked before turning to the Grimms with a wave of his hand. As he slowly approached the hushed and sullen Iairos, he commented, "You are very quiet mud-born. I do not know what to make of it."

"The Prince will make of it what he will," Iairos trembled while the pained shrieks of the frostbitten Aslan echoed off of the walls as he was drenched by the water from the barrels. In mere moments, the water had frozen against his body and the puddles in the cell were solid. Succumbing to the freeze, Aslan fell over and bashed his head badly on the stone floor.

"What did you think of the fire-born's story?" Horatio asked Iairos curiously.

Iairos was cautious to answer, yet replied honestly, "I think a mother's pain is a pain with no equal."

Satisfied, Horatio nodded and approached the cell of the other Westerner, Dimitrios, "I do not get the impression that you and your hold-mate care much for one-another?" He nodded in indication to the cell over, "You seem very sure of yourself, while he seems very aware of the seriousness of the situation. The two views seem to be at odds with each other."

Dimitrios offered a moment of contempt with an eye-roll before returning to a cocky smile, "He scares easy."

"Does he? He doesn't seem particularly afraid. Just... aware."

Dimitrios shrugged.

"Where was Prince Hector found?"

Again, Dimitrios shrugged, but this time, with a chuckle.

"Remove your shoes," Horatio commanded.

Dimitrios, shivering, laughed with a shake of his head.

"No?"

Still laughing, he remarked, "No."

Horatio looked to a Grimm and made a motion with his hands, one from the other, as if indicating length before returning to speak with Dimitrios, "Your kind are very good with poisons. We don't have much use for poison here. It is a hard weapon for an honorable kill, and the cold can fatigue the mixtures, causing them to degrade if one isn't too careful. We are, however, excellent with two weapons: the broad sword, and the pike."

With a laugh of impudence, Dimitrios instigated, "Being able to use, and being able to use well are two different things, Grimm. The poison is just one of our skills."

"Ah, but we kill bear here. I would say we know what we're doing." Into his extended hand, a long pike was placed by one of the guardsmen. "Are you rich, and he's poor? Is that the great divide between you?" He nodded over to the wall that served to separate Dimitrios from Iairos. "Is your home somewhere near The Sepal?"

With a puff of steam for a scoff, Dimitrios nodded, "Of course it is."

"So, this is about you thinking he is beneath you?" Horatio stepped back and glanced to Iairos, who did not have much of a reaction. He turned back to Dimitrios, "One more time: either remove your shoes, or tell me where you found Prince Hector."

Dimitrios shook his head and stood his ground. His dexterity was badly compromised by the cold and he could not get out of the way of the quickly approaching pike from Horatio's thrust. He was pierced and left to dangle in excruciating pain while the pike's ends rested on the cross-beams of the steel bars.

Horatio approached little Valerian and quietly commanded, "Remove your shoes."

In terror, Valerian took his shoes off and tossed them between the bars despite the pain of exposed feet.

"Where was Prince Horatio found, wind-born?"

"He was found before I joined up, sir."

"Joined up?"

"Yes, sir." He was clearly hesitant to elaborate and Horatio found it interesting that he would protect something when faced with such certain doom.

"Was the Prince in the poor condition that he is in now?" Horatio asked, turning to take a sip of ale from a crystal glass on a table near Banquo, who listened closely with folded arms.

There was a clear, pregnant pause, as if fear suggested to Valerian that he should say a thing that his mind preferred to keep concealed. After the pain shooting

186

through his legs became critical, he surrendered a damning statement, "Mowbray had him and kept telling him that we were going to help him find his brother. He told us that we were going to take him to GoldCloud Castle for what happened with Princess Lavinia. Well, he told me that."

Horatio glared at Mowbray.

Valerian continued, "Mowbray got to beating on him pretty bad when he started to think we weren't going to help him find the brother. I don't think that brother was ever part of it, but the kid believed it for a long while."

"Mowbray told me that we were going to ransom the young Prince. And that he wouldn't hurt him," offered the otherwise silent Iairos.

"Is this so, Mowbray?"

"You would trust these foreigners over your own kind, Prince, sir?" Mowbray pathetically whined. "I'll tell you this: that Easterner, Valerian, he did most of the beating over that Princess story."

"So, you did tell him the Princess was killed by Prince Hector?"

Mowbray, a fool in most respects, shook his head and looked around with a confused frown.

"Most of the beating?" Horatio looked to Valerian. "His condition is due to you?"

Valerian did not answer and found that the floor had begun to turn his feet black from frost exposure.

Horatio exhaled a long sigh and glanced at Iairos, waiting a few moments before speaking, "You have no home. Am I right?" He gathered from the way in which Dimitrios, who carried himself like a wealthy, but bored Westerner, treated Iairos, that the difference of class, and possibly loyalty, caused a wedge to be present.

Iairos met his glance and shook his head in a slow, hopeless way.

"Tell me why."

"There is nowhere for me...anywhere. I joined the revolutionary unification movement, The Coadunation, as they call themselves, to make the world better, not to hurt children."

With a high-raised eyebrow, Horatio was interested to hear that revolutionaries may be organizing against all of the Holds. He leaned closer to Iairos' cell, "I am considering amnesty. In exchange for your life, you provide me with everything you know about what happened to Prince Hector, everything you know about this unification movement, and everything you know about the Western defenses on the border to the North. Would you find this as an agreeable arrangement?"

Slowly, and after obvious contemplation, Iairos nodded, "I would."

"Even if your friends and family in the West may die?"

"I have neither, sir."

"Die?" asked Banquo.

"We need soil. They provoked us. We react. War," Horatio replied before turning to the turnkey. "Have Mowbray put to the pole. Somewhere near the East so the ghost of Lavinia can have her revenge for his lies."

Mowbray collapsed and began to scream in horrible shouts, causing Horatio to wince and speak louder, "Kill the rest. Send heads to their Crowns. Except that one," he pointed to Iairos. "Clean him, feed him, find him proper clothing, and deliver him to my office."

"Heads to their Crowns? Lord Commander..."
Banquo began to speak on his disagreement.

"If it proves problematic, then perhaps their Crowns will like to answer for their presence in this Hold. It is a warning against trespass."

# Chapter XIV
## *Of Coadunation: Magomed*

It was a place where the hot and dry air of the South moved with the winds of the East. The moon glowed as a huge red orb overhead as waves of heat distorted the celestial illumination. The border city of Magomed, one of the great outpost burghals of the South, sat in an unusual silence while a cloaked figure stole along the steep and narrow alleys as they bent and sloped. Keeping to the darkness, the practiced footsteps padded out nearly no sound. The occasional scuffing of sand against rock was met with an exasperated huff with each occurrence. She had less reason than usual to guard her stealth: most of her neighbors had made for Tephra Keep to attend the upcoming Jubilee of Flame. Yet still, Izledo grew frustrated with the racket that was of notice to none but herself.

She walked up five stairs, along ten paces, and down eight steps before turning a hard right into the back-passage that led under a shop that, when open, sold spiced tea, coffee, and wine. Her destination was reached: the aroma was unmistakable. After pressing a series of recessed stones on the cellar wall, a set of gears began to click away. A doorway was revealed and, after striking a torch aflame, she slipped down into the dark tunnels beneath Magomed, heading east. After a short time, the mechanism triggered within the wall. It returned to conceal the pathway. She pulled the parcel bag at her hip closer to her chest and pressed on.

The cavern was a well-worn path taken by those

traveling between The South and The East from the revolutionary resistance of the Four Holds: The Coadunation. Rats, cantankerous and hungry, watched her as she advanced along the passage which gave up the luxury of any crafted architecture soon after the entrance. She had noticed over the span of a few months that the starving rats were beginning to forsake caution. They did not scamper away but rather watched while upraised on hind legs, wringing their hands, panting, and smirking. Their behavior concerned her greatly and many-a-night's rest had been betrayed by the waking-dream of being overpowered by a legion of rodents while in the commission of her duties as a Shadowfoot: a Coadunation border smuggler of goods and persons.

The Southern Shadowfoots had the best obscured trails of any Hold. Grottoes connected the cities of Itzal and Demai to the West, while caves formed from ancient volcanic gas bubbles linked both the cities of Bahasin and Magomed to the East. The West and East enjoyed the well-camouflaged travel on their southern borders, but found great difficulty in passing into the North Hold's vast, wide blankets of white. Only the native Northerners or the most skilled of foreign members ever chanced the locale. Operating in the harsh North was an ongoing challenge for the revolution.

Izledo shot glances to the off-shoot pathways and chambers as she passed, taking inventory on whether any Coadunation refuges lingered for transport. She had many to cross into the East on her last visit, and was not overly surprised to find herself alone with the rats. Sweat bled from her pores as the faint echo of humming finally reached her ears. It was melodic and soft. She ran her free hand under the strap that held on her hooded dark brown linen short-cloak and lamented the moisture. The night was far hotter than anticipated and dehydration was a grave concern. A damp thickness grew on the air. She let out a whistle, calling to the hum.

The hum hushed. Footfalls followed. Along the approach from before her, the sound of something heavy being dragged punctuated the booted steps. The only light came from the torch she held. Her dark hand tightened the grip.

"Nothing?" A man's voice called toward her. Melodic and soft, it was clearly the vehicle of the humming.

"You sneak through the dark as a phantom. Why should you have no torch, Osvald?" Izledo scolded as the Eastern man, Osvald, came into view.

He had behind him a large woven sack which he labored to drag along the floor of the cave. With rosy pink cheeks, a thin little nose, and blue eyes, he had hair nearly as dark a brown as hers. "It's raining on my side of things. Everything was wet. I couldn't keep a fire alive."

She shook her head.

"Explains this muggy mess down here." He nodded toward her over-saturated clothing.

"The night is an unusual one. Large and angry was the moon." She frowned before pointing to the sack, "What do you bring?"

"Oat and wheat," he smiled with a lift of his shoulder. "For the travelers."

"The travelers would thank you, but to store it: I do not know. The cave vermin would have me attacked and robbed like cut-purses before I drift out of your sight."

"Oh, come on, Izledo! I brought this so far! Could it

be stored in your town?"

Flatly, she replied, "Magomed? No. The Red Spines are making checks on the homes and on the shops. This I can not do." With a growl, she continued, "People, they starve and here you have a sack of food and I can do nothing with it. This irritates."

He quietly took in the words while watching her with knowing eyes: she, too, was starving. She was smaller than the last time he saw her. She was thinner and clumsier. Turning away the goods could not have been an easy thing. The pressure from The Red Spines must have been immense. Osvald released the huge bag and slipped a hand into a pocket of his coat. "I brought you a gift."

Easing away a headache, Izledo offered an interested nod of her head before a smile of appreciation washed over her features. It was a most welcomed gift. She accepted the loaf of bread and bottle of water with an eager bow. Proving her state of famine, she quickly devoured the offering before even opening the water.

"I can't bear the sight of you like this," Osvald muttered. Flipping his thin coat aside, he pulled the strap of a parcel bag over his head. It was identical to the one Izledo carried. They exchanged the two. It was a familiarly choreographed dance.

Izledo flipped open the flap of the bag and spied the contents: addressed messages intended for various Coadunation members currently in the South Hold. After giving the bulk a look-over, she remarked, "More than usual."

Osvald nodded while securing the bag he accepted in the exchange across his chest, "Well, there would be, wouldn't there?"

She shook her head with a disgruntled sigh, "In-fighting: this is not the way."

"It isn't about in-fighting, Izi. He has overstepped."

With wide eyes, she protested, "This is about Valko, then? All of this?" She raised the bag in flummoxed annoyance. "You whine and cry: he has grown too big! Yet he only grows big by the act of his name filling a mail bag. This is a madness that I can not understand, friend."

"Many think he killed the Eastern Princess, Izi."

"I hope he did," she spit on the floor before bobbing her chin with words, "but he did not, did he? If he had, why would this be a cause to hunt him so? Against the divine-born: this is what we stand for!"

Osvald frowned while resting his weight against the cave wall.

"But you do not want death for the Princess?"

"I don't want death for anyone."

"Ah! Not for anyone except Valko?! This, do you see? This is the problem. Many like you say: no, he has broken tenants. He is too well-known. He is too well-loved. He must be destroyed. And now, to act now, because this Princess is dead? Why now?"

Osvald said nothing.

"Is this a love for this Princess? Are the brothers and sisters of the East so divided?"

"It's a separate issue."

"Is it? You bring up this Princess, not me."

"Killing is not the way."

Izledo rolled her eyes and took a long drink of the water.

"For sake of argument, let us set aside the mention of Princess Lavinia completely. Make that utterly external to the issue of Valko. It has been a growing problem, Izi. He has far outgrown his place."

"His place? This sounds like noble-talk, Osvald. Do you hear yourself? Have my brothers and sisters of the East forgotten so easily? Most of them...most of you are in the resistance because of Valko. Valko brought you in! He need but smile and rows and rows of new faces line up." She placed the torch into a nearby brazier.

"This is the problem, Izi."

"How is this a problem?"

"He wields far too much leadership in a movement that is against the role of 'leaders'." Osvald's words were almost apologetic and sorrowful. "He is a dangerous man, Izi."

"That a man is well-loved: this is no reason to kill a man."

"Perhaps it's the best reason." His shoulders slumped, "It's hard to express, Izi. You've never met the man."

"No, but you have, sweet friend. This makes this talk all that much harder to understand. You know him. You've known him. How could you wish him death? What must he have done, so egregiously, to merit such violence from you?"

"By the Veil, I would not wish violence for him. Some soft sleep. Something painless and simple."

"To offer such affection with assassination, you sound like a Unicorn." She extended her arms, "I can not understand."

Osvald folded his arms and overturned a finger, pointing in indication to Izledo, "Did you not, at just our last meeting, suggest that the band traveling the North, with Aslan in it, should be killed?"

She frowned, knelt, and looked to the ridge of dirt beside her sandal, "There is no comparison between these two things."

"Really? You're chastising me for mentioning that Valko's magnetism may, at some time, turn against us. And so, kill him. While you think that a group of five of our brothers is so weak that they should be snubbed. So, kill five. How does this make sense to you?"

"That mission: fool's work. At the time I said it was a thing that should not be done. They will be caught and they will be tortured until names and places are revealed. They are a handful of fools that came up with a poor idea. And those Grimms? Ferocious. Merciless. No word has come from those five in weeks. Weeks, Osvald! They have been caught, and will talk. They are dead either way. Best to have a small cell slip in and end them before the words flow."

"The idea to sway the Northern Princess?"

Izledo nodded with a disgusted scowl.

"I think it's a good idea. Maybe they're okay. Maybe she protects them."

"Again with the adoration of the Crowns! They are nothing, Osvald!"

"It could help with unification."

"They are why no unity exists!"

Osvald huffed, then smiled and knelt to sit next to Izledo, "We don't need to argue."

Still vexed, Izledo remained quiet and glared at the ground.

"We don't need to fight, Izi."

"All we do, all the movement is, is fighting. You see

196

now that fighting between us is harm?"

Osvald waited until her gaze met his before nodding.

"He is one man, Osvald. One man."

"He could win an empire if he set his mind to it, sweet sister. It frightens me. He is my friend, and I have loved him enough to travel across my hold for little more than a meal-length visit. But I tell you, with no sway in my heart, that what his charisma could win for him terrifies me."

"He has given The Coadunation much, Osvald. You forsake a man to whom we owe much. It is a thing that a Southern mind naturally struggles with. Praise would suit his deeds, not death."

"Some worry that he gathers followers of his own, Izi."

"For what, eha?" Galled, Izledo insisted, "There would be little point. Yes? What would be the point? He commands much power with the resistance – so much so that some would wish him death – to what end would he waste the energy to strike out?" She raised both hands, "It is a broken stone: this argument. It can not be placed back together. You feel as you feel, some agree. I feel as I feel, some agree. If he should die tomorrow because a cloud falls from the sky and opens his head, The Coadunation would suffer. He is a man to protect, not a man to hunt."

"Let us talk of other things before I venture back to the gusty rain and you back to the sands," Osvald held a low tone of voice and looked to his own hand while he spoke, "The Eastern villages near the border have noticed the funerary fires of late. Huge plumes of smoke plunging into the sky; many rumors have suggested the worst. The

197

volume of ceremonies has not passed unnoticed."

"Death has struck my people rapidly. A sickness travels unchecked. People are too weak from lack of food to fight off this plague."

Osvald looked to the grain sack with shame.

She followed his attentive expression, "You must take it back. I can hide it nowhere." Izledo was filled with regret and envy. "When found, and it would be found, there would be great suffering for all involved: me, whoever offered a place to store it, those who ate it. Is too much."

Replying under his breath, Osvald muttered, "I can divide it. Leave it at a couple of friendly Inns for when they cross."

With relieved gratitude, Izledo reached to his forearm, "Good. That would be good. Very helpful."

Although filled with woe, Osvald offered a smile, "You are a very kind person, Izi. Do you know that?"

"I do not know how kind I truly am. I tire of watching children waste to bone because one Crown would rather bow to another than extend assistance to the very people placed in their care. Poaching? Poaching from the West and East borders was common only a generation ago. Now, you will publicly die by a blade if caught. One horse does not wish to upset the other for the way the grass grows. This is why I am no more Izledo I'Magomed to those who truly know me. I am just Izledo. And to my good friends, Izi." She offered a faint smile to Osvald.

"What we do matters, Izi."

"This is so. It is very true. It matters. I am a good Shadowfoot."

"That you are."

"I once thought to join The Wanderers, you know."

Quietly, Osvald listened.

"I wanted to leave. Just go. I wanted to slip away and cared little where I would end up."

"Why didn't you?"

She thought for a moment before responding, "There is nothing for me in the past. To live with those who love nothing but what has already happened? I could not do it. My heart would break under the weight of blindness."

Osvald felt her sentiment deeply. "While on one hand, I've never met a Wanderer I didn't like, on the other, I wonder how much of the problem they are."

"Problem?"

"They are a walking altar to a history dictated by oppressors. They are a celebration of everything that we are not."

She lowered her head with earnest agreement.

"Be that as it may," Osvald chuckled, "they are often in the act of a good drink or good smoke or good tale or song; they are difficult to dislike."

Izledo smiled, "Perhaps all Wanderers are truly from the East, no?"

"It does sound that way, doesn't it?" He stood and tapped the bag filled with messages, "I should get these in the hands they're meant for. And I have a sack of grain that weighs as much as three of me to get back to my mule."

Izledo stood with the help of Osvald.

"Will you be alright, Izi?"

She lifted a shoulder, "Who would complain. All will be fine." Her words trailed off while noticing that his face held an unusual expression, "Something else worries you?"

Crestfallen, he looked to the glowing brazier, avoiding the question.

"What troubles you, my friend?"

He was hesitant with his words. Careful in the crafting of a response, he measured the need for honesty. He thought that he could concoct a lie, but soon somberly realized that for Izi, he could not. "I'll be away for a while."

"Away?"

He nodded with shame.

"For how long? Who will see the people across? Who will guard the messages? Not for so long? No?" The news disturbed her. She couldn't conceal her disappointment.

"For a few full moons, Izi. There is a young woman who I've been training. Her name is Livia. She's a good girl, Izi; you will like her very much! I've been teaching her the paths and the places to find informants and assistance..."

Izledo interrupted, "Why would you go?"

Osvald shook his head, "There is something I feel like I have to do."

"Oh? Something you have to do? Just you?" She challenged in dismay. "What is this something, eha? Tell me, then."

He offered an incriminating sigh.

"Valko?"

A nod was his only reply.

"To find Valko? To kill Valko?! This is what you have to do?!"

"Please don't be angry, Izi."

"I will die before you see me again, Osvald. Is that a

thing you can understand? Surrounded by death, surrounded by the sickness, likely I am already dying. I have given everything I have left in my life to this resistance. Everything for the people of The Coadunation and the hope – the possibility – of seeing my only friend at month's end has kept my feet moving and my eyes waking. Please. Do not leave me to die alone."

Osvald struggled against the guilt of his decision, "Something has to be done about him, Izi. Someone has to get to him. With every day that passes, I feel that he grows in influence. He has to be stopped."

"By you?"

"If I can, yes." He took her into his arms. She seemed so small to Osvald, "I love you, my sweet friend. Find an apprentice, but try to outlast my absence. I can't fathom this being our last moments together. We promised to watch the rise of the revolution together. This has to happen for the revolution to survive."

# Chapter XV
## *Of Unicorn: Myth, Fable, Distort, Control, Lie*

Sullen was the Prince Regent, Nyseis, in the magnificent royal dining hall. Usually a bustling place, filled with laughter, drink, and music, the room was veiled in a sheet of tense sighs and frowning. Nyseis, having been made more saddened by the twang of memory from each note the instruments sang, sent the musicians away with apology and faint explanations. So fine was the music, he claimed, that his heart would not stop its weeping. With his fork, he poked at a piece of asparagus and proved very poor company for the only other person in attendance: the Purpureus Councilor and his relative, Reileus.

The Councilor had been eating well, before he finally leaned back in his chair and wiped his mouth with a square of cloth, exhaling, "This melancholy will be the death of you."

The only response issued from Nyseis was the acknowledgment offered by an extended stare. He held his gaze and frowned at Reileus for some time, unmoving, with his elbows on the chair's arms and forearms draped together in a convergence over his lap.

"You won't even try to eat?"

"I have the opposite of hunger as an affliction. There is an impenetrable sadness filling my gut." His words were barely a whisper: at best, a mutter.

"The Wanderer accepted. Should you not find some happiness in that?"

"She did not accept the invitation to dine," he remarked. "Her face: she was very harmed by her retirement."

"Nonsense!" Reileus exclaimed jovially. "If I could garnish a mere fraction of the pension that a Wanderer received at retirement, I would..."

"What would you do? Quietly farm and build an impressive library of your own hand-marked words, like a Wanderer in their twilight. Or even become a lovesick idealist, bent on roots and family. Would you be like that?" He was not as confrontational as he was skeptical and with a deep breath, he muttered, "I don't want to hear about how you don't have enough wealth."

"I wasn't saying that." Reileus popped a small tomato into his mouth.

"No? You were saying that the meager living wage and strip of land granted to a retiree would suit you. And I think you were alluding to how she ought to be grateful. And that her sorrow of the death of a life she chose for herself could be cooled by the refreshing tokens of the court?"

"Why did you offer if you mourn with her?"

"Same reason I've done anything since the last full-moon: because I don't know what to do. I have a growing list of regrets and mistakes." He unfurled his arms and inched the plate away from his presence a bit with a thumb. "I am adrift and lost."

"This will pass, cousin." Reileus authentically worried at the depth at which Nyseis felt emotions and began to frown along with him. "It will pass. As unhappy as the both of you are, Morigan may well help us to find the root of this plague. It is a noble and important task. She knows this: there is no other reason under the sun that she would have accepted. That is a thing you could read from her sorrow: she must know how important it all is. As difficult as her retirement was and will be, she is here with us." He watched as a slow nod of acceptance was offered by the Prince Regent before continuing, "You will have to come out of this darkness, Nyseis. Your people need you."

"My father's people. My mother's people. Those people would, in an instant, trade my one life for both, of even just one of theirs. So often, lately, I have wished to find a way to arrange it. They grieve as deeply as I do. And with the lack of bodies to honor, and with the thing that may or may not have stolen their lives still rampant, and with the unhappy Prince that convinced himself that his parents would never die, eternally ruling, never with an end..." He sniffed away tears, finding it difficult to continue at all.

Reileus never found it particularly difficult to set aside his usual political scheming when alone with his cousin, for whom he had great affection and closeness. Although he built a shield around the Prince from knowledge of his own underhandedness, he searched for a morsel of a thing to say that would help with the grief. He concluded that the best possible thing to offer to the new ruler would be a gift of information couched in a metaphor of a tale. It was a difficult and guilt-dripped gift that he would never have mentioned otherwise. "Once, many ages ago, there was a child of Unicorn whose royal parents were ripped from her by a war. Savagely, she was left alone and frightened."

"This is 'The Founding of the Purpureus Council'?"

"This is that story, yes." He nodded and took a drink of wine to coax his throat into storytelling form. "She was the Princess Aniea. Your direct ancestor from your father's line."

"I know this tale well, Reileus."

"It would suit you to hear it again." He readjusted his posture and permitted a slight slouch. "She was a child of seven. The borders were mere checkpoints then: traders, travelers, dignitaries, kings and queens passed as easily as the rest, as easily as any Wanderer now. So too did spies, criminals, and assassins. On a particular night when the Festival of the Berry was underway, foreigners of every ilk comprised the revelry as thickly as Unicorn's natives. There was dancing, and the King laughed and made merry with a noble from the South who was insistent on his leaving the royal table. One freshly filled glass, one sip of wine, and the poisoned Queen crumpled at the feet of her terrified little girl. Chaos. People fled from The Sepal into the forest. Trails of blood from one kind killing the other in fear and accusation. The King, understandably, ordered his daughter to be swept away, into the highest tower of the keep at the Satyr fortress of Chloris, which still stands in its glorious central position, nearby to here. There she sat and waited, years, absorbing all she could from The Satyrs, who deeply cherished the child of Unicorn. Her father, the King, rode into battle against a force of both Northerners and Easterners in the Northern Hold, as his campaign kept pressing deeper and deeper into the ice-lands. Then, once having reached the dreaded Dark Tower, poised to deal a fatal blow to the armies of both The Grimms and The Magpie, from behind, a pack of wolves descended on the rear-guard while at the front, in a coordinated effort from high atop the keep wall, archers from the East peeled away layer-after-layer of Westerners until all that remained was ruin and death."

Nyseis nodded his head while carefully listening to the legend that he had heard a million times before, as if some new pearl of insight could come within reach.

"The West seemed doomed. All were in despair and the sadness stretched far across the lands. Through every door and across every stone: dire sorrow. Until finally, the Princess Aniea emerged from Chloris on the back of strong white horse."

"One," quietly, Nyseis remarked.

Reileus nodded, "Whose name was One." He overturned a hand while continuing, "Flanked by those Satyrs who loved her so, and by that time the age of ten, she marched and gathered strength to her army. She selected those that proved the most clever from the people who wished to fight but could not, and requested that they stay here at The Sepal: those, the first five Purpureus Councilors. With the Council's carefully planned communications of advice and strategy sent to her moving and growing war camp, she secured both the borders and dealt strong blows against the North and South. She, a small heartbroken child on the shining back of a white horse named One, became more than what she could have been before. She was hope and strength and power. She was what you must become."

"I am not fighting the world, Reileus. Our enemy is an invisible and mysterious one. Sneaking unchecked and preying on anything it touches. I know you don't spend any great deal of time with the common-folk, but I do.

There is a woman I know very well from the village of Selvans: near-to the Veil, near-to the border to the South. She tells me that this sickness has claimed the lives of several from her village and that of those afflicted, death is not the end. "

"The weapon for this war is Morigan, cousin. All you need do is find a shining white horse and sit upon it. The people need you to be a champion."

"A champion," Nyseis mused dubiously. Silence was held for some time while the Prince tried to think of himself in the way that Reileus suggested. While in the act of finding the image difficult, Reileus quietly spoke.

"There is a matter of which you should be aware," secretly, he whispered just loudly enough for Nyseis to hear by straining. "I have heard a rumor that has disturbed me greatly. But I have kept it quietly away from all others out of fear for what speculation can do to an already fragile time. I can not say this unless I am made to believe that this melancholy will part to the rays of the sun of your destiny. I will believe for you - in all that you will become. But I need you to start to believe it with me. These are not words for the ears of an unsure and awkward Prince. These are words for the ears of a King."

"You would have me take the Crown?"

"I would have you hear me as a ruler would and not as a heartsick son."

Unsure and saddled with the discomfort of the obvious seriousness in the sudden shift of Reileus' demeanor, Nyseis' curiosity made the decision for him, "I will try." He had never heard Reileus speak in such a hushed, fearful way.

"I have been told," with the utterances of conspiracy,

he began, "that the South is in turmoil. An informant of mine, a Satyr, said that she knows of a man that was threatened into providing a huge amount of poison to a Red Spine."

"To a Red Spine? Why would a Red Spine have any contact with a citizen of Unicorn?"

"This, I don't know. But it had been enough contact that the wretched Red Spine threatened the man's lands and family. The Satyr told me that the man had thoughts of poisoning the Southerner, himself, but was made to believe that the absence of the officer would cause alarm to his brother-in-arms, and retribution would be swift and horrid."

"So, he delivered this poison to the Red Spine?"

"A vial of Shiverotoxin."

"A full vial?" The Prince exclaimed the question. "A full vial?" he repeated in awe.

After Reileus shushed Nyseis with a finger to his own lips and a quick glance around to the still empty room, he nodded, and whispered, "Enough to lay low the majority of the South, yes. If they could ever be cunning enough to divide it."

"Oh, mercy of the horn." Nyseis, overwhelmed, rubbed his face and fretted. "Where is this poisoner: the fearful man that supplied the Shiverotoxin?"

With the dismal eyes of the liar, convincingly, Reileus replied, "He told the Satyr, then when assured of anonymity for the sake of his family, who knew nothing, he killed himself. The Satyr then told me."

"Does anyone else know?"

Reileus shook his head, tapping one ringed finger against another.

"I should speak to the Satyr."

"I see no need. All that could have been learned has been. She took the death, committed right in front of her, very hard."

"He killed himself right before her?"

With a nod, Reileus remarked, "I imagine he felt that there was no other way after admitting what he had done. And frankly, as sad a tale as it is, he was correct: illegal trading across the border is a serious offense. Especially of weapons that may trigger war by their very volume. His family would have been wrecked had he been made to face his crimes."

"You said it was a rumor, yet to hear you speak, you seem very sure of its authenticity."

He shrugged and continued to tap his rings together, "It is the sort of thing one believes because of the possible outcome, Nyseis. I don't want to believe it. Truthfully, the Satyr informed me of the possibility of hoax: the man was badly in personal debt and something of a coward. Having a valid reason to kill himself would set his surviving family up in a good light. However, if he spoke the truth, the idea of that much poison floating around the South in the hands of some disgruntled Red Spine is a story worth sharing – to a king, and very few others." Every inch of Reileus' words were a fabrication carefully designed to protect his own actions while still informing of the possibility of conflict. He leaned and lifted a shoulder, "It could be nothing."

"It could be everything," muttered Nyseis with a scowl.

A grin slipped across the lips of Reileus and he nodded in agreement, "It could be everything." His coercion of the Prince was starting to succeed.

"It is wise that General Barro travels to the South with The Wanderers. I admit to having not been fond of his plan to escort with the bulk of the Satyr forces before you told me what you had." Suddenly, an expression of urgency crossed Nyseis' face, "Should we not notify The Wanderers of what they travel into?"

Quickly, Reileus shook his head, "I wouldn't."

"But..."

"It is nothing more than speculation at the mere possibility of a thing, Nyseis. It would be a foolish act to implicate where there is no evidence. This is why I cautioned you. It may be a hoax, yet. We have no way of knowing. And truly, they frown on cross-regional politics. They want to hear nothing of innuendo or accusations from one Hold to the other. They want nothing to do with the politics or the schemes. Let us not annoy The Wanderers further. They're likely wounded by our request for that bright thing: Morigan. We should take our gain there and sit on our eggs until they hatch." He dipped his chin down with a point and wink.

Mumbling a remark while in thought, Nyseis said, "I'm sure you're right."

"I'm sure I am."

"I'll have a dispatch sent to Barro to re-emphasize the need for caution."

"Oh, I'm sure he will be thorough, Nyseis. The entire point of the escort is the looming threat of the sickness. His Satyrs will be ready at any point for any threat."

"Even so, we can not afford to lose him. No, nor any Satyr, if possible. A suggestion of vigilance and an indication of complete support from the Crown would help me rest more comfortably."

"Complete support of the Crown?" Reileus scoffed with an impressed smile. "Very kingly, cousin. Very kingly, indeed." He raised his glass once Nyseis submitted an embarrassed and slight chuckle. "It suits you. I knew my faith was not misplaced."

After a few moments of friendly calm, Nyseis commented, "I find uncertainty disquieting."

"Everything is uncertain: that is the nature of existence. One never knows, from one moment to the next, what would happen. All we can do is grab the threads before us and make as much a marionette of life as possible."

Nyseis nodded and ruminated a bit, staring at his untouched food.

"Will you have a coronation?"

"Should I? Neither the King nor Queen have been recovered."

"I think," Reileus was cautious and pondered on his words before speaking, "I think that if the absolute worst happens, a king already on the throne would be better than a prince on the steps."

"There are some convinced that I betrayed my parents, Reileus. You know this."

"They are unlikely to ever believe otherwise. Besides, of that lot, some applaud your assumed sneakiness."

"It harms me almost more than their absence. That my love and affection could be so easily doubted."

Reileus rolled his eyes and sighed, "Be that as it may: you are the only one who may fill the crown. There are dark times on us now, perhaps more on the horizon. You could give the people, most of whom adore you, some sunlight before the clouds grow too thick."

The Prince placed interlocked fingers to the back of his neck and stretched, "I wonder at the amount of sunlight, Reileus. How much is required? How much is expected? How much could I truly provide? A head in the crown does not bring the sick back to health."

"Your doubts are exhausting," he groaned, growing quite irritated with the flippancy even as it was fueled by Nyseis' naturally kind and heavy heart. "You could marry. Fill both roles with one motion. Weddings are celebrations. If you want flower petals dancing on the air, then that would be one way."

Nyseis scoffed a chuckle.

"What? You have several amorous relationships. Pick one."

"Just a queen and king? A pair of kings? A king, queen and...harem? Two queens and a king, the exciting list goes on." His laughing subsided into a grumble, "Oh, I am ill-suited to rule. I can never decide on anything."

"I don't think anyone will take issue with a line of lovers, cousin. No one has yet. This isn't the boring East. Can you not just pick one?"

"I truly, really do not think I can! Say I think of it in terms of who would be best as nothing more than a figurehead: an image. I can not honestly tell you, when pressed, as I am now, who would be best for that role. I want what is best, but the whole of it is overwhelming."

"Then what will you do?"

Nyseis shook his head and contemplated. With a deep breath in he spoke and his words filled Reileus with a sense of victory that he had never before known, "I'll take the crown, although I had wished to never have to.

Alone, for now. For stability. Besides, I have you to aid me."

"That you do."

# Chapter XVI
## *Of Pyrois: Jubilee of Flame*

"Highly irregular, is it not?" Queen Gabija remarked while pulling her face away from the woman who had been applying powder and tint.

"I informed all that needed explanation: I must see you. The Red Spines, your daughter, all who barred my approach." The voice was stern and filled with immediacy as Nusair I'Na'if, head of the House of Na'if, bowed with a hand to his tunic covered chest.

With a sigh, the Queen waved away the women who were preparing her for the grand event of adoption: The Jubilee of Flame. The whole of the Hold had a bulk of representatives in attendance, even the Houses of Itzal and Raquour, who were nearly on the verge of riot.

The event was peculiar in a host of ways. In addition to the adoption and introduction of her last heir, the Queen's festivities would double as the platform on which Prince Mugdi would wed Zillah I'Itzal, the newly appointed house head in replacement of her slain father, Tibon, forever forsaking the crown for the promotion of peace. However, the unrest between the Houses was unprecedented and tension and paranoia ran rampant, even brewing in the minds of individuals far removed from the actual families affected by either the sickness or the assault. People were on edge and small cells of violence had broken out in the outer pathway corridors of Tephra Keep, keeping The Red Spines on constant patrol and causing a fray in their patience and understanding. A normally celebratory festival had landed right on the lap of chaos.

Queen Gabija tilted her head as silvered curls bounced with the soft jingle of jewelry and hair accoutrements while she watched the downcast face of Nusair I'Na'if, one of her closest and oldest friends. Her forehead creased at the sight of his posture, crinkled with the weight of worry and ill-news. She had no way of knowing what hounded him when he arrived, and thought he brought little more than well wishes. But to witness his physical sorrow as he would not lift his eyes filled her with foreboding. Had there been a king of the South, if would have been Nusair, and his apprehension was of notable concern. "Nusair?" she covered her mouth.

"News. I have news." Before he could say much more, his mind quickly triggered to clarify, "Your children are fine, Gabija. Nothing has happened to your children. The child of another, this is why I am here."

Relieved far more than she could have anticipated, her body finally permitted a breath. With a close of her eyes, she shunned the unimaginable horror of what was possible and steadied her words, "By your demeanor..."

"It is not so much removed from what you dread. Apologies for the fright, but I can not bear to look in the face of a mother when I deliver word of the loss of another."

"A mother's loss?"

He nodded slowly and with a dry throat and regret he remarked, "Word has crossed the border. The East has announced a public funeral, and a public coronation."

With a frown, Gabija lowered her shaking head. "The Princess of Pegasus?"

215

"This would seem so, yes. The only heir from the union of the Eastern King and Queen."

She drew in the news with a hushed sadness and contemplated the wounds of loss.

"This information: it is not an official statement. It was learned by a nephew of mine that makes poor choices when traveling. The fool loves a girl in the East, so he would say. Weeks on end, he would vanish to come back exhausted and full of drunken longing."

"He should not be crossing the border, Nusair. It is a crime."

"And I have told my Queen. This is how important this is." He clenched his hands and begged, "But please, he is a fool, yes, but please understand: the boy is a fool for love and because he is a fool for love, this information you now have. Give clemency and hear my words. Please, Gabija. Please, Queen, he is just a fool. As I was just a fool."

Gabija softened and smiled with a huffed exhale, "Yes, a fool. But not just a fool." While studying his slumping shoulders, she requested, "Please, continue this story that does not place your nephew in harm's way."

"Sparse are the details. The people from the village of the fool's girl say that the Princess had been dead sometime and that GoldCloud, due to the normal rate of decomposition, had to release the news before they got answers as to why she died."

"Why she died? Assassination?"

"The understanding is that it was not natural causes and not accident. It was not sickness and it was not an animal attack. Some people say she had a Northern lover, while others say that the town she was found in is well-known as a revolutionary town."

Gabija stood and crossed to a large desk with the movement causing her crimson gown to flutter behind. She opened a drawer and pulled out a large rolled parchment map while inquiring, "This town: do you know the name?"

Nusair I'Na'if finally raised his gaze with a slight apology to his voice, "No. It was Falcon-something, but my nephew could not recall."

Hunched over the map, she scanned the township names before muttering, "Falcon's Perch. So close to the North Hold that I would think they dine on snow at supper. I could see where a rumor of a lover could come from. Especially if the border to the North is as tight as their border to the South?"

With shame, Nusair shrugged with his palms raised upward.

"However. It is in these border-towns where the unification radicals live most comfortably. Sound argument for either rumor could be found."

"Would a unification radical murder a princess?"

"Possibly. But, so too would an angered lover. Either is possible. Although," her inflection rose a bit while she drew away from the desk with a thought, "...one would wish for the body of the Princess to be found, the other would not. How was she found?"

"This I do not know. I know where, but not even when – although recently enough to still offer a public service. In some manner that was clearly murder, I gather."

"Tragic," she muttered.

"Yes, Queen. Tragic, but advantageous."

Astounded, Queen Gabija looked hard at I'Na'if with a scowl and narrowed eyes. "To suggest what I think you suggest: this is not so?"

With outstretched arms Nusair commented, "Consider the scope of things, Gabija."

"Queen," quickly she corrected his way of addressing her when speaking such madness.

"My Queen, consider the opportunity."

"What opportunity, I'Na'if? You would have Red Spines spilling into the East while the people of Pegasus still have tears in the eye? This is the opportunity on which you speak?"

"If nothing is done, there will be revolution in every village, in every Hold. This collective gains strength by the belief that the Holds are weak."

"There has been no war in ages."

"There has been no trade in ages, Queen! There has been no contact or diplomacy in ages! Our goods of metals and ore do not feed our children. Let us show the world the might of the South so that the world comes to us for weapons again."

"You would have Pyrois attack the back of a weeping Pegasus?"

"I would have Pyrois fed, Queen."

Unwilling to bend, Gabija uncomfortably shifted the focus, "Who is to take the crown? You said coronation? Who, then?"

"The King's younger sister."

Overwhelmed, she stood in amazement for some time before, with carefully cupped hands over her coal lined eyes, she muttered, "Bloodshed is not a thing I care to entertain. Be it in thoughts or dreams or wishes or dread:

it repels me, or I repel it. My reign will not be for an eternity and by my age, it shortens daily. To set my people on the path of struggle? Who could do such a thing?"

Without a cogent response, Nusair I'Na'if extended a hand to the door behind him, "Commander Sule escorted me. She waits in the hall. She asked that I not take long: she has been busy, I think."

"Does she know of this?"

"She would not have permitted my visit otherwise. She knows some, yes. I mention this as I think, perhaps you may wish her presence in this?"

Sule was the commander of The Red Spines. The most senior and decorated officer of the South, her service to the royal guard began when Gabija was a child. It was with her hesitant blessing that the arrangements were made with the temple to allow recruitment to extend to the Queen's adoption program, twenty years ago. She was stern, respected, and admired in the hold: little girls would spend huge amounts of energy learning, running, and play-fighting as often as they could to measure up to the great idol. She was a champion for Pyrois, and a dear, life-long friend to the Queen.

Gabija enthusiastically waved to I'Na'if to allow her into the dressing room, "This should have been known as a preference!"

In her red and gold ceremonial armor, Sule entered and removed the helmet that resembled a lizard head. With a deep bow, she said nothing, but her slightly fidgeting hands suggested she had things which needed her attention elsewhere. Her dark face bore deep lines of well-earned creases, and her short hair glimmered a spectacular silvery shine.

"She is annoyed with me, I should think," Nusair I'Na'if remarked to the Queen before he lowered his head and softly muttered to the commander, "Apologies. I said it would take but a short time."

Breathing angrily, she offered no notice to I'Na'if, but rather lifted her eyes to the Queen who stood in a space between the desk filled with maps and the table overflowing with cosmetics. "Your Grace," again she bowed her head.

"Sule, do you know on what matter he is here?" Gabija pointed to I'Na'if who had begun to cower a bit.

"The Princess of Pegasus? This he told me," she responded with a quiet and confident voice. "Has this conference concluded?"

As much as Gabija wished it were concluded, she felt the need to extend, "If a show of force were needed, how prepared are The Red Spines?"

"A show of force?" Sule questioned.

"To open the border for trade," added I'Na'if, confused as to how the plainness of his plan was not immediately accepted as obvious by the Queen. "To show them that we are still here. And they need our weapons as we need their game for food."

"To attack, so to show that they should arm, with our arms? You would have The Red Spines invade and then arm those we are invading?" Sule asked with incredulous amazement. She shook her head and turned her attention back to the Queen, "We are strong. Ever-ready, yes. But this is the wrong way."

"Give me the path to the right way." The Queen nodded, far more pleased with Sule's line of logic than she had been with the proposal from I'Na'if.

The commander shook her head and searched the floor while in quick thought, "They have suffered a loss, no?"

The Queen nodded while Nusair shrugged in some measure of agreement.

Sule nodded, "Offer a gift. Follow the gift closely with diplomacy. Official business is permitted to cross the border. Have your diplomats travel with the royal seal."

"No, they would be robbed and killed when on Eastern soil. This is too risky," I'Na'if protested.

"The loss of a handful of diplomats: that is grounds to attack. But, if they are not lost, then we do not overextend and all may proceed without the initial loss of countless Spines. Peaceful, this is the peaceful route. Besides, Pyrois would frown on sneaking onto a saddened Pegasus. We are not the North; that is not our way. Besides, the East would know that they are in a weakened state and we of the South come with open hands rather than tight fists? It is a good gesture."

"I prefer Sule's approach," Queen Gabija remarked.

I'Na'if shook his head, "Opening trade again: this is all I want. But I wonder, who would be so willing to risk so much as a diplomat to such a plan? There is a chance that those Magpies will attack on sight."

"Your nephew seems to travel with some freedom, Nusair," the Queen quipped. "He will have an official court title and he may travel with whatever companions he wishes. Two, I think, would keep him company?"

Nusair, with a frown of worry and guilt for all that he had brought upon the day, nodded once before a compulsory bow, "You honor the House of Na'if, Queen."

After the bow, he staggered through a slight pause with a remark, "He will be told right away."

"His name, Nusair?" Queen Gabija asked as I'Na'if had begun to dismiss himself.

"Idris I'Na'if, Queen." He sullenly bowed again before leaving the Queen and Sule alone.

"What I do not know," Sule began once Nusair was out of earshot, "I do not know what calm this would bring to the recent distress."

"Houses of Itzal and Raquour, you mean?" Gabija asked.

"It begins there, but has spread throughout. People have begun to kill each other for the slightest infraction. There is much rage. Even on this sacred day, with a wedding and the adoption, many are angry and lashing at all around them."

"Mirza I'Raquour spoke of a sickness. Noted the fury within Tibon I'Itzal as a symptom serious enough to strike him down over." Gabija overturned a hand while pointing to Sule as she spoke, "This was the odd thing. I have known him my whole life. I had never seen him in such a way."

"Perhaps many are ill?"

"Perhaps many more than we thought," she muttered with woe before bowing her head to the commander. "Surely, your hands are full. I have to finish preparing for my one son's wedding, and the other's birth. Has Basem been alright?"

Sule nodded when asked about the candidate not selected by the queen to be Prince. "He has taken to the training well. We offered the detail of personal guard to the new Prince Daim. He was very thankful."

The Queen nodded and with a smile said, "Thank you," while the sound of quickly shuffling feet made their way up the corridor.

In response to the swift approach, Sule stepped into the hall and took in that the footfalls were of no threat, just attendants who had come to collect the Queen for the festivities. She turned back to the Queen and bowed before leaving, "You honor me with the plan of diplomacy."

"You honor me, Sule. It is a good plan."

\*\*\*

Signifying the approach of the Queen, drums and double-reed woodwinds rang through the air at Tephra Keep. Grand stone doors opened wide as the great Southern matron emerged and made the slow, ceremonial walk to the lip on the balcony to join her other children, the Princesses Creo and Yuma, and the young Prince Fazil. Over the side of the ore-etched balcony were steps that were quite wide at the base and top, and pinched toward the middle, like an hourglass. The crowd of citizens was partitioned to each side of the long walkway, behind barrier ribbons and intermittent Red Spines on watch. At the base of the stairs, looking up to the royal family, stood a single young man, dressed in the red tunics of the House of Pyrois. To his left and right, two figures in gold faced inward, looking past him and to each other: the bride, Zillah I'Itzal and the groom, Mugdi I'Pyrois. The three were veiled. The crowd was loud, and had been filled in equal part with cheers of joy and shouts of discontentment. All volume simmered to a mutter once the Queen began her address.

"Over twenty years, in the glow of our great fire steed, Pyrois, I have been given the honor of your trust. Over twenty years: and from that, four children, so exact in the specifications as to be as the colts of great Pyrois, himself! And here: as I give my first son to the path of peace, I bring my last son to the path of your hearts."

She took a pause, and allowed the cheering to surge a bit before continuing, "I have heard that you are angry. This I can see, in your faces, thin and tired. I see fear where no fear should have ever been known. Heard, have I, that The Red Spines, who love and protect us so well, have been worked to the bone to keep raging brother from brother or sister from vicious sister. This is not the way. To be vengeful to a whole House due to the act of one: this is not the way. To riot and harm. To destroy, to kill? This is not the way of Pyrois. Your anger, your hunger, I see this, and I have the medicine." Again, loyal and proud Southerners applauded their Queen's grace.

"I first give you my son, a quiet scholar and brilliant man: Prince Daim I'Pyrois!"

All but the royal balcony and the marital couple, who were standing on ceremony, erupted into chants and cheers as Prince Daim I'Pyrois carefully began to climb the stairs to the Queen. He knelt before her as she removed his red veil. His dark eyes nervously darted around before landing on the face of Yuma, who sweetly waved and mouthed, "Hi." The young man smiled and felt calmed by her instant kindness as he stepped forward and accepted an embrace from his mother, the Queen, before taking a spot to stand next to the little Princess. Quickly, Yuma took his hand into her own, causing a greater swell of cheering from the people.

"Next," the Queen called, triggering the crowd to quiet again, "Next, it is my honor not to welcome a bride to the House of Pyrois, but rather, to send a groom to the House of Itzal. Mugdi I'Pyrois and Zillah I'Itzal, approach."

A temple priest followed closely behind the gold veiled pair, who came to the base of the stairs and turned to the Queen while ascending. Once at the top, both knelt and the Queen, fighting back tears of joy and sorrow, unveiled the two. Mugdi, although still deeply wounded by the Queen's decision to send him to House of Itzal, loved his mother and smiled at her. Zillah, a beauty with long locks of coal colored hair and the dark rust colored eyes of her father, Tibon, bowed in deep honor for the gesture of allowing her to marry the blood of Pyrois while claiming the head of her own house.

The priest stepped forward, "Here, on the sacred steps of Tephra Keep do two souls fix into one. Here, in the sacred glow of the fire, do we celebrate the health and unity of House of Itzal, who on this day finds that not only does their family grow, but also grows their fortune and prosperity. Mugdi I'Pyrois: Pyrois gives you to Zillah I'Itzal. Zillah I'Itzal, Pyrois gives you to Mugdi I'Pyrois. And together, Pyrois gives you to the House of Itzal: forever may you live your days in the arms of your House, Zillah and Mugdi I'Itzal!"

The Southerners were moved by the act of the Prince forsaking the crown for the betterment of an ailing House, and as such, gave an ovation of adoration. Loud and cheerful, they offered shouts of love to the adorable couple while Mugdi offered Daim a secretive glare of

225

darkness. The couple slowly turned, and raised their hands with smiles and waves back to the people as the Queen stepped forward to speak once more.

"And on this most festive of days, this Jubilee of Flame, I give but one more decree. To better heal this suffering, and to better feed these children, I am appointing the honorable Idris I'Na'if as The Speaker of Pyrois: an official court title allowing him to cross the border to the East and re-establish good faith relation and trade."

At this pronouncement, fewer cheered than before and some even loudly decried the appointment as 'doing the will of the revolution'. The House Heads, however, began turning to their kin to whip up vocal support for the initiative. If for no other reason, each one perceived the good that it could do for their house's coffers.

Soon the jeering was overpowered and with a signal from the Queen, the musicians commenced. The feast was nearing its start when a young girl brought over the ceremonial wine. With a lift of her hand, Queen Gabija called, "You are welcome, my dear friends, to Tephra Keep!" Upon the official proclamation, she drank. As quickly as the wine hit her throat, the Queen, witnessed by all her people, began to convulse, vomit, and choke.

Alarm, shock, and pandemonium broke out as quickly as wildfire and began to engulf the already edgy masses. Yuma screamed and fell to her knees at the side of her mother's body while Sule and a small force of Red Spines clambered to grab up every member of the royal brood. Mugdi looked to his siblings, then his new wife, Zillah before loudly remarking over the hysterics, "Your House!"

House Heads frantically tried to locate and collect their own members while the Red Spines who had been assigned to guard the respective families fought against other families in complete chaos. Zillah I'Itzal, fresh in the role of leader, grabbed her husband's arm and ran into the crowd in search of her House mates. With a glance over his shoulder in complete confusion, Mugdi watched the last breath of his mother leave her body just before he fled.

*****

*Rise and thrash, you of no notice.*
*Rise and crash through the chains and walls.*
*You, abandoned,*
*You: perdu.*
*You, forgotten,*
*You: traduced.*
*Rise and thrash in Coadunation.*
*Rise and fall as one.*

*Come you ice of Winter,*
*Or, earth of Springtime.*
*Come you, flames of Summer,*
*Or, winds of Autumn.*
*Rise and thrash in Coadunation.*
*Rise and fall as one.*

*-Pamphlet Found in town of Havfrve, North Hold.*

# Chapter XVII
## *Of Coadunation: Falcon's Perch*

In the Eastern border town of Falcon's Perch, Nest
Twig Inn was situated straddling a long, thin, winding
mountain river. It was the same river in which the body
of Princess Lavinia had been found. Raised on log stilts,
the Inn was a long row-house with a large watermill to
supply power to the attached brewery. The rapids of the
river rushed along over slick rock-faces. A spattering of
patrons huddled in small clusters around tables of oak.
Their quiet voices whispered over the flames of candles,
while they clenched knit-gloved hands and their noses
ran from the tears of heavy sorrow.

The bard's over-cried blue eyes were transfixed
through a window on the turbulence and undertow at the
base of the water-wheel. The ginger-brown haired son of
the East lamented deeper and longer than most others.
His folded arms, clad in a tattered wool sweater, had
grown numb from the duration of his trance. He was
unusually handsome, with a strange and slight dimple
poked at the end of his nose. A strong round face was
punctuated by his closely cut beard of a hue more orange
than the dark of his short mane.

"You have to shake of this," quietly remarked his
companion who sat across the small round table. She was
hooded to conceal her hair of sunshine, and dressed in
the autumnal fashion of the East, although a woman of
the West. Woven knits covered the majority of her golden
skin while the sleeves of her dark orange tunic sweater
covered her hands as gloves. Her bright green eyes took

in the sight of his untouched food and lager. "Valko, eat something," she urged.

Valko blinked and shifted his vision to attend her words, while still frowning. He had held with the silence for a long while but only because he hadn't wished to speak first. "Why?"

"Why? Because all living things need food."

"Is this living, Leda?"

With a sigh, she placed a hand over her eyes and groaned. She was empathetic to his heartache, but had begun to run short on patience. Although Falcon's Perch had become something of a haven for members of The Coadunation to gather and meet, the recent death of Princess Lavinia, Valko's secret love, had triggered a heavier than usual presence of Magpies. While the natives were shocked with the proximity of loss, the covert foreigners had to exercise more-than-usual levels of caution and discretion. And then finally, that morning, word had arrived from GoldCloud Castle: there was to be a public service for the death of one princess and the coronation of another. "We should go north. Follow up behind Leontes."

"I thought you were defending him," Valko muttered while capitulating to take the cup of lager into his wide hand.

She shook her head and looked down into the churning waters below. She didn't particularly wish to discuss something so delicate in public, even with the room as thinly populated as it was, but she knew how profoundly the emotions of Valko, her friend, ran. She lifted a shoulder and cracked out a few whispered words, "I don't know."

230

"You don't know?" Valko pressed after a swallow of the drink that was the same temperature as the surrounding air. A healthy dose of anger and betrayal tempered his mourning and came through in his words.

From the North Hold, Leontes crossed the border many months before. He said he was a disenfranchised Grimm looking to sign up with the revolution. Once that gained little traction, he shifted his tale to claim nobility and still found himself avoided by nearly all of Falcon's Perch. Valko offered him shelter and friendship when no others would. And through carefully placed socialization, Valko won the trust of those sympathetic to the cause of The Coadunation for Leontes.

As much of a multi-mouthed beast as The Coadunation was, the core philosophy was the bait on the hook that seemed to catch most of the fish. Unity, freedom, equality: it offered all things dazzling in theory. The movement grew and swelled but suffered badly from an aversion to a central leadership, and often functioned in small groups led by an arbitrarily defined internal hierarchy. Completely comfortable retired Wanderers would sign up if for no other reason than to be a part of an important movement. It was attractive to myriad walks of life: the scholars, the traders, the laborers, and anyone else who ever wanted more than what they had. It promised community, adventure, and progress. But for every good-natured idealist, there were three scoundrels filling the ranks of The Coadunation. Valko woke to the possibility that his friend and swiftly-sworn-brother, Leontes, was less a like-minded philosopher for peace, and more a vicious and jealous villain.

It started after a tryst with his beloved Princess

Lavinia: a night filled with sweat and lust spied by the covetous gray Northern eyes of Leontes. Before the sun rose, she prepared to leave and whispered her concerns that they had been watched by Valko's guest through the airy fabric curtains within the hut that served as crude divisions of the otherwise single room. His initial response was to laugh off the worry, but her insistence planted a seed of sober concern. She left and moments passed before Valko decided to follow along the path he knew her to travel. There he saw the creeping, sneaking Leontes traveling between the two in some presumed prowling wickedness. Swiftly, he caught up to Leontes, confronted him and was eventually swayed to the prowler's side of the events: Leontes claimed to follow the Princess in an effort to protect her.

It was a flimsy and foolish thing to have believed, Valko presently convinced himself. But with event after event misconstrued and misinterpreted, Leontes' darkness should have been obvious and in retrospect, it truly was. Valko was firmly convinced that his false-sworn-brother had betrayed him and murdered Lavinia. The morning that Leontes mysteriously vanished was followed by the nightfall her lifeless body was found afloat.

Leda unfurled like a great crane in repose in an effort to soothe, by sight, the horrific pain within Valko. Days had passed with her claiming Leontes' innocence by way of unhappy coincidence and misunderstanding. Even after hearing of his pursuit of the Princess, still she offered a perspective misaligned with Valko's beliefs and her words were like a thorn to his heart. She and the few other members of The Coadunation cell of Falcon's Perch were opposed to his relationship with the Crown, even though that relationship predated the presence of the revolutionaries. But, as the most highly respected native of the town, he took something of a leading role in their small collective, and to Leda's silent mind, it really could have been anyone wishing to distance him from the capital. Surely he was a few sweet words from marriage, and then, the throne. It wasn't a loss that The Coadunation members would take lightly. His soft, natural charisma captured the revolutionaries as easily as it captured the love of the Princess. "Valko," she began while studying the brightness of his brilliant and sad eyes, "No one knows what happened. I wasn't suggesting we track him, I was suggesting we join him."

"It would be tracking. And I would kill him."

"You're going to find ghosts in every shadow, my friend. What happened, happened. It was horrible, but you can not let it drown you."

"Somehow, I don't think you really believe it was all that horrible," he growled while taking another sip of his drink. "I mean, not really."

With a scowl, Leda bristled at the accusation. While it was true that she disliked the political system of the divine bloods, she would never wish the death of anyone, much less the death of a person for whom a friend had such love. She did wish he would have seen his time spent with the Princess as contrary to the revolution, but would have never desired harm to acquire that outcome. "Ghosts in every shadow, Valko."

"Where else would they be?" he rubbed at his bearded cheek and looked back onto the water.

Hopeful to shift the conversation, she leaned closer

and remarked, "Did you hear about those that found the little Prince?"

He extended a finger pointing north and waited for an affirmative nod to comment. "A panoply of stupidity."

Leda sucked at her teeth before a scoff of a laugh, still conscious to keep the conversation quiet, "How do you mean? They saved the boy. They're taking him back to his mommy and daddy."

"Oh, pony balls. You don't actually believe that, do you?"

"Of course, I do! Why can't you just accept a nice gesture when you see it?"

"Because I don't see a nice gesture. I see a ransoming. And I don't think they're going to get to mommy and daddy, they have to get through the coffin nail of a brother first."

"The Grimm?"

He nodded, "They both are. I mean the oldest one, Horatio. Whatever, maybe they'd catch a break and bump into Edgar first. I hear he's an understanding sort. It doesn't matter. It really doesn't."

"Why is it making you so mad?"

Valko's frustrations were obvious and made more intense by his complete lack of cheer, "I really don't care about any of it. It was stupid. What they did was stupid. It is going to hurt everyone. Everyone on our side, everyone not on our side: everyone is going to be hurt by that stunt. But really, I really don't care. Who would decide that it would have been a remotely good idea? So stupid."

"You wouldn't try to reunite a foreign Prince with his family?"

Scratching his head in anger, Valko groaned, "Stop

talking about it."

"Well, alright," Leda remarked while glancing over her shoulder to observe a scrappy little boy talking in something of an exhausted panic to the barkeep. "But I still think I may go into the North."

"Why?" Valko narrowed his eyes and folded his arms across his chest, "Why would you possibly want to do that? The border is almost a deathtrap and if you get past it, the damn snow waits to finish you off. There's nothing up there but ruin."

"Maybe Leontes went up?"

"Unbelievable. So what if he did? It would be better for him if he had really just vanished. If you go north and find him? What clearer sign of guilt do you need?"

"Maybe that's what I need to find out. You want to go, don't you?"

"Nope."

"Nope?"

"No."

"Why not? I think it would help."

"Help what, Leda?"

"Help you."

Valko shook his head and exhaled a taciturn sigh.

"Why are you being so impossible? I can't do anything right with you. I tell you I think Leontes had nothing to do with it: you fume. I tell you I'm willing to entertain the possibility: you pout. I am trying to help you, Valko."

"I needed her, Leda. I needed her and now she is gone."

"She is gone."

Injured by the phrase, Valko recoiled and rested his

head against the sill-frame of the window. After a few silent moments of thought, he nodded out a whisper with tears in his eyes, "You do know that many, many, many people say she was killed by a lover?"

Wordlessly, Leda indicated she knew and was still listening.

"She only had the one," he muttered. "It's an act of the winged-god that someone hasn't pointed a finger at me, yet."

"The people here love you, Valko. They won't turn you over, even if they thought you had done it."

He rolled his eyes with spite, "Gross negligence of priority."

"Is it, though?" she argued with furrowed brow. "You can be so ungrateful sometimes. You know what: be sad. Mourn, take time with it. Be angry, fine. But don't belittle people who choose to protect you."

He shook his head and moved his attention to the barkeep and frantic child while still speaking to Leda, "I'm..." the words for Leda trailed off as the barkeep made intentional motions to Valko as if pleased to have his attention.

"Ah, Valko!"

"What?" His arms were still folded over his broad form. Leda turned her hood-obscured eyes toward the call of the barkeep.

"This little boy has a remarkable story he's telling me. Say, your horse had a deep neck cut, didn't she?"

"Yea, a while ago. Why?" Valko asked curiously while Leda noticed a Magpie through a window on the side wall and began to slip away with a knowing glance to Valko who quickly followed her indication of the sight for

236

himself.

"Well, throat cut, actually," Otver exhaustedly muttered while seeming like he would fall over at any moment.

"I thought you could help, seeing as how you've patched your own mare up."

"Um, yea." Valko wanted to flee, but did not. He stood and gave an earnest look out of the window to the Magpie and the old gelding who was carefully bandaged and laying across a barely intact lowered cart. "That looks pretty bad," he offered down to Otver with sincere sympathy. After watching the dirty little face for a few seconds, he crossed to the barkeep and handed a few coins over, "Send some soup around to my place. And mutton." He looked down to Otver and placed a hand to his shoulder, "You like mutton, kid? Of course you do. Come with me."

Nervous and badly shaken, the Magpie swallowed dryly as the man descended the stairs with Otver. She extended her hand and was grateful for any sign of assistance, "Magpie Eileivia Morninglight, sir. This is Otver. We really appreciate anything you can do to help. I don't know how much more I can do..."

With a raised eyebrow to the ominous statement, he took her hand into his and replied, "Valko Cidershine." He nodded and moved to the cart. "Did you two pull him here?"

Both Otver and Eile nodded.

In impressed disbelief, Valko questioned, "From where?"

"A terrible place," Otver began as Eile interrupted, "In the woods."

237

With the slight confusion of curiosity, Valko nodded once and chose to not press as it seemed they were hesitant to discuss any of it. He motioned that they should cover their ears and once they had, he shouted, "Wanion!" His voice ringing through the town was fairly common in Falcon's Perch and presently in response to the call, a stunning gray mare with a thick neck scar and black mane and tail appeared. She stomped and pressed her snout near his head with a familiar huff, causing him to flinch. "Help with the cart?"

"Is she yours?" Eile asked with a quiet amazement.

"I think I'm hers, actually," Valko remarked while lifting the rope from the cart bracers to Wanion's back. "How long has he been like this?" He nodded down to the gelding.

"His name is Raccoon," Eile offered before answering the question, "A couple of days, we think."

"You think?" Valko asked while helping to lift the cart so that the full weight didn't rest on Wanion. Without delay, several townspeople came over to lend a hand.

"Day and night sort of blended together," Otver admitted quietly while watching an old lady offer Wanion a quickly accepted carrot.

Playfully, Valko scolded the old lady, "What are you doing?" The distraction was good for his mood even with a mysterious Magpie around. He called over his shoulder to both Eile and Otver, "The town stable is near to my house."

"Is that where we're going?" Otver asked while watching the cart move with ease from so many hands.

Valko nodded before inquiring, "Did he bleed much?"

"Um -" Eile muttered before fainting to the alarm of

238

all present.

"What happened to you two?" Valko questioned Otver while quickly checking the Magpie for a pulse. Once he found one, he waved a few people over to carry her body to the cart where she was laid next to Raccoon. "Are you going to do that, too?"

"What? Fall over?"

Valko nodded with concern.

"I may," Otver answered while his eyes rolled around a bit.

Grabbing him at the ribs, Valko lifted little Otver and sat him on the cart. Quietly, he turned to a couple of young women as they continued on with the cargo, "I'll need a moment at the stables to look at the wound. Could you get these two set up at my place? I have soup on the way but they may need to rest."

The young women smiled and nodded with an indication that it would be no problem.

"Keep an eye on the bird," secretly, he whispered with a nod toward the Magpie before looking back to the rushing river with a reoccurring heaviness as they continued on to the stables.

The expected amount of time passed. Valko arrived at the door of his cabin with an interested expression for the two women who were asked to watch the pair.

"She's still sleeping, I think. The little boy isn't saying much," the more vocal of the two offered with a lift of her shoulder. "How'd the horse make out?"

"He'll live. Thanks, you two." He smiled and filed past the duo while climbing the stairs.

One called over her shoulder after the parting of ways, "The soup is on the fire. It was just delivered."

"Potato?" Valko asked hopefully.

She shook her head, "Cabbage."

He grumbled under his exasperated breath, "Piss-all, I hate cabbage." He lifted his hand before slipping into the hut, "Alright, thanks again."

An awkward quiet was held between Valko and Otver, as the child turned to the sound of the entrance. They watched each other for a time. One sized up the other and at every instance of a conversation nearly happening, a breath or expression from the other would cause them to restrain the utterance. To the man, the child seemed far too mature and guarded, while to the child, the man appeared far too approachable and almost juvenile.

Eventually Valko lost the battle of attrition with a bashful chuckle, upraised eyebrows and a shrug with overturned palms, "You're looking at me like I'm a bear or something. I think Raccoon is going to make it. Wanion is staying with him."

"Do you mean I seem threatened? I'm grateful. We're grateful. It's just..."

He muttered as if to clarify, "I mean, maybe you're looking at me like you're the bear."

Otver, intoxicated by the wafting aroma of the cabbage soup, shook his wan head.

"You're not going to try to rob me, right? Are you a thief? Is that why you're with the authority figure over there?" He nodded toward Eile, who had been splayed onto his bed as if she leaked in through the roof.

With a weak and terse response, Otver said, "Not going to try to rob you. Not a thief. No, that is not why she is with me." He leaned hard against the back of the chair that held him. "But I'm really glad Raccoon is alright."

Valko waved at the soup scented air with a disgusted grunt, "Do you want some soup? The faster it's gone the better." By the sight of the emaciation, he knew the boy would eat. With a swoop of movement, he strolled through the space between Otver and Eile, breaking Otver's doomed stare briefly. "You said that she is with you? Not that you are with her?"

"Hm?" Otver had barely been listening but his attention was quickly won by the sight of Valko dishing soup from ladle to bowl. "I'm sorry, what?"

"Thus far I have discovered that you are..." Valko turned and set the bowl of steaming cabbage soup on the table near-to Otver. He handed a wooden spoon to the boy and changed the point of his words quickly, "Want some bread?"

Otver nodded emphatically, suffering the heat of the liquid for the swift consumption.

Valko reached into a burlap bag, brought out a small loaf, and tossed it underhandedly to Otver before folding his arms and continuing, "...that you are kind, courageous, a little intimidating, not a thief, very hungry, and someone who would have a Magpie in their company, rather than the other way around."

"How do you think you know I'm kind?"

"What kind of person carts a half-dead gelding into a town filled with strangers?"

Otver glanced to the unconscious Eile and remarked, "It was her idea, actually. I haven't been the most helpful since it happened."

Valko nodded and gave a distrustful glance to the Magpie in his bed.

"Scary?" Otver questioned with interest.

"What is?"

"You said you were scared of me?"

Valko laughed gently, "Did I? I don't think I did."

"I think you did."

"I believe I said 'a little intimidating'."

"So, you are intimidated, but not scared?"

"You weigh as much as a sack of grain, kid." Their rapport was quickly developing and as a smile and chuckle was shared, Valko spoke with cooled honesty, "You looked like you would take my head off if I came in here with designs to harm your little bird friend, there. It was clearly stated. Your eyes are the eyes of a fierce and loyal thing."

Otver issued a single slow nod while chewing on bread, "I didn't know I did that."

"Maybe that's why I believed it."

Eileivia shifted a bit and rolled to her side.

"Should we wake her?" Otver asked with earnest concern.

Valko shook his head, "I wouldn't. Let her sleep, you two can stay and recover. I don't have any plans." His words came as something of a surprise to his own ear. He was decidedly not comfortable in the presence of a Magpie, but felt that the opportunity to ingratiate himself to the boy could offer some cover from later troubles. It was a fascinating arrangement: the little boy important enough to have a Magpie all his own. It may have all been ignorable, or something easily overlooked, had the pair not arrived with a heavy half-dead horse that was worth less in value than a bowl of soup. Valko was beguiled by the humane absurdity of it all and welcomed the distraction.

"I don't even know how we got out," Otver vocalized his thoughts, not altogether meaning to make the statement aloud. His glum and dour face read annoyance at his own muttering while a slimy oversized leaf of cabbage slipped from his spoon with a small splash into the broth in the bowl. His dark eyes searched the room for a thing on which to fix a conversation. The state of clutter was of interest to Otver's notice, as it seemed recent. It was a dust-free place, yet mounds of empty cups and piles of fabrics, clothes he thought, here and there. Otver gathered that the disorder was fresh: something very troubling must have happened to their host. But that wasn't a thing he could bring himself to ask about. A diversion presented itself as he spied a cluster of well-kept stringed instruments in the otherwise chaotic home, "Are you a musician?"

Valko had been holding his body tightly within his folded arms. The growing tension was evident from his chest, shoulders and neck, drawn and taut. Having watched Otver studying his home just after mumbling a thing he clearly wished he had not, Valko too was anxious for a conversation to break the seemingly inflexible discomfort. He nodded with subdued zeal while casting a glance over-shoulder to the indicated instruments, "I am! Yes."

Again, silence played on the air, vexing both.

"I thought you might have been the mayor, the way everyone seems to treat you."

"There isn't a mayor of Falcon's Perch. There was. There isn't now," Valko offered while sneaking a nervous glance over at the sleeping Magpie. "Besides, if I were the

243

mayor, I'd have had mutton delivered when I asked, and paid, for mutton."

"What happened? To the mayor, I mean." He frowned while watching the squirming of Valko. Otver understood the mistrust and wondered how he would have felt to have a stranger show up with a Magpie, had he had a home of his own. "We've...we really appreciate all that you're doing. We've been through a lot."

"That's pretty obvious, boy-o. A badly battered horse. A blacked-out Magpie and a half-starved boy with the eyes of a Wanderer turn up. Yea...obviously you've seen your share."

Otver nodded, thankful to have understanding. "So, what happened to the mayor?"

Valko drew in a sigh and with a slight lift of the left side of his lips, he surrendered to the question, even while it edged the limits of what he wanted to talk on, "He killed himself after killing his family."

"Why would anyone do that?" Having never had a family aside from his sister, young Otver was shocked.

"You ask a lot of questions." Valko tried to appear unattached from the topic and took a seat at the table across from Otver, who had paused his eating due to the surprise.

Unnoticed by the others, Eile groggily woke and opted to lie still, listening.

"The...thing. With the...Princess. He felt, I don't know...responsible, I think."

"Responsible? Did he...was he the one that..." Otver carefully asked. He noticed that Valko's blue eyes fought against making contact with any one thing for very long.

"No," the response was a quiet one. His face quickly

filled with the heartache he had been trying to mask. "He, I think, worried that he hadn't done his job well enough. If he had been more vigilant maybe she would be alive."

"Do you believe that?"

"I don't know." He shifted and exhaled to avoid crying. "I think the guilt, and honestly, the fear over what the Crown would do to him, terrified him."

"But to kill his whole family?"

"It is a great shame to be in charge of the sight of... what Falcon's Perch has become. I don't know, I'm rambling. The point is that he really wasn't a very good mayor. He had a lot of years to enjoy the status without every really doing much to earn it, aside from the outstanding ability to turn-a-blind-eye to anything, ever. I think he felt it all catch up with him. I don't know what he felt. Maybe he should have been better at reporting what he saw, rather than just permitting everything. I don't know."

"What do you think he 'saw'?" Eileivia asked finally while pulling herself up to sit on the bed.

"So, you two are here on that 'official business'?" Valko, feeling deceived frowned over to the Magpie. "Are you alright?" he asked, shying from the topic. "There's soup, although I'm sorry to admit – it's cabbage."

"Cabbage soup is fine," she groaned, wincing with the motion of standing. "Is Raccoon alright?"

"I wouldn't classify him as 'alright', but he's patched. No infection. Alive. Cuddling with my girl. Come have some terrible but hot soup." He stood to retrieve the food and offered her his chair, although two others were available.

"How do you feel?" Otver quietly asked.

She sighed with a sickly moan, "Not the best." With a louder comment she aimed her voice to Valko, "Your bed is very comfortable. Thank you."

"So I have been told, and you're welcome." He set a bowl of the soup on the table along with a small roll. While turning to pour water from a jug into a trio of cups, he mentioned, "I told boy-o that you two could stay a bit..."

"We can't stay," Eile remarked quickly.

"Oh, what a shame," the feigned disappointment came swiftly as he handed a cup to her.

Otver protested, setting his spoon down, "Eile? Why not? What are we even doing?"

"I don't know how much of that we should be discussing in front of our host, Otver," Eile sternly groused while biting into the bread.

Valko raised an eyebrow and decided to turn his back while in thought. He stirred the soup in the cauldron over the fire.

"If you're suggesting we go back to GoldCloud, I can't go back, Eile." As quietly as he possibly could, Otver demanded, "How am I supposed to go back?"

"I could step outside, if...you...two...you know. Okay, I'll be outside," Valko offered with a slight smile before exiting the cabin. While shivering off the gust of cool air, he turned and situated himself below a window, in complete anticipation of eavesdropping.

"What did you tell the bard, Otver?"

"I haven't told him anything!"

"There's something rotten about him."

"I think he's nice."

"Did you see how quickly everyone rushed to help? As

if, it was because he was involved? No one helped us until the Inn, when he got involved."

"He seems very nice. I imagine he has a lot of friends."

"And now you're an authority on niceness and friends?" As immediately as she said it, Eile regretted her venomous words. "I'm sorry, Otver."

Otver shrugged, frowned, and sulked with a knit brow.

"I just don't know what to do. I don't understand what happened. I'm scared."

His pain melted enough for his body to lean forward with surrendered words, "I know your family is from a village, Eile. But, the capital – life in the capital seems to make people forget that there are things outside of those cliffs. I only know it because I ran into the forest at every chance I got when my sister died. The people below are not like the people up high. They aren't even much like the villages, really."

Eile nodded in defeat and took his words in.

"They were bandits. That part of what we agreed on is true. They were bandits: we were attacked while lost in the forest."

"We should have never strayed from the path."

"Will you just listen to me? All of that is true. But we can't go back to GoldCloud without having finished what we started. Or, really, I can't. You can, I think."

"I can't. I have to go wherever you go! The letter the King wrote can only be delivered by a representative of the Crown. That's me, your Magpie. Our only chance to cross the border at all is for me to be with you."

"Oh, come on," Otver scoffed in disbelief. "People

find holes, Eile. People cross without help. Everyone knows that."

"How am I supposed to go back alone, Otver? You want me to tell them I lost you and the Prince?"

"Prince?" Valko mouthed while deeply absorbed in the secret conversation. He spied a small boy passing and waved him over.

"What are you doing outside of your house, Valko? Did you lose something?" the boy asked while getting hushed and chastised for his volume.

"Trovy, go to the stables for me and – you know that cart that the travelers brought the horse in on?" Valko frantically whispered, pulling the little boy close.

Trovy nodded, pleased to be part of some scheme of Valko's.

"Okay, on that cart, which is in the stall next to the one with the patched gelding and Wanion, there should be a satchel of some kind. Not like a goods bag, but like a proper traveler's purse."

"Wanion hates me!"

"She hates everyone. Take an apple. Tell her I said it was okay...but also take an apple. In that satchel, there should be a letter. Do you know what the Pegasus seal looks like? Kind of a golden-orange wax with a figure of a wing pressed in it. Find that. Bring it here. Quickly." He gently smacked the boy away while resuming his listening of the conversation.

"I don't know what to do. Going into the North? Still? This is what you want?" Eile asked, completely unaware that ears other than Otver's were listening to her words.

"None of it has ever been about what I want to do," Otver lamented. "I'm scared, too. I mean, go home and admit we failed, facing who-knows-what now. Especially with the sisters having him. And they said they were going to the Queen and King? So, we could hope to out-pace them, maybe?"

"They were gone in an instant, Otver," Eile sadly remarked. "He could already be there for all we know."

He shook his head, lowering his face into his arms as they folded on the table, "This should have never happened. I wish it had never happened."

Trovy, out of breath and impressed with himself, returned to Valko and shoved the royal missive into his ribs to gain his attention. "Found it."

"Did Wanion give you a hard time?" He looked the letter over as if it were a rare treasure.

"Nah, I handled her. The apple worked."

"Handled her!" He scoffed and playfully kicked toward the boy, "Go home. Thank you, and go home."

Trovy nodded and jogged off while Valko, with a wince and a slightly shut right eye snapped the wax of the royal seal. He began to read and with an amazed breath, fell against the banister at what he saw.

"How long before Raccoon is well enough for travel? Did he say?" Eile asked before the opening of the door silenced her question.

"You two," Valko proclaimed while holding the missive in the air, "have been had."

Outraged, Eile shot to her feet once she recognized the paper and shattered seal, "What have you done?"

"I have liberated you," he replied while pointing to the chair from which she stood. "Sit down. I shouldn't open a royal missive, I know. But, sit down." His tone had changed from the awkward uncertainty used when speaking to Otver alone. He was serious and stern.

"Sit down, Eile," Otver gently urged.

"You two are being sacrificed," Valko commented while looking the inky words over again. "It says that the boy, that's you," he pointed to Otver, "is 'a rogue orphan criminal'. It continues: 'although his actions do not reflect the wishes, demands, or desires of the Eastern Hold – out of undying loyalty to Pegasus, he reacted in the belief that Prince Edgar had seduced Princess Lavinia...and murdered her when she rebuffed his unholy advances'... that's what it says. THAT is what it says. It goes on to beg clemency for the Magpie warden who is delivering the criminal – but that there is an understanding if the Magpie 'finds penal destruction' as well. Penal Destruction! Exact quote!"

"This can not be." Amazed and sorrowful, Eile extended a hand to Valko for the letter, which softly, he surrendered.

"I'm sorry. It is exactly how it is," Valko muttered while releasing the note into her hand. "Sacrifice."

While Otver quietly wept with bitterness, Eile, with tears in her eyes read over the words, before uttering, "How could you?"

Appalled, Valko questioned, "How could I what?"

"You broke the royal seal?" Eile asked while overturning the letter with ruin in her eyes.

With a confused and unsure laugh, Valko tilted his head forward, "The thing most forefront in your mind – the thing that upsets you the most – is that I broke the royal seal? Not what the seal was sealing?"

Eile had no cogent response. She wondered if she had assumed the possibility of treachery all along, or worse yet, fated to permit it by her unquestioning obedience. But a thought pulled at her heart: her love of the East made it clear that it could not have been expected. It was a painful shock and agony to consider.

Valko studied Eile's despondency and after carefully weighing his options, said, "A Magpie no more?"

"What kind of question is that?" Otver demanded with a protective roar. "You think this is her fault? I'm the reason she's here! I'm to blame for all of it."

"You're not to blame for the quickness with which the King would discard you. Neither of you are," Valko replied before quietly remarking, "The interesting thing is, this letter that brought you such woe, actually brings me some welcome news."

"How so?" Eile asked.

"The only way, I think, that the King would assert some claim that the Prince had anything to do with Lavinia's death is if he actually believed it. Otherwise, since he seems so eager to be rid of the two of you, he would have just said 'this dumb kid killed your dumb kid. Me and mine had nothing to do with it.' It's almost instigation by accusal."

"Princess Lavinia," Eile corrected with scorn before the sight of his bashful dismissal triggered the realization, "Wait – you're the lover? You are?"

Slowly, Valko nodded with a shrug, "Forgive me for suddenly not being overly concerned about being arrested. I don't think you're in the best position to be dragging in suspects, especially if the ex-King is convinced the dead Prince did it. Besides, I didn't kill her."

"Ex-King?" Otver questioned.

"His little sister is taking over." Valko placed both hands behind his back while leaning against a side table. "You two appear to be marooned. A dandy pair of fugitives."

Otver and Eile shared a glance of doom.

"So? Still want to go to the North?"

"I do," Otver quickly answered.

"Why?" demanded Eile. "The whole thing is over, Otver. What would be the point?"

"I would have done it even if the King didn't send me. It was my idea. I owe it to his family."

"Would you still do it if it were a cobbler's son?" asked Valko.

Without delay, Otver nodded.

With an impressed nod, Valko pressed, "You know they'll kill you, right? If you even make it to the castle, I mean. Why not write a letter? Didn't bandits swipe the Prince? Let it be the bandits' problem, now. You have two people to answer to for it: one, the King, who wanted you killed for it, and the other is you yourself. Don't toe the King's line and want death for yourself. You're a young kid with a full life ahead of you."

Eile quietly listened and started to see the sense in Valko's very persuasive argument.

"But, I took a life. I took a mother's son," Otver replied.

"The mother is a bitch and her son was known to skip across the border to rape and pillage. Did you know that when you shot him? You did the whole Hold a favor. The King should have rewarded you."

"Prince Edgar came over the border often?" asked Eile.

"Frequently, with a little band of Grimms. Our mayor knew. One of the only good things he ever did was report it. To Magpies. Guess the news never reached you?"

Eile shook her head slowly.

"Listen, kid, I can't tell you what to do. But I can tell you with *complete certainty* that I do not think crossing into the North is a good idea. But, that said, if you'd like to go through with it, I'll help you get as far as I can."

"What? You don't even know us! You'd go across the border with us?" Eile asked.

"Us? Yea, I have an acquaintance I think I need to locate. A friend said she wanted to go up and if you – two – apparently, want to take the trip, then I don't see why not. Us? Really?"

Eile nodded and muttered while looking to the bright eyes of little Otver, "I promised."

# Chapter XVIII
## *Of Hippocamp: Provocation*

"The news blows on the wind as fancy and light as snowflakes," an old man, the tall bony image of a withered leafless tree, spoke. "He has a head full of nothing! There is a sickness that forces an absence of reason to the boy's mandates."

"Now, now, honored Lord Polonius. The boy is the Prince, Lord Commander of the Grimms, and failing all else, he is your grand-nephew." With a soothing scold to her voice, Lady Helena Menteth, Thayn of Rindr, reached from her chair and set her soft hand atop the cadaverous fist of Lord Polonius Cade, uncle to the Queen and Thayn of Sorrowmore. The gesture wore the mask of kindness when in actuality it was a threat colder than the darkest winter's ice. "One should not so easily besmirch blood," she indicated to the throng in the war room to which they had all been summoned: King, Queen, Thayn, and Justice Prime alike. She would prefer to not attach herself to such treason.

Pockets of chattering conversation were scattered throughout the room. The majority of attendees were thayns, and as such, Grimm commanders: deeply loyal to their Lord Commander and whatever had caused him to collect them into a single place, with only very few outliers. Black filled the room: gloved hands creaked around goblets, wolf or bear fur cloaks hung lazily, and boots, heavy and thick, shuffled with movement.

The war room was low in the belly of Bleak Spire palace. Light blue and crystalline, the ice walls glimmered and lifted into a fantastic spiraling shaft up to the distant ribbon laced night sky. The table was long and draped with white pelts on which oil lamps illuminated the event. Silver flecked glints everywhere: the lamps danced with their reflection against the platters that held the food, cutlery, ale, and jewelry. It was the hypnotic flicker of light against King Alistair's ring which appeared to so completely captivate his seemingly simple attention. However, although his eyes devoured the sight of the trinket, his ears dined on every breath around every word from every set of lips. Yet no sound came from the mouth of the Queen, as both she and her King-husband recently received word from Dark Tower about a near-dead son, a missing son, and a son whose quill bled the ink for the message.

Queen Isobella wondered if Horatio called the meeting of the thayns to beg forgiveness for his incompetence in protecting his divine brothers. While she waited, she simmered: her anger a poison. Perhaps he would admit to his part in the loss, she thought. Perhaps he would announce a quest for some ancient magic to right his wrongs.

Justice Prime Rosalind Grey was the Grand Judge of Forseti, and, as chief executive to a team of judges, she ruled over the final execution of law for the full North. She was not a Grimm, and made little secret of her ongoing concern for the blurring of boundary between the role of the Grimms' policing and Forseti's courts. With a somber, puckered expression, she silently sat in the chair to Thayn Helena's right and endured the banter between the Rindrian and Thayn Polonius as it crossed past her more than a few times. Thrice by that point had she scooted her chair back away from the table to avoid being reached over. In hostility, she wondered to herself if she would end up half-way up the wall before the Lord Commander arrived.

"He would see me removed as Thayn!? Had you heard word of that?" Polonius demanded.

"I have not, no." Helena replied with a hushed voice, urging the old man to lower the sound of his discontentment.

"This pup, this little pup, barks and barks," he rambled. "You know what yipping pups do when they find their teeth? They use them. On everything. So, this pup would turn his teeth on me?"

"Sir, that is enough," Helena remarked, offended and embarrassed. "I am certain he would not seek to remove your titles."

"Oh? There is a young upstart: a Grimm too young to have had his balls drop, by the name of Corin, who seems to act on behalf of some scheme." He took a quick and hard drink of his ale before slamming the goblet to the table.

"Scheme? A scheme for Sorrowmore?" Helena, against her better judgment, asked in disbelief. "Princes do not scheme." While she did not want the room to witness the unraveling of Polonius, the accusation intrigued her.

"If I may," Justice Prime Rosalind Grey sat forward to interject in the conversation that had been thoughtlessly thrust against her for some time. "Were the Prince in the mood to remove you, Lord Polonius, as Lord Commander, he need do little more than appoint another to the position of Thayn of Sorrowmore. There would be no need to scheme, as you say." Her words were secretive and low, a thing for which Helena was grateful as she glanced to the silent and statuesque King and Queen.

The King was the image of distance, while the Queen held too much fury and sorrow to even quake from it. Few knew the state of things for the blood of Hippocamp. Too little time had passed for the news and rumors to begin to circulate. No one even truly knew why they had been summoned to the war room at Bleak Spire; it had not been used for actual war-time strategy in ages.

Some speculated on a possible announcement of an engagement to marry. Many of that mind felt that it was a thing long overdue.

Some expected news of important advancements, promotions, and retirements. It was the ardent worry of Polonius as he wrung his cold hands and thought on what to level against Horatio as leverage.

Many were simply surprised and open to the possibility of any cause to gather at Bleak Spire.

And then he arrived. Dour and cold as the ice of the underworld, Prince Horatio Aquilo, Grand Lord Commander of The Grimms, cast a long and scornful, towering shadow of silhouette at the entrance of the war room. He was alone, and in full uniform with every ceremonial metal he had ever been awarded pinned with precision to the breast of his coat.

All but the King and Queen stood to receive his entrance; even the King's pair of wolves sat in attention. The Justice Prime was a bit slower to rise, but rise she did. Then, with a wave of acknowledgment, the awareness of Horatio's humorless and stern face swept down along the table. His usual joy and charisma was hostage to an imposing intimidation. His eyes elicited fear. The posture that he learned, developed, nourished, and so carefully groomed to use against the enemies of the North, effortlessly attacked those very nobles in the room who awaited him. He was dread. He was made of a nightmare.

Queen Isobella, incorrectly convinced that she was witnessing a performance, frowned at the display. She leveled her gaze at him. Sensations, previously unknown whilst examining her eldest son, began to manifest. She felt scorn and disappointment. But more unnervingly, she felt challenged and subordinated.

Thayn of Lockfrost, Banquo, had been in mid-sip when Horatio entered and still his goblet lingered near his chin. Having been in the Lord Commander's company the most recently, he was best prepared for the possible sour turn of Horatio's mood. Yet, the depth of ambition painted across the Prince's niveous face could never have been expected, even by one so close as old Banquo.

Silent was the room. Cold and silent. The Thayn Grimms, locked in a fist-to-chest salute, kept their eyes low in amazed uncertainty. Grand Judge Grey maintained a brave eye on the Prince, concerned that the rumors of a soul-shifting sickness may have been true, and that Horatio was infected. The King, with steady breath, offered the same sad glance he would a corpse, while Queen Isobella elected to finally speak.

"Why have you convened this assembly, Lord Commander?" She called him neither Prince, nor son.

"It is a war council, Mother," he replied while removing his gloves. The word war sent ripples of surprise and consternation through the Thayns courageous enough to mutter among themselves. Banquo sat down as if he had been thrown to his chair.

"A war council?"

"It is." With disgust, Horatio spied the large spread of rich foods along the table. "Remove this opulence."

Reviled, Queen Isobella replied, "Mind your place." She held a hand up to halt the servants.

"My place?" Furious rage exploded through his words. "My place, Your Grace?" With stormy handfuls, he grabbed at random platters, food sliding through his fingers as he slammed all he could onto a serving plate. Once the dish had a small mound of various bits of cuisine intermingled, he held the plate high, "This is twice over what a single villager – in your Hold – may eat from one full moon to the next! A child could be driven to murder for even a whiff of so much! The old are starving! The infants are starving! Women, who should be fat and round with child, are skeletons begging at the hooves of Hippocamp for enough to birth a thing with a heartbeat!" Violently, he threw the plate of food into the fire while considering if he should succumb to his rage and continue his words. With only a moment's delay, he raised a finger of accusation right to the face of Thayn Polonius, the uncle of his mother. "You. You of all know better the curse of which I speak. You conniving, worm-meal villain."

"Only one here speaks with the tone of the villain, my poor addled nephew," Polonius coughed nervously. He looked to his royal niece for assistance. No assistance came.

"Where is Corin of Sorrowmore, old man?" Horatio demanded while a couple of Grimms bristled at the treatment. "Did my message not distinctly order you to see that he arrive here, at this meeting, alive-and-well?"

"It did," Polonius offered.

"And he is...where?" Horatio pressed to no reply. "I asked you a question, Grimm! Where is Corin of Sorrowmore?"

"You have him digging around for answers that do not exist, Horatio. I know what you promised him! I know you would have me gone!"

"If I would have you gone, you would be gone." The Lord Commander looked over his shoulder and lowered a hand causing those in attendance to reclaim their seats. With the same hand, he then waved at the entrance to summon in a pair of young Grimm initiates that traveled with him from Dark Tower. "Clear this food and lay my maps."

The pair obeyed and took to the task.

"Does he live, Polonius?" Horatio turned back to the angry, yet cowering old man. "Corin, that is. Have you decided to have him killed?"

Polonius shook his head. He had wanted to have the young man killed, but hadn't yet gotten to it before the sudden meeting had been called. "It is a terrible thing you do, Horatio."

"My, how tones change!" the Prince remarked. "That sounded nearly sincere and sentimental."

"A terrible thing."

The Prince, while responding to Polonius, offered his mother a glance while unrolling a parchment map, "It would appear that I was made to do a great many terrible things."

"Why do you look this way when you speak such

filth?" Queen Isobella snarled. "You killed your brothers, Horatio! You failed them!"

The only other person present who knew about the state of Hector and Edgar was Banquo and, with measured caution, he kept silent. He watched as the Queen's words drove into Horatio as spears would a bear. The Prince fought under the weight of the attack and exhaled through a frown. He said nothing.

"How could you..." She began to weep, which Horatio quickly took as an act of emphasis to sway the loyalty of the Grimms present. It was not that he did not believe her grief, it was that he knew she would never let others see her cry. A quick, silver glance to Banquo preceded a scan of the faces of the thayns. They were horrified.

The Queen glared at her oldest boy. A slight tremble to her dimpled cheek displayed to Horatio that his silence harmed her. "You could have saved them," she hissed. "You should have saved them."

The rage of Queen Isobella Aquilo was legendary and the chamber held a crypt-hush that lingered like a disease. The thayns, high-ranking Grimms that swore blood-oaths to their Lord Commander held, within each mind, a swirling pandemonium. They had their allegiance to the order, but also swore allegiance to the Crown. The tension and uncertainty grew.

Grand Judge Grey was not shackled by divided loyalty. While the information and accusations were severe, she, with a balanced observation between the Queen and Prince, finally spoke, "Is this the matter on which we have been gathered? These terrible things that you have been made to do: do those things include the murder of your brothers, Prince Horatio?"

"It is not the cause of this assembly and I did not murder my brothers," with a deep, cold, and quiet voice, Horatio responded to the Grand Judge while staring into his mother's face from across the table.

A number of thayns exhaled in relief and softened their posture.

"Had you any awareness of impending danger to your brothers, before their demise?" Grey continued.

"I did not."

"Neither is truly known to be dead," Banquo offered, which drew the full attention of the room his way. "Little Hector was found in the custody of the rebel thieves, The Coadunation, in the state he maintains: a perpetual slumber. Prince Edgar has not been found."

"Where is Prince Hector, now?" The Grand Judge looked from Banquo to Horatio for an answer.

"He was carefully and secretly transported here," Banquo remarked before issuing a comment to the Queen directly, "He sleeps in his own bed, my Queen."

Horatio, aware of the history and esteem between Banquo and the Queen and King, tilted his head and watched his mother for a reaction. It had been by his own order that Banquo was tasked with the duty.

Queen Isobella held her breath and wished to rush to the side of her ailing son. She longed to see his condition with her own eyes, or even witness his breath, but her hostility toward Horatio would not allow her to give him the satisfaction of an exit. The two maintained a locked stare while King Alistair heaved a series of sighs to punctuate the quiet of the room.

"You say very little, Lord Commander," Grey remarked, fairly annoyed by the awestruck and subservient Grimms who held their words hostage out of either dread or woe. "The journey here is not a small affair for some present. I wonder if you would speak to the cause? Are we to discuss The Coadunation?"

"Those guilty of having Prince Hector in their possession have been executed. All but one," Horatio offered.

"Executed?" Grey asked with disapproval.

He nodded, "Executed."

"Without trial?"

"They had a trial."

"A Grimm trial? That is not good enough, if you will excuse my saying."

"I shall not excuse your saying, Grand Judge. While I respect and honor the need and value of Forseti, it was a uniquely Grimm affair."

"The well-being of two from the royal family in this Hold is within Hold jurisdiction, Lord Commander! It is a matter for the whole of the Hold!"

"My brothers were abducted while on Grimm business, Grand Judge." Before Horatio could offer much more, Rosalind Grey raised both hands and shook her head. "Do not dismiss me," he demanded.

"I was not dismissing," her tone was a call for calm. "I grow uncomfortable with The Grimms' involvement with punishment...ever, Sir. Yet, this is clearly neither the time nor place for such a debate. What is done can not be undone. But hear this: you could have never given justice as the injured were your own brothers, Prince. One becomes clouded, you see. I never allow a Judge to sit on a trial where the Judge has a relationship with any involved. What you did was wrong."

"What he did was act as Lord Commander! He was protecting Grimms, brother or no..." Banquo's bark was interrupted by Horatio, who said, "Be easy. She is right."

Grey offered a skeptical lift of her chin.

With a nod to the Grand Judge, Horatio continued, "It should have been a thing managed by Forseti. This I know. While, however, it is a thing that I know, those under me look to me to lead them. They believe in me. They are asked to trust in me and pledge their lives to me. Even these esteemed and accomplished Grimms here in the room with us, even they would expect me to act as I did. It was not only a pair of princes attacked, it was The Grimms."

"Why did you execute them? Is that expected of you, too?" she asked.

"It is. And because I told them I would. All but one."

"Surely law enough has been broken to strip this pup of his responsibilities?!" Polonius foolishly croaked.

Horatio had nearly forgotten he was there, "Which brings me to you, Uncle."

"To me? We are talking about you and the liberties you take!"

"I take no liberties that are not demanded of me. Notwithstanding, you will retire tonight. A Grimm will escort you to Sorrowmore to collect your belongings and with you, bring Grimm Corin back to Bleak Spire."

"What?! On what authority do you dare...?" Polonius demanded.

"And if Corin can not be found, or, if he is found dead, then you will be surrendered to Forseti." Horatio turned from Polonius to Grey, "This is, I trust, acceptable?"

"What is the reason for his removal?" Grey questioned with curiosity.

Banquo guffawed, "Have you seen the state of Sorrowmore? I swear, all veins from all outhouses and latrines flow to Sorrowmore."

Horatio added, "Grimm Corin was tasked with uncovering answers about a missing priest from Maregill Temple. What he found was deep corruption, abuse, and all manner of sadistic behavior implemented by Lord Polonius."

"This is an outrage! Again, the pup oversteps!" Polonius shouted. His full frame of bones shook as he took to his feet.

The Queen sat in dark distraction and, like the King, failed to react in any way to the exchange. The thayns, however, began to show physical signs of having chosen a side by sneering and fuming at the way in which Polonius spoke to their Lord Commander and Prince.

"Truly your anger must confuse you, Uncle. You act as if this investigation shames you alone. By mere association, I am made filthy. You are a stain of kinship," Horatio quipped. "The way my mind has been forced to lean lately, it is a wonder I don't remove your head from where you sit."

Polonius wore an expression of injury and shock. The contortion of features pushed the offended Horatio deeper into anger.

"This face. This look of amazement. From where does it come, I wonder? Did you think what you did would find excuse in your pedigree?"

"Again, I must ask my lord: of what do you accuse him?" Grand Judge Grey asked.

"The lightest of possible crimes involves Thayn Polonius forcing combat-games in Sorrowmore for the prize of rationed food. So, if in theory, you have ten families: nine would have a month of starvation while mourning the death of the family member slain in the hope of winning enough food for three people. It's barbaric. The temple at Maregill supplies the food to the region that includes Sorrowmore, and for nearly a year the stocks have been so far depleted that it's amazing the North Hold is home to any people at all." Horatio flipped a hand while explaining, "Then there are all of the details I have omitted: that Sorrowmore is home to far more than a mere ten families. That there is an entry-fee to participate. That those that do not win are forced to form ill-equipped hunting parties in an area rife with more predator than prey. That bodies are left to rot outside and away from their namesake tombs. That children who have lost a father at one month's games, and a mother on the next, may either choose to participate (if they can afford it and have hands big enough to wrap around a sword hilt) or yield to the service of the Thayn's Manor, where their hands are required to wrap around far less girth."

"Does the Lord Commander speak true, Thayn Polonius?" Grey asked with a crack to her angered voice.

"The boy embellishes..." Polonius offered, quickly receiving a shout of a response from Banquo.

"The boy is your Lord Commander and Prince, you old fool! You should be cleaning his boots with the kisses best reserved for dying mothers! By all rights under Hippocamp you should be executed for egregious crimes against the people of the North! He has shown you a great

266

mercy and here, you spit complaints?"

"Mercy, in this matter, is not necessarily the Prince's to give," the Grand Judge decided.

"Oh?" asked Horatio with a suddenly agreeable flutter to his voice. "How better ought we proceed? He is a Thayn. A Grimm. You would suggest Forseti?"

"I would. His alleged crimes were not committed against other Grimms. He harmed the common people of the Hold. It is for Forseti to judge him," Grey remarked. "I trust there is evidence that Dark Tower would surrender to the judges?"

"Certainly, Grand Judge." With an obedient bow of his head, Horatio grinned in satisfaction. He felt his relationship to Polonius barred his ability to do much about the crimes and welcomed the intervention. "Four of his subordinate officers have also been implicated..."

"Give the names and they, too, shall be collected. What of the other Grimms of Sorrowmore?" Grey asked.

Horatio replied, "Aside from the Thayn and his four brutes, it would appear that most were complicit only through coercion and abuse. While not instrumental in the acts against the people, Dark Tower has decided to relocate all The Grimms but the newly appointed Thayn Corin. We will replenish a presence with fresh faces. Many selected are already familiar with young Corin as peers of his through his initiation. It bodes a stable foundation. All so long as Corin actually lives? Has he been killed, Polonius?"

"No!" Polonius demanded while stringing along words of outrage and protest. He turned to the Queen and begged, "Niece! Reel in this conspiracy!"

The Queen, while silently watching her son, shook

her head to the words of her uncle. She would not help him.

Over the loud words from Polonius, Horatio leaned to a page and muttered, "Away to Sorrowmore with two others. Have each bring a sled of provisions from the palace kitchens to the town. Find Corin and deliver this news to him. Instruct him to stay at Sorrowmore and do what he may to protect and ease the people. Do this task well and with honor and you may well find a reward of a place of worth alongside the young Thayn." He nodded and gripped at the young Grimm's shoulder. With a smile, he added, "Beware of bear."

"At once, Lord Commander," she bowed her head.

Grimm Perdita Goneril, Thayn of Vimuk, a city near to the veil, stood. Nervously, she squeaked her gloved hands by wringing them and looked to her colleague, Grimm Richard Bianc, Thayn of Rime Hall for support before submitting her address to the room, "There is a thing, Lord Commander, that bears mentioning."

Thayn Richard, with arms folded, nodded her on. The ancient settlement of Rime Hall was further from the veil, located on the eastern border of the Hold.

"What is it?" Horatio asked while watching Polonius contend with an armed escort out of the room. Almost flippantly, he placed his hands on the map on the table and waited before finally adding, "There are matters of grave concern for the Hold awaiting their moment to discuss, Thayn. Say your piece so that we may proceed." As he raised his gaze he noticed her fright and softened his approach, "Perdita?" he looked from her to Richard and back again, "What is it?"

Perdita, who in the span of a week had lost a

grandchild and husband, could not make sense enough of her own thoughts to reply. She babbled a deal before the Thayn of Rime Hall stood while lowering her into her seat.

"Apologies, Sire," Richard offered as he assisted Perdita. "The respected Thayn of Vimuk has suffered great loss by the matter we wish to mention."

"No apology is necessary. Our condolences on what is clearly a painful thing, Perdita Goneril. What villain has caused such suffering?" Horatio, sincerely concerned over the display, turned to cross the room to Perdita. He took her hand into his own while looking to Richard to explain.

"There has been a plague of sorts, Lord. The people are calling it the ice-curse. The belief is that small and evil things fly unseen on the cold air and enter otherwise healthy bodies."

"Such is an apt way to describe most sickness," Horatio offered.

"But Lord Commander, it is most certainly not like most sicknesses, I'm afraid," Richard continued. "My own scouts have come back from tracking missions and have begun to tell stories of phantoms and smoke-spirits seeping from the veil. Full-fledged, hard-seasoned Grimms are filled with terror when the tales are told. Often, it has been those who have seen the things, and told such tales, that have been the first to fall ill. And once ill, the damage seems done. All is lost."

"How do you mean?" Horatio asked while the room flooded with interest and worry.

"The body seems to roam, Lord. After it expires, it roams."

With a frown of disbelief, Horatio tilted his head before looking down the table to the King and Queen. The Queen was clearly still furious and paid little heed to the words but the King intently listened and offered Horatio eye-contact to indicate his mental presence. "How does an expired thing roam, Sir?"

"In violence and destruction, Lord Commander. It is a thing the like of which I have never known. This is why some are hesitant to call it an illness in the place of a curse."

"How long has this been going on?" Banquo asked Richard.

"It has recently shown in Rime Hall. Half a week, at best."

"How many have been lost to this sickness?" Horatio questioned.

"Just over eighty, Sire," with quiet shame and fear, Richard replied.

"Eighty? In three or four days' time?" Shocked, Horatio drew back. "Have you asked the temples for guidance?"

"I have. Some of the priests admit to ignorance and dread while others claim that it is a purging of souls that have displeased Hippocamp."

Perdita looked away and began to weep more forcefully. In response to her obvious disturbance, Horatio remarked, "This is not the way of Hippocamp. This is no purge."

"Lord, there is another thing to this: Thayn Perdita sent word to Rime Hall requesting assistance once an outbreak had taken hold of the people of Vimuk. At the time I received the message, no sign of the plague, at least none that I knew of, had manifested among the people under my care. My scouting parties were still out and not a word of the veil phantoms had yet come to my attention. In that message she commented that Grimm-Prince Edgar had come to Vimuk. By the time the message reached me, the Prince was in Rime Hall."

Horatio nodded while listening.

"This was just a week hence, Lord Commander. Having listened to all that has been said, it seems that the timing of his appearance at Vimuk and Rime Hall may have a meaning to the situation regarding young Prince Hector."

Horatio muttered his thoughts aloud while quickly snapping a glance to his parents, who by then had both issued interest in the conversation. "A week hence? Edgar would have collected Hector by then. Why was he at Vimuk, and then Rime Hall? Was he alone?"

"He was, Lord Commander," Perdita sniffled and remarked. "He rarely came to Vimuk, but mentioned he was on his way to Rime Hall. And he was not himself, Lord."

"You believe him to have been afflicted."

"I do, forgive me, I do," she cried.

Richard interjected, "I agree: he was not himself, Lord Commander. I could have brought word no sooner than this moment. Every messenger I have sent to Dark Tower has gone missing. I nearly lost my own life on the journey here, just yester-night, to a pack of wolves that set upon my party and claimed two young Grimms."

Richard looked to Perdita, the stricken Grimm. He nodded to her and she supplied her tale, "When Grimm-Prince Edgar came around, a few were already sickly. I told myself that sickness was normal and could be contained. Then ten died. Then those who came into contact with those ten died. Then those first ten escaped the crypts and began to sneak through the ice bluffs and set on others as would owls on mice. I sent word to Rime Hall and the Dark Tower on the same day. Then I sent more word. Then more. Nothing ever came back. Then my Charles died and came back and tore to shreds my granddaughter who went to the door to greet him."

Taken aback by the ghastly account, Horatio turned back to Richard. "What happened to Prince Edgar, Richard?"

"He vanished the night after he arrived, Sir. But his eyes, I remember his eyes were so black."

"Clearly, you are mistaken, Thayn. None of my children have dark eyes." The Queen broke her silence, insulted by the suggestion that Edgar had any attachment to the ordeal.

"The eyes turn into The Veil, Majesty. I have seen it and would never suggest it had I not known it to be so!" Richard proclaimed. "Forgive me, Queen, but I came to know Prince Edgar very well. He was oft at Rime Hall. This last time we met, I scarcely recognized him. His demeanor was not his own. He would flow past me and others who normally he would greet and join in a meal."

"He would have never abandoned his brother. He was better than my eldest in that way," the venom forced the words to sting and bite at Horatio, who, while dividing his energy between the disappointed barbs of his mother and the comfort offered to an old friend and subordinate, began to unravel a touch.

"He was not himself, Mother. This was plainly said,"

Horatio offered.

"Do not call me mother, Lord Commander." The hostility of her demand was as stubborn and suffocating as the sea.

Horatio shook with anger and contemplated the many paths that could have sprung from that moment. A step away from Perdita shifted his gaze first to Thayn Richard before Forseti's Grand Judge Rosalind Grey, who abruptly offered him a shake of her head in an effort to dissuade his anger. He then took in the many faces of the other Thayns who appeared to hold their breath in their chest for terror over Horatio's response. He staggered slightly, pulled his sword and handed the hilt to Banquo before turning to face the Queen and King.

Quietly, evenly, Horatio replied, "I have, with diligence and care, cradled this nation of grand antiquity in my arms like the simpering infant it is forced to remain. This Hold, which you yourselves have abandoned into my care. Abandoned? No, too light an image for the reality of your thrusting onto me the full scope of expectation normally afforded onto a fully staffed kingdom and professional government. I have loved none so well as I have loved the snows and ice of the North. My affections have been aimed always to my duty to serve the North Hold."

"Hold your tongue, Grimm," the Queen growled.

"I am no mere Grimm, Queen! I am the Lord Commander and I am the beast that you have designed! I am what shields your people from the monsters and you from your people! And I will not be doubted in my ability to protect those who do not foolishly sneak off in the night, as Edgar did."

The Queen shook her head, "Stop."

"The blame for Edgar's choice is none but Edgar's. Far too often had he skulked away from accountability. Your disappointment is better aimed at the missing son who, had he been any other Grimm, would have been marked for disobedience at best and desertion at worst. He was not where he should have been and Edgar's entitlement placed Hector in the possession of thieves from the revolution. The Coadunation. A handful of whom I ended up murdering in the name of the Crown for little reason more than Edgar's choice to slip away on his own. He was prone to compulsion, Edgar. He was very poor at thinking things through before acting. He wanted to go – so he went. And what Edgar wants, Edgar gets. He was not accustomed to waiting or asking permission. A blame, my once-upon-a-time mother, that truly should be set to you."

"I shall have you arrested for this insult!" Queen Isobella shouted while leaping to her feet.

"You'll do no such thing, and you'll sit you down while remembering you are surrounded by men and women who would die for me."

Grand Judge Rosalind Grey sunk a bit in her chair, shrinking away from the astonishing exchange.

Horatio continued, "It is by a very delicate and thin thread that you remain seated unchallenged on the throne. Both of you. I need but think of ruling and rule would be mind. So, change your approach from one that you would test on a usurper."

"I will have you put to the pole," the Queen hissed as she sunk back into her seat.

"You'll do no such thing, Your Grace. For I have made

274

clear that I do not seek to unseat you. You would respond with threats?"

The King folded his arms and smiled. The Queen, furious, trembled.

Horatio continued, holding up a finger with each sibling indicated, "One charming, yet vicious son: missing, presumed dead for how poor his survival skills were. One son too young to reach whatever potential his wretched parents would put to him: almost dead, sleeping. One sick and swooning daughter buried under conspiracies: in custody. And two forgotten creatures, in the form of children, huddled together, in the dark, shielded from all the world, with one hand gripped by the other."

"What do you mean in custody?" the Queen asked feverishly.

"Oh, I had not yet mentioned, had I?" Horatio laughed. "The very strangest thing, you see. Princess Eleonora is either a target of The Coadunation or an active member."

"Your sister is not part of the rebellion! How dare you punish her with no reason!" exclaimed the Queen.

"There is a difference between custody and punishment, Highness."

"For what reason would you do such a thing?"

"Corin of Sorrowmore's report detailed your Uncle Polonius' indiscretions only after his activities crossed into questions about Douglas, the missing priest of Maregill. Douglas was precious to our sweet Princess Eleonora, and likely sick with this plague that Thayns Perdita and Richard have mentioned is currently sacking their cities. He had begun acting erratically and saying

275

things he probably should not have been saying: gold from the treasury at Alberich being filtered through Polonius into The Coadunation. He was killed, or died, but probably killed and it was explained that from where his body lay, the tattered bloodied rags of his robes remained while his corpse danced off into the icy night. The little white ermine was found dining on those soiled robes when Princess Eleonora went around to see if his body had yet been discovered."

"But you said that this Douglas was precious to her?" Grey interjected.

"And likely dying," Horatio nodded. "And exposing little secrets with every breath he exhaled. Secrets involving some noble backing of the rebellion." He glared at the Queen and shook his head, disgusted by her disbelief.

The Thayn of Alberich, Henry Gargrave, had grown pale and uttered a shaking, "I had no...I had no idea."

Horatio lifted his chin, "Neither the investigation nor my rebel informant indicated that you had any idea. You'll need to look into your accountants, though."

"Yes, Lord Commander." The relief from Gargrave was obvious.

Horatio turned to address the rest of the room, turning his back on the Queen and King, "And that was some of the cause for this assembly. The rest of the cause is as follows: Our Bearing Shrines are depleted. We have poor relations with the West, from where the soil comes, and even less to offer in trade. We will march on the West and lay demands."

"You would start a war?" the Queen asked.

"I would not have the North starve," Horatio said. "I

will not." He indicated to the map on the table and remarked, "There is a small pass, here to the west of a great bog. We will enter there and hold ground until an audience is granted between their Prince Regent and I. I will secure means by which to feed our people."

"What will you offer?" asked Grey.

Horatio sighed with a shake of his head. There was a sad apprehension to his voice, "I will offer to cease hostilities against his people in return for what we want. Meanwhile, I have already sent an envoy to the East. They have suffered loss. The Princess Lavinia died, and we're to understand that the King and Queen are stepping away from the throne to make way for the King's younger sister. She, I have been told, is barely a woman – but, the possessor of some ancient magic or wisdom. She will likely be open to negotiations for relations. If she brokers a treaty with the North at the onset of her reign, she will garner much sway as a peace-seeker among the people of the Wing-God."

"What is on offer to the East?" asked Thayn Richard.

"We were once great builders of ships. We will reopen the shipyards of the North and offer the means to travel the sea by wind to the Easterners in exchange for provisions. Wood. Food. More food."

"There hasn't been a campaign in eons," remarked Grey.

"I wish there was no need," quietly Horatio remarked before concluding, "I'll need every able bodied Grimm in fighting form as I sweep to the West. The army will be compiled and collected as I go. Thayns and Thayn councils remain intact and at the appointed town or village. We can't risk the rebels taking advantage of absence."

"Does the Crown support this campaign?" Grey asked the Queen.

"It would matter not." The Queen glowered.

# Chapter XIX
## *Of Pegasus: To Ascend, to Descend*

Dawn crept. Once the first morning-wisps of sunlight broke over the crest of the elevation, the procession would escort the body of Princess Lavinia to the Cliff-Tower at The Great Stretch of GoldCloud for her sky burial. It was not yet the time. And in those last dark early moments, a million mourners held each other in their traditional gray mourning garb. The winds joined in the soft songs of sorrow and carried laments up over the ground and out to sea. Queen Etvera trembled as she looked down to her dead daughter while King Voreto could barely stand from emotion. Lavinia's long fawn-colored hair had been curled under a crown in large waves which fluttered with the overhang of the winding sheet. The curls, dark and rich, lifted and danced on the breeze before resting again on the viewing plank, the sight of which buckled the King in grief.

Princess Lavinia was nearly as beautiful in death as she was life. Her body had been carefully prepared for the memorial: a task made difficult by the corpse's exposure to the waters of Falcon's Perch. The temple extended all of its focus and energy in the event and here, at the customary viewing of the deceased, many priests silently congratulated themselves on a job well done. She had been drained and dehydrated to a degree before being cleansed and anointed with black sunflower and juniper oil while her likeness had been molded and cast for the statue that would reside in the royal shrine crypts in the catacombs of GoldCloud Castle. The design of the

Princess' memorial statue was to be seated with a Pegasus foal in her lap and arms. She had been secretly pregnant, and all promises that her father and mother made to each other to accept the death with solemn grace began to crumble. There was an added anguish, darkness, and sorrow.

The ornate funerary cart, guided by six Magpies in ceremonial gold, began to approach the viewing plank while following behind a single high priest. A veiled woman from the temple trailed slightly. She carried one orange silk bag and one gray. When they would arrive at the Cliff-Tower for the greeting of the rising sun, she would be tasked with the honor of collecting into the orange bag the Princess' clothing, crown, and shroud while into the other, her shorn hair. Even she, seasoned to the duty through generations of loss, wore the paleness of personal heartache.

The East cherished their Princess, Lavinia. She was regal, yet loving to the people. Interested in the lives of the subjects and receptive to interaction, there was little wonder that a great populist folk hero like Valko could love her, even if clandestinely.

The Magpies lifted the viewing plank before placing it onto the cart with great care. From the gathered mass of citizenry, wailing began. Many approached to touch the body and muttered prayers to Pegasus. The finality of the scene proved too hard for some as they buried their tear-stained faces into the shoulders and chests of near-by loved ones and neighbors. The King looked away. The Queen could not.

"Horrible." The Captain's voice was private and quiet as the creaking of the gold armor suggested an uneasiness. The wing-engraved spaulders on his shoulders groaned at his efforts to shift his arms back before tensing again into a position of attention. He stood on the royal platform next to the adviser, Marvis, a good distance from the grieving King and Queen who had begun to prepare for the long walk of the funeral procession.

"Your discomposure is suspicious, Captain Birchbark," Marvis said while barely moving his lips.

"More suspicious than your composure, Lord Marvis?" Valé Birchbark, commander of The Magpie, asked while unable to look upon the beginning of the long march for more than a few seconds at a time. He was haunted by the unanswered questions in the death of the Princess only slightly more than he was haunted by the misery of his King.

"She is going to The Veil. Blessed be Pegasus and the creator," muttered Marvis to an unseen eye-roll and frown from Valé.

"The Veil seems to be a popular place these days. So many are rushing into the dark embrace."

Marvis raised a cautionary eyebrow to Valé.

He shook his head, "Many deaths."

"On that matter, I have continued to withhold the information from the King and Queen. I anticipated bringing it to the court's attention once the Princess had been laid to rest at her sky funeral, but having actually seen her caused far more distress for them than I had anticipated. They seemed almost accepting at the news of her demise before seeing her. Then, seeing her triggered the King to wish to step down. It will be addressed as an urgent order of business with the new Queen. We can not have rumors run wild of a magic-curse killing and reanimating people."

"Preoccupation is not acceptance, Lord Marvis. I don't think it's a thing they could ever accept. I don't think any parent ever could. Noble or common." He grumbled while continuing, "Besides, it isn't a rumor. I don't know what it is, but it isn't a rumor."

Taken aback, Marvis questioned, "You speak with such authority! Have you fathered a lost child, Captain?"

"I have fathered no children," Valé huffed though a sigh. He was annoyed that his remarks about the mysterious sickness passed unnoticed.

Marvis folded his arms, silently urging Valé as if there had been more to the statement.

"I have known many parents who have suffered loss. Many who serve the Crown, Sir. The sorrow is not particular in the death of either pauper or princess."

"This sorrow, as you say, is particular in that it was murder."

"Or suicide," Valé muttered the general consensus held by The Magpie.

"You would silence such notions, Captain. That is not a reality that suits The Hold."

"As you like it," Valé responded. He watched the funeral march. It had traveled along the path away a good distance.

Ushers worked to clear the royal platform of any hint of death while readying it for a coronation. Valé held his distaste for the itinerary silent. By rights, his place should have been by the side of the King and Queen to honor the Princess at her sky funeral. But the King and Queen made the choice that by the moment the first bird came to the corpse of their daughter, they would renounce rule. The Captain of the Magpie should be present at the crowning of his new Queen, and so stayed behind rather than seeing his Princess off.

"You seem like a hunting dog left in a barn, Captain," Marvis observed while drawing his dark gray robe up around the back of his chilled neck.

"I feel like a hunting dog left in a barn," he nodded with a longing to his gaze.

"Well, you look spectacular," Marvis indicated to the ceremonial armor that had hardly any wear.

Valé offered the shallowest of smiles and sighs before remarking, "Your compliments usually come at a cost. What now?"

"Queen Nova will be crowned within the hour."

"That she will be. May she reign with the wind. What of it?"

"She will be needing a husband."

"I think the word 'need' is an overplay. Don't you?"

"Not at all! She is very young and in-so-far as I am aware, has never truly been groomed to rule."

Valé's shoulders slumped in an uncharacteristic fashion. "I was made to understand that Voreto is staying on as High Chancellor to Her Grace?"

Marvis interlaced his fingers and inched his hands into the oversized sleeves of the robe. "This is true. He and Etvera will remain here at GoldCloud in residence. He has accepted the position of High Chancellor."

"So then you have the most qualified man at her right hand. None other know policy so well," Valé muttered in a flustered flurry of words. "And would it were not so: she has an excellent relationship with Etvera, does she not? I fail to see the need to use the word 'need'. Her young Majesty is in need of very little."

With a shake of his head Marvis frowned and made obvious his disappointment. "So little ambition from such a well-decorated man is a paradox that I will never comprehend."

"I'm sure that there is very little that you do not comprehend. You can detect the slightest change in inflection or tone of words and gather the root motive of whatever is before you and you need me to tell you how absolutely I do not want the crown? You must know I don't want to sit on the throne. Or, even less than that, how little I want a bride. Or even less than that: a child bride."

"Why such an aversion to the throne, Captain?"

"I dislike sitting."

"You dislike sitting?" Marvis mocked with a scowl. He was unsatisfied with the remark and made every effort to have it known, "I wish you knew how many times I moved the pieces on the game board to keep you from direct harm."

Valé did not care for the comment and bristled with a perked eyebrow, "You?" He had no way of knowing the truth of Marvis' remark and all the manipulations that went into keeping him from many errant quests based solely on the Captain's value while alive-and-well. He was the most skilled, celebrated, and honored warrior of the Hold and did not take the suggestion that his success hinged on Marvis lightly. "You want to feel brave and big over all that you've done for me?"

Intimidated, Marvis quickly regretted having said anything at all. Before he could let even a whisper about how close Valé was to the journey into the North with Otver escape, he silenced himself and nodded with overturned hands, "You are correct. Of course, you are correct."

"I have a Hold that weeps and mourns. Mourners do foolish things. Bakers stay closed for weeks, people begin to starve. Hunters stay in bed, predators grow brave and draw close. Those with no heart prey on those with broken ones. There will be an increase in crime before all is said and done. And then there are The Coadunation and all those that would give shelter and aid to them. And then this sickness that is no mere rumor, Sir. I have seen horrors in the villages near-to the veil. There is something stirring that needs to be addressed."

Marvis nodded, "It shall be. You have my word. I will deliver this concern to Queen Nova myself."

"Do," Valé remarked before suddenly noticing that the small cell of officials that were standing in a cluster to receive Nova scattered. A rider approached from the direction of The Great Stretch.

"What is this?" with concern, Marvis whispered. "They ride into the crowd!"

The collection of mourners divided and provided a path with terror and confusion. The rider, although moving quickly, took care to not trample the people.

Valé shook his head once and watched closely while drawing his bow. He nocked, marked and nearly drew on the swiftly approaching rider when suddenly he realized that it was one of The Magpie assigned to the procession. He lowered his bow and stepped to the edge of the platform, before glancing over his shoulder to his squire with a motion to fetch his horse. Placing the arrow back into the quiver, Valé shouted, "Report!"

"Oh, Captain! Pegasus help us! The King and Queen: Four Magpies have tried to detain them. The King gives fight, Captain. He is in a frenzy! One Magpie has fallen. The temple priest and woman are dead!"

"The King has killed a Magpie and two from the temple?" Marvis asked in fearful amazement.

"No, Lord," cried the rider. "Princess Lavinia has."

Valé shook his head once in denial before shaking himself from shock, "Lord Marvis, see to Nova."

Marvis was unresponsive and trembled.

"Marvis!" Valé grabbed at the adviser's robe until he gained eye-contact, "See to Nova. Lock the castle. I'll post Magpie at the lift." He nodded a few times as if checking for any acknowledgment. "Go. Now." He shoved at him to move him along.

Marvis nodded, muttered a few convoluted words and moved toward the lift.

"How close to the Princess did you get?" Valé asked the rider.

She was hesitant to respond and stammered, "Not very."

"Not very?" Valé was stern and demanding, "How very is not very?" He looked for his horse.

"Not at all, but, Captain..."

Valé looked to the Magpie while adjusting the stunning, yet uncomfortable and stiff ceremonial armor.

"The King, Captain. He tried to embrace her. All was as it should have been. She was laid on the slab at the top of the Cliff-Tower. Her hair was taken. Her clothes were taken. We stood back to await the birds. The birds, they came. The vultures first while the crows lingered at the walls of the tower. They pecked at her shoulders, her chest, then her abdomen. From her womb...from her womb...they took...they ripped out a small...the fetus...no bigger than a coin purse. Such a little thing. She woke. The Princess woke and ripped the birds to shreds quick enough to catch them before they flew away from fear. The King ran to her. Reached for her. She pushed. She did not look like Lavinia. She changed."

"With an opened womb she woke?" Valé asked softly as if the words were too offensive to offer with any real volume. "And Voreto went to her?"

The Magpie nodded with horrified sadness.

"And the fetus?"

"She has it. She wouldn't let it go."

"Wouldn't? She still stirs?" As quickly as his horse, Leafcut, arrived, Captain Valé Birchbark was atop her.

The Magpie nodded and wept.

"Go to the lift. You are to guard the lift. I'll have those at the city gates seal all of you in. You are certain you did not get close to the Princess?"

The Magpie nodded and sniffled. "But the King, Sir."

"Guard the lift," he demanded before Leafcut flew into a gallop toward the Cliff-Tower.

***

The light blue of Princess Lavinia's skin flooded with crimson blood. Her arms and legs seemed so much longer than they were. Unnaturally lengthened somehow with great bulging elbows and knees like the ancient hinges in the deepest part of a fortress. Her eyes were black and as big as fists. Her nose had been removed, presumably by a vulture. Her mouth hung slack and played the role of a gateway to the most scornful and harmed sounds. And she cried and screamed while cupping the unborn Prince or Princess in one hand against her chest. She was tortured anguish and roared at those that had been her parents while stepping back, closer to the cliffs.

Her mother, Etvera, had gone limp in the arms of a Magpie, while three others gripped at Voreto to keep him away from whatever Lavinia had become.

The creature screeched and snarled when suddenly Voreto produced his sword and slashed against the Magpie closest to his right. The other two backed away. Voreto stabbed into the wounded one's chest, killing him.

The Magpie who held Etvera began to panic and considered quitting the scene altogether. She trembled and cried, having heard the rumors of the sickness but having never actually seen it, she quaked and quailed. It was too much. The scene was impossible to understand. The Princess, bleeding and half-mangled from her sky funeral, screamed as a creature that vaguely even resembled a human. She began to hyperventilate and witnessed another Magpie die to the blade of the King. They refused to draw against him. There was one left.

She realized that neither she nor the Queen had come anywhere near the rest of the group or the creature. When the vulture began to rip at the Princess' womb, the Queen turned away and strolled to the spot where they were then before fainting into her arms. Seconds later, the Princess appeared to wake and the King rushed forward. They had been far from the scrum. She found courage in the hope and with a steadying breath, convinced herself to stand. She tried to carry the Queen, but could not, and so dragged her as well as she could toward a horse that was clever enough to meet them partway. The horse had been one of two that towed the funerary cart but was cut away from the harness when the rider took his companion for a swift return to GoldCloud.

Captain Valé Birchbark arrived and dismounted as quickly as he could to position himself under the Queen's arm to assist. He did not question the Magpie about proximity but received the information without delay while hoisting the Queen across the back of the horse.

"We wasn't nowhere close, Capt'n," The Magpie admitted while Valé looked deeply into her eyes for any hint of deceit.

He quickly nodded while drawing his bow, "Ride back to the castle. The gates are barred, tell them I sent you and the words to speak are 'flutter finch'. They are ordered to not open without these words.

The Magpie bowed her head and lifted herself onto the horse, careful to hold the body of the Queen. She gave one more look to the creature before retreating to the path to the capital.

Valé measured the situation carefully while pulling an arrow. He watched as the beast continued to back itself toward the high cliffs and found the behavior curious. It was not lashing and attacking as he heard they often did. The sight of the thing was horrific. It seemed to degrade quickly from any human appearance: quicker than he would have expected from reports. He watched the thing it had cupped against its chest and fought to keep his bravery. "Voreto? King? Can you hear me?" he called over to the King.

King Voreto did not respond and lunged, missing his blow, toward the other Magpie that was trying to restrain him.

The creature screeched and began to kneel before cocking its knee and lurching upright again. It was very close to stepping off the cliff.

Unwilling to let the thing fall into the sea and risk an improbable survival, Valé adjusted his aim for the distant face of the monster and let the arrow fly.

It took the hit, seemed to die, and fell over the ledge, still cradling the bloody mass.

Voreto fell into a deeper madness and with furious frenzy, slashed into the leg of the near-by Magpie before turning to run toward Valé. His eyes were half black: the King was surely gone.

Captain Birchbark lifted an arrow to the enraged approach and leveled him with a single shot to the forehead. Wordlessly, he drew again and finished the Magpie with the severed leg. In the silence of the morning sun, he stood still and stared as the awareness filled his mind: she must have already been infected. How many of the millions that gathered to honor her had drawn too close? Quickly, he started to return to the capital.

*****

*Queen Fire,*

*We hope this finds you well. The forts at our warmer border have reported conditions dryer than expected. The weather of yours must be harsher than usual. The penning of this missive is poorly-timed, and for that we must apologize.*

*Our border arrangement must expire. It is well-known that the South Hold (much like those in the North) have difficulty in procuring proper sustenance, but from our position, little more can be done. Small pockets of Southern hunters here-and-there may pass unnoticed, but the volume of armed Southerners entering the East is beginning to cause panic. The agreement to simply ignore the activities has proven sound – as now we may turn our attention to the state of things and act with clean hands.*

*We apologize. Long had we hoped to foster a trade relationship between the Flames and the Clouds, but no more do we find this possible. We are deeply wounded and disappointed in the lack of the dearly promised weapons of Serpentronum. We are even more severely saddened by the lack of a simple ore sample, (which had been requested to secure your request for initial provisions – provisions you received whilst we waited with empty hands) or charted schematics and plans. We have exhausted the ability to wait with hope and must finally address the woes of our people who are uneasy with fear of raiders.*

*It occurs to us to mention that a hungry people are often a willing people. Perhaps the motivation of hunger is just the spark needed to make more efficient your miners and metallurgists? If the time should come that you feel able to uphold your end of the bargain, we may still be willing to entertain the possibility of opening actual trade. However, it would take a great gesture to splint this break, you understand. Far more than previously discussed.*

*There is also a seed that seems to have found fertile ground. Something appears to stir between Unicorn and Hippocamp. Grimms have been apprehended at our border to the North while in the possession of Western-crafted armor and potions. This is not only a warning to you and your Hold, but also an added explanation as to why security must come into focus.*

*The Queen is with child. We can not look away anymore. These correspondences must cease 'til you send word of a preparedness to fulfill your oath. We do wish you health, friend. I am confident you will find a way to serve your people best.*

*-King Wind*

*Well-worn letter found in South Hold, hidden in book, 'Histories of Architecture'*
*Age unknown*

# Chapter XX
## *Of Unicorn: The Delver*

Morigan hunched over a mountain of tomes and parchments strewn across an irregularly shaped trunk-base table. She had been issued the highest chamber in the highest tree tower on the north side of The Sepal. Whereas her new country-folk of the West would dub the quarters nearly uninhabitable, the daughter of the North found the shrill bite of the night air a comfort and didn't at all mind the lack of sun-exposure during the day. The fit was good and the room did much to ease her into her new life and weighty responsibilities.

She hadn't yet come to the point in her comfort to dress the part of the Westerner. The fabrics of the West, especially at court, were sheer and light. Thoughts of various flower petals would cross her mind while watching people come and go at a pace so leisurely that it nearly bordered on lazy. Some, men and women both, would have vine or tree embellishments just over select areas of the garment while the rest of the fabric would serve as little more than a window to the luscious golden skin. They were a naturally beautiful people, to her eye. She often wondered if how attractive they seemed had anything to do with how opposite they were from those she knew in the North.

She found that the Westerners would spend obscene amounts of time and energy on gossiping and social games of manipulation. Rumors circulated that her retirement and place at court actually originated from the strangest of fabricated events. Impregnation by General

Lysander Barro was a popular view while others gathered that at-least one (and at most, three) of the Purpureus Council had taken her for a lover. Some people felt that her time with The Wanderers was so short that she was still a loyal subject of Hippocamp, but not so loyal as to turn away the advances of The Prince Regent for information and intelligence. The presence of the young Satyr Caradis provoked even more bizarre twists of illusion and fictions. The tales and variations were limitless. Morigan stopped trying to make any sense of it and found fulfilling distractions in the combing of old books and fables. She had been sworn to a duty, after-all.

Most nights found young Caradis curled in a tight ball, in a chair under layers of fabric in a sleepy bid to get warm. In her short time with Morigan, she had already learned to read twice as many words as she knew before they met, gained a deeper understanding of the mythology of the gods of The Four Holds, and even how to discern a general region and age of a text based on the ink used. The education reminded her of her time at home at Ljudot with her retired Wanderer parents. It was satisfying beyond any Satyr drills or training; Caradis was glad to have been given a place by Morigan's side. This night she did not slumber in the large chair. Caradis had been sent to quickly fetch any Purpureus Councilor she could find.

The small bells and chimes at the hem of the silken drapery tapped and sang. The sound of breeze ripping at the flame of oil lamps triggered a twitching in Morigan's forehead. She looked over her shoulder to the arched door-way, waiting. Her fingertips began to drum a ripple of a rhythm. A feeling governed her: the feeling of having captured something that could escape at any moment. She was a cat outmatched by the feisty fat rat in her mouth. Every second that eclipsed the one before it gave her worry that what she had would slip away. She could not allow it to escape, and so turned back to the mound of reference works and arched her hands over illustrations and words, muttering to herself: recapturing and securing.

"Lady Morigan! Lady Morigan! I found Lord Reileus, Ma'am!" Caradis exclaimed with Reileus loosely in tow.

With a nod of faint appreciation, Morigan smiled to Caradis and requested, "Fetch water." Any other Purpureus Councilor would have been more welcome as something about Reileus always caused Morigan a feeling of unease. She was hopeful that Caradis would have brought back old man Honeios, but there stood a seemingly surly Reileus.

"Wine," grumbled Reileus while slamming down into a chair. He was dour and wrapped in a robe over night-clothes. Clearly, he had been woken. He squinted one eye under the glare of the amount of oil lamps apparently necessary to study words through the long dark night. "Wine will do, yes?"

"Wine is fine, Sir." She bowed her head to Reileus before nodding Caradis away to fetch some wine that wasn't in her own personal stock. "I think I may have discovered something about the sickness!"

"I do not think I've stopped drinking," Reileus remarked. "There was party. I went. I only just returned. I only just closed my eyes."

Morigan shook her head a single time and with a blank expression, exhibited that she had no idea how to address what had just been said.

"Ease into it, please. While Nyseis would leap across this table and pull fireflies from his ass over the glee of hearing this information, I need just a hair of time to gather my wits." He sighed, "I shouldn't have said that. You didn't hear that said."

"No, certainly not."

"He's just very eager, you see. Little else concerns him but this sickness. For him, it's personal. For me, I have a host of other worries. The sickness is just one of many. I am very tired. I hear you have caught the interest of a score of suitors?"

Morigan offered a quiet grunt of annoyance while glancing at a haphazard pile of gifts that had recently begun to accumulate near the door. She didn't want to talk about parties, gifts, or suitors. The notion of romance, and Reileus' interested mention of it, vexed her deeply. "I think I may have discovered something about the sickness," she flatly repeated.

"Does your position expire when you complete the task, I wonder? Surely it doesn't? I don't know, but I would hardly go rushing into the conclusion without savoring the journey, were I you."

Flabbergasted, Morigan clenched a fist and listened before remarking, "You are not me."

"No, I am not. That is certain." Reileus' blonde hair stood in the strange way that only having been oiled and set against a pillow would allow. He tilted his head and began to sink slightly in the chair. "This is proving even more exhausting than trying to sleep, my Lady. I will tell you what happened and we can both part ways by the quickest of paths. The royal hunting party was poisoned."

Morigan recoiled, "Poisoned? Is that what you think?"

"It is what I just said."

"If you think they were poisoned, why am I even here?"

"The Prince Regent wants certainty. He is hesitant to believe the most obvious evidence."

She shook her head, "It wasn't poison, Councilor. I read all the statements and looked over all the evidence, and truly, I think I know the root of the malady and that root is not poison."

"While we're alone, you may call me Reileus, and it was poison. I think I know poisons."

"Listen, there is an antecedent! I have found, through reading..."

"My, you've become quite the extraordinary little fly, haven't you? Buzzing about from page to page. I would happily call you a butterfly for your inherent beauty, although you seem to have refused to find your wings. Why are you still in Wanderer gray?" he nodded toward her with a flip of a finger.

"What?" With confusion she looked down to her clothing. While frowning she grumbled, "Please stop interrupting me."

"Stop being interruptible." He reached for the wine offered by the silent Caradis before she withdrew in reaction to his dismissive glare.

Morigan drew in a deep breath and pointed to a scroll, "Three-thousand years ago all Four Holds documented a great calamity. It was a time of war. The East is the only one that recorded that the battles took place after the event. The other three Holds claimed that the calamity resulted in warring for one reason or another. The North, West, and South contended in their histories that the hostility of man drove the gods to cause the calamity."

"Leave it to Pegasus to be contrary," remarked Reileus flippantly.

"The time-frame is so compressed that the order almost doesn't matter. As the warring and the calamity go hand-in-hand in every account, which came first is almost an afterthought. Especially as it takes time for any one thing to spread. If an event is documented by all Four Holds, particularly in a time of great segregation, more often than not, that event is noteworthy."

"Three thousand years ago was before the era of the common-tongue. You can read ancient dialects?"

Morigan nodded with vaguely embarrassed, yet enthusiastic pride. "Some are harder than others. The North has much of the ancient words rooted in every-day life: places and such. The East's words are often elegant and lofty, while the South I can read, but would struggle to speak. Very throaty."

"And the West?"

She struggled, "Very pretty words."

"Pretty?"

"Sensual. Every word looks like a lie or a promise on the page."

"Well, that hasn't changed much," he remarked before yawning. "So you feel that this event, this calamity as you call it, is related to that which I call poisoning and you call a sickness?"

"I do, yes. There are accounts of symptoms and..."

"You've seen one of them, haven't you? When Barro

found you? The hound boy?"

She frowned and nodded, unhappy with the memory.

"If I happen to be wrong and it isn't a poison, and you happen to be right and it is a sickness, how do you know you haven't caught it?"

She had no words to offer in defense.

"So, in a way, if you're right, you may already be lost to it. How tragic. And, now me too, since I'm here with you. How doubly tragic." Reileus took a sip of wine to conceal a smirk, "Luckily you're probably wrong."

Her gazing gray eyes dropped to the parchments, scrolls, and books with dread and worry.

Reileus grew slightly ashamed of the harsh treatment offered to the scholar. He sighed and mumbled, "I'm not used to speaking to such a soft heart."

"I'm not a soft heart."

"I don't know what to call you! I can't speak without risking your ire or tears. I was apologizing."

Morigan nodded with trepidation.

"I'll set aside what I already know to be the answer, and hear your explanation. Clearly you've worked hard. You look like you haven't taken sleep in a week."

"You're doing it again."

"I don't mean to." He pursed his lips. "Just go on."

Morigan took a book and opened it to a diagram of events. While placing her finger at the start of the time-line, she said, "The first recorded case of this sickness, from all four accounts, is an Inicune, 'a divine blood' from the West. It doesn't say if this royal is a King, Queen, or child. Although with the lack of an actual name, I suspect it was a child, and not the first born."

"Inicune?" Reileus was careful with the

pronunciation of his ancestral tongue. It was a thing he had seen on tapestries, but never before heard spoken. He treated the sound as if it were a fragile and precious thing.

"Inicune," Morigan nodded once, suddenly entranced by the sight of a Westerner's mouth dancing with native sounds. "Ellai," she nodded again.

"Ellai," he repeated as if in the warmth of a reunion.

"It means yes in that you are correct. Yes for consent is a different word. So is yes for the acceptance of something offered." She was pleased in his interest, "The word for no is trou. With a roll on the r."

"I'm shocked to learn my ancestors even had a word for no," he laughed softly, clearly warming to her company.

Cognizant of his change in disposition, she smiled uncomfortably and quickly snapped back to the topic, "The point is that I imagine the calamity, or what we're calling the sickness, was likely floating around the common people for some time before finally reaching the capital of any of the Holds. History doesn't often extend to cover the death of the poor, unless the death of the poor profits or benefits the..." she trailed off.

Reileus raised an eyebrow with a knowing grin. He was part of that broken system, and in many ways, relished it. "Go on."

"The sickness takes root in the body of a living being. Contrary to what I thought when I started all of this, it can not infect and control an already dead thing. The host has to have the spark of life when infected. It may breed or hibernate in a dead thing, but I don't think that dead thing will wake without having had the sickness before death."

"What causes it?" he seemed genuinely interested while clenching his robe from the chill on the air.

"That, in itself, is what they called the great calamity. It was believed that the sickness was caused by The Veil."

"The Veil?"

"Well, came from The Veil, not really caused by The Veil."

"The Veil? Where we all go when we die? The land of the gods? The great house of our mothers and fathers?"

"Yes, that Veil."

Reileus rubbed his face in disappointment, "And I suppose it was inflicted upon us all to punish us for some stupidity?"

"You don't believe in the gods, Lord Reileus?"

"Would it surprise you?"

"A bit, yes."

He shook his head and groaned, "Even if I did believe in the gods, why would they wish to punish us? What would be the point?"

"To learn from our mistakes?" Morigan was authentically amazed. A doubt in the actual existence of the gods was fairly common among The Wanderers, but almost never seen anywhere else in the world. "So you don't believe in Unicorn?"

"Unicorn is a great symbol of my people, Morigan. I believe in that symbol."

"But The Veil?"

"What about it?"

"It is a physical thing, surely you believe in The Veil."

"As the afterlife?"

She nodded.

"Certainly. I have seen spirits come and go to The Veil. That has no bearing on whether or not gods turn up to guide them on their way." He shifted in the chair. He didn't want to discuss his personal views any further, "Yet, these writings state that all Four Holds felt the sickness came from The Veil?"

"They called it The Yawning Veil, or The Yawning of the Veil depending on which you read. It was written that Malotetch..."

"Malotetch?!"

Morigan nodded sheepishly.

"The great dragon at the center of The Veil?"

Again, she nodded.

He placed both hands to his face. "Why can you not just accept that it was poison?" There was an absence of a response during which Reileus peeked over his fingertips, "Alright." He reached for the wine, "So, Malotetch, destroyer of the world: go on."

"Malotetch sighed and on his breath was the sickness."

"What a bastard."

Morigan sighed and took a seat, "It means something."

"What it means is that three-thousand years ago a nasty sickness swept over the land and started to matter when it took the life of an Inicune and in an effort to explain it: dragon and gods. And truly, a nasty sickness in a time rife with war? I am shocked."

"I think it's a fungus."

Reileus' sarcasm cooled at the sound of her comment.

With confidence, Morigan looked to Reileus and continued, "I think it comes from The Veil. I think it's a fungus that spreads by spore. The person inhales it, or has it on their skin and hair and has no idea. I think it changes something in their minds."

"So, it is a poison?"

"In a way." She continued, "I think you can set aside the four gods and Malotetch but you can't set aside the distinct possibility that it comes from the land within The Veil. All the writing seems to suggest that the densest areas of infection were in the lands nearest to The Veil. I imagine that it's the same now. A wind, or Malotetch's sigh, carries the spores. You can't see them, you can't protect or defend from them. They enter the host and grow. Host dies, the fungus takes over. All the while anyone close enough to the host to have contact with the spores may be infected. It's terrifying. It's truly terrifying."

"How is it destroyed?"

"My first thought was burning..."

"No Westerner would permit the burning of a body. That's a Southern tradition. Barbarians."

Morigan sighed, "...but burning would be more likely to disperse the spores rather than destroy them. Like paper lanterns, the heat from the flame would send them flying."

He rubbed his chin in thought.

"I truly do not know how to stop this. But I feel like I have come close to understanding the process."

Reileus nodded, "What about the physical changes? I have heard the sick turn into monsters?"

"From the histories: the more sick, or the longer a body had the sickness in it, the more deformed after the death. Eyes always turn ink-like. Lips and eyelids recede.

Ears and nose usually fall away. I think the fungus destroys the muscle tissue, eating it in a way, causing the body to seem to be little more than bone and skin. But they have such power and move so quickly, I don't know about the muscles. It's just a theory."

He drew in a deep breath, "Nyseis should be briefed."

"You believe me, then?"

"It doesn't matter what I believe. You believe it."

"We should send word to the other Holds."

"No."

"No? Why not?!"

"We're in no position at the moment."

"What does that mean?" Morigan demanded while standing. "You have an obligation to inform the other Holds. I have an obligation!"

"You? Your obligation is to The Sepal." Reileus stood and finished the wine.

"You can't keep this silent. People are dying. People will continue to die."

With a sigh of acquiescence, Reileus looked squarely to Morigan, "Nyseis will soon assume the throne as King. No messages are to leave until he does so. At that time, I will pen the notes and you will sign them as witness. We will have to make every effort to display stability and strength. There is no better time to launch an invasion into a territory than when that territory is sending out messages about supernatural plagues. There is too much risk involved."

"How long will that take?"

"Soon. When Lysander Barro returns. That would be a good spot to point to. I'd very much like to have fuck-with-us-not levels of Satyr at post rather than the handful currently on duty."

She nodded with a frown. Waiting was not something she was willing to do. "Thank you for hearing my theory, Lord Reileus."

He bowed, "Thank you for the wine."

# Epilogue
## *Of The Veil: All Returns*

And there, within The Veil, The Snatcher Sisters made a crude camp and huddled around the corpse of Prince Edgar Aquilo. The speaker: Calaeno, wide-eyed Ocypete, large-eared Aello, and beak-nosed Podarge all sat and swayed with troubled minds. Indecision instigated their retreat to that place in The Veil. The initial intention to deliver the Prince to Hippocamp shifted under the concern of possible outcomes. They wanted to win the favor of a god who was as real to them as the people they spent centuries observing. But the people of the North Hold were not well-known for welcoming gift-offering travelers. It did not augur well. The sisters regrouped to contemplate their boon. They were unaware of the hidden pair of eyes drinking their peril. Although Podarge's keen sense of smell suspected something near-by, the state of the Prince's decay, which had since been held at bay by The Veil itself, overpowered most any distinguishable aromas.

"We can not risk coming from the bush to only have a wolf pounce," remarked Calaeno ruefully. "While we peek and see something sweet, it is what we do not see that we must consider."

Aello nodded in agreement.

Ocypete indicated north with insistence.

Podarge was distracted and starred at the lifeless body at the center of their sitting circle.

The unseen eyes, shimmering from brilliant hues of blue to silver to white, blinked. They watched.

"Ocypete, sweet sister of sight," Calaeno remarked, "we can not know how Hippocamp's children would react. We should have not stolen this boy! What will we do with him? This treasure is a cursed one. We are rich from the value but poor from the worth. We should be rid of him! But how? How to destroy a thing from the gods without offending the gods? Oh, this curse is a grave one." She shook her aged head and grumbled, "We took the wrong boy."

Ocypete lamented with a nod, remembering Otver.

Calaeno continued, "And he has in him the Sigh of the Dragon. He is Veil-touched." She groused again, "We should have taken the other boy. The half-born veil child: Otver. We should have taken him."

"What is this woeful dread that hounds you?" A voice belonging to the unseen eyes drifted over the crones, causing alarm. "Poor feathered ones of the East."

"Hidden trickster with ears like sponges! How dare you set upon our dismay!"

"Nae, not set upon, stumbled upon more like. Nor trickster neither." From the surrounding misty fog, a smoky form began to take shape. "Stay your cruel intent, or I would remain intangible and unseen."

"No, come forth so we would know who would prey on our troubles!" Calaeno demanded.

The partially formed mass lingered a small while, silent in contemplation. "I would not give myself over to danger any easier than you four would. Perhaps I ought to hover and watch more?"

"Come from your cloud, beast. We've no interest or energy to offer you harm."

"I am no beast, crone." The fully formed figure was a

lithe body of the lightest blue clad in linens which seemed to be little more than frozen sea-foam. She was a salt-sidhe, and although Veilkith, she was as much a part of the north as The Snatcher Sisters were of the east.

The Snatcher Sisters panicked a small measure. Although they were known to spirit children away, it was an incriminating thing to be caught in the possession of not only a young adult, but also a northerner. They were not known to ply their craft in regions not their own.

Calaeno spoke, "This seems strange, I suppose."

"That it does, speaker." The salt-sidhe crossed her arms and swayed her weight to her left hip. "I would hear your tale then ascertain how I may best help in your troubles."

"Why should you help, watery woman?!" Calaeno remarked with scorn.

"Because he is not yours."

"He was found in The East! He is ours!"

"He was born to The North. He is not."

The thick and dense fogs swirled, carrying the voices unsafe distances.

Calaeno sighed and groaned while pulling her skeletal body from the dirt and dust covered ground. "With quieter words, perhaps a bargain could be struck."

The salt-sidhe nodded once, but said nothing.

"A boy and a royal guard Magpie arrived at our cottage. The Magpie had the soul of a champion. The boy had the soul of The Veil. They had, with them, this dead blood of The North Crown."

"You wanted to impress the boy with the soul of The Veil?"

The four Snatcher Sisters nodded. Calaeno added,

"We hoped to win favor."

The salt-sidhe took a moment to process the tale. "Why was the boy with the soul of The Veil with the Magpie?"

"To deliver this Prince to his home. The boy killed the Prince."

While in calculation, the salt-sidhe again nodded when suddenly her thoughts were interrupted by Calaeno's confession, "We doubt he knew what he was."

With confused amazement, the salt-sidhe questioned, "How could that be so? Was he not like you? A thing of the Eastern Veil? How could he not know what he was?"

"All things said to him seemed foreign. We saw him as Pegasus while he saw us as little more than strange old forest folk. He is not fully Veilkith, yet partially is. We should have brought him back rather than this cursed lump. Damn this foolish lot!"

Having heard Calaeno's words, the salt-sidhe looked down to the pale face of the corpse with a frown of mourning, "I know this boy well."

"Is he truly of Hippocamp?" Calaeno eagerly asked while the other three leaned nearer.

The ringing of the words on the fog had drawn the attention of something else. Curious and suspicious ears listened on much like the salt-sidhe had moments before. But this eavesdropper did not attend the conversation out of mere interest like the salt-sidhe. This eavesdropper paid heed with rage.

"This boy is the second son of the ice-crown. He is called Edgar," the salt-sidhe began. "He was a tortured boy: caught between an older brother of pure nobility and a younger brother of pure poetry. He was adrift yet always protected. When he was small, he would see me reflected back at him in the ripples of the warm-spring fountains in the castle. We would poke faces at each other. I always have enjoyed the laughter of children. He was often alone yet never out of his mother's grasp. He was a tortured boy." She paused and wondered if she should continue. Before long, there seemed to be no reason to stay silent. "He grew into a monster. He stopped seeing me in the water, or snows, or ice although I would call to him. I believed his heart was good, but his mind was bad and I wanted to understand and help this poor mortal. But a monster he became. He would charm for pleasure. He would kill for pleasure. He was untethered: still adrift and always protected. I tried to save her and have been roaming since."

"Save her?" Calaeno questioned while the other three sisters, as well as the unknown onlooker, listened closely.

"These matters of mortals interest you?" asked the salt-sidhe.

The Snatcher Sisters emphatically nodded in unison.

The salt-sidhe shook her head before speaking, "The girl from The East crown. He held her beneath the cold waters. Then she died."

Some sense of loyalty to the East as a whole dictated Calaeno's response of disgust, "This boy killed the Princess?"

"And many more before her. He had his gloved hands around her throat and I could not pry them away. I was water. All I could do was cradle the poor sweet girl. I held her as a mother would a child. For such fragile things, mortals can be so vicious."

Silence fell around the ethereal beings.

"What should be done with him?" Calaeno asked of the salt-sidhe while simultaneously noticing her three sisters grow agitated.

"What could be done?" the salt-sidhe remarked. "What has been done is done. The life left this shell. All that remains is the Sigh of the Dragon. Should he leave the security of The Veil again he would surely reanimate as one of those things. One wonders how you got him here at all."

"Worthless! We thought as much!" Calaeno griped before giving pause again at the sight of her sisters stirring.

The secretive onlooker, all of bitterness and animosity, came closer.

"You should not have brought him here," muttered the salt-sidhe. "You should not invest yourselves in mortal affairs."

"Something prowls. My sisters are uneasy," remarked Calaeno. "Something comes."

"He comes to see the wreck of his body. His soul was drawn by this thing you stole." The salt-sidhe folded her hands and took a step back, "What will be done, will be done. It is not for us to say."

In fear, The Snatcher Sisters huddled. The Void was home to all manner of spirits, but never before had they come in contact with a ghost of a body in their possession. The horrible anxiety of having been caught with a thing not their own triggered a frenzied terror.

"What is there to fear?" the salt-sidhe asked. "Have you been so long outside of The Veil to not remember what dwells here?"

Surrendering all claim to their bounty, The Snatcher

Sisters quickly retreated to the east.

The apparition slowly approached the corpse which was left at the foot of the salt-sidhe.

"A quicker death than you earned, Edgar," the salt-sidhe offered with a soft salutation.

"Why am I there?" the voice asked.

"Death, Edgar."

From the mist formed the faintest of figures. The ghost of Edgar loomed. The sight of his own dead face held words from forming.

"What will you do, Prince?" the salt-sidhe asked.

"What can I do, Undine?"

"You remember what I am?"

"I might," he remarked. "I remember stories. Moments. Water."

"There would be a way," she nodded while quietly speaking, "but that body has the Sigh of the Dragon in it."

"Is that a sickness?"

"It is."

"A terribly awful one?"

She smiled sadly at his familiar way with words. "It is. I doubt the cure would even work now. I could place you back in that body for a price, but that body may not hold up against the illness."

"There is a cure?"

The salt-sidhe nodded, "The sap of the great tree has within it an oil. The oil can fully destroy the Sigh, if the thing infected is fully submerged until the Sigh is eradicated."

"The thing infected being my body?"

The salt-sidhe nodded.

"Submerged?"

She nodded again with a lift of her shoulder.

"Why would you not do this for me, Undine?" With a stern frown, the ghost of Edgar insisted.

"Many reasons come to mind. Water is only present in The Veil as mist: not enough to submerge a body. Getting the sap would be a chore. You were a monster. And I do not know if you'd be willing to agree to my terms."

"Fae terms? I was always cautioned of making deals with immortals."

"You were cautioned from a great many things in which you indulged."

The ghost was speechless.

"My kind, the Veilkith of the North, are not like those sisters of The East. They thrive in air and wind. If not in The Veil, I am made to return to the waters. I am not able to live as freely as others. I am without a soul while you are, currently, nothing but. The only way I would assist would be if we fused our fates. You would make a promise to me and I to you. I would get a soul and walk freely and you would return to life. We would be united. Eternally united. But if ever you were to betray me, your suffering would be unimaginable."

"Marriage? Is this the promise you seek?"

"Is that an eternal union?"

The spectral Prince offered a nod.

"Then that is it. Do you agree to the terms?"

"...I do."

The salt-sidhe smiled and bowed her head, "Then it shall be done. Stay with this body and I will return shortly." She began to fade into the misty fog. "How odd a thing it is: he who murdered you came from a union just like ours."

## Appendix
### *Maps of the Four Holds*

The following pages contain maps detailing The Four Holds. In order:

Map of the East Hold

Map of the North Hold

Map of the West Hold

Map of the South Hold

Legend:
- ● town
- ○ fort
- ✕ temple
- ⚲ inn
- ‖ Wanderer's Path
- – – Traveler's Road

Linger Leaf
Evermeath
Ballad
Apple Run
Strum Tavern
Gale
Sunclimb Bluff
Quiveret
Dinlet
Tracker's Den
The Rip Trail
Ruby Brook
Howling Hare Inn
Goldcloud City
Plum Pond
Snowshimmer
Faint Drop
Twelve Quail
Falcon's Perch
Nest Twig Inn

N

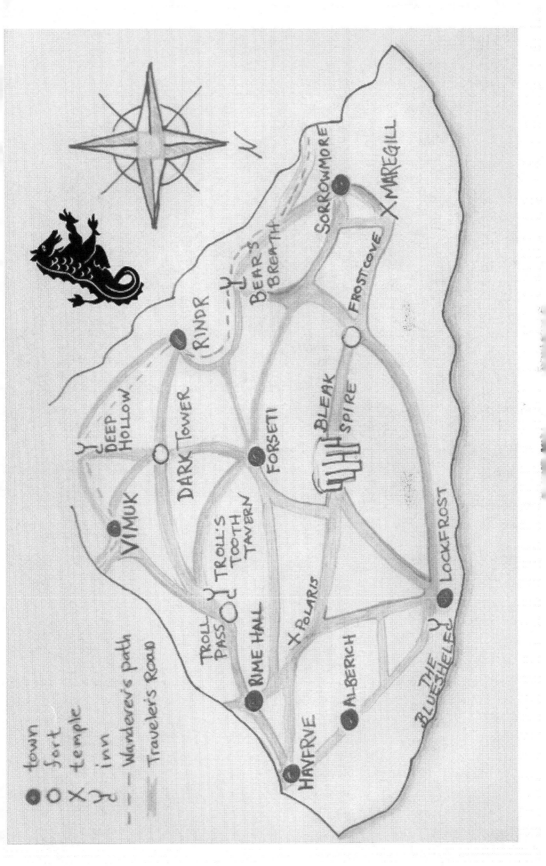

Legend:
- ● town
- ○ fort
- ✕ temple
- ♀ inn
- - - Wanderer's Path
- ── Traveler's Road

THE PEAT WASTE

BRIAR BAY

THORN BUSH
• Lyulot

MOSSGLEN

HONEY BUSH

MAGNOLIA CUP

TRAVELER'S JOY

RAMARIA

HEMLOCK LAKE

OLD MAN'S BEARD

FOREST OF DISMISSAL

PRIVET

THE SEPAL

CHLORIS

BOLETUS

PETAL FOLLY

THE HORN

TYRIA

TOAD'S GROTTO

LEPIOTA

BOG REACH

RAKE'S REST ♀

GROTTE CLUSTER "THE UNDERWORLD"